They had suited up, closed and secured their face plates, turned on the air tanks, and were running across the beach, almost to the water, when they heard the helicopter. Judging from the *chub-chub-chub* of the twin rotors, the Mi-12 was coming straight at them.

The Death Merchant kept right on going. Soon he was in water up to his hips. He dropped the plastic cylinder and threw himself forward in the water, pulling the line of the cylinder with him. By then, the Mi-12 was 200 feet up and close enough to open fire on them. The starboard gunner did so, getting off a long burst from a 14.5mm KPV machine gun.

Hundreds of slugs started hitting the sand, then throwing up tiny spurts in the water. Hushan turned and attempted to throw himself to one side. A 300-grain bullet hit him in the shoulder and almost amputated his left arm. Another projectile exploded the gas bottle on his back. A third and fourth projectile stabbed through his back, came out of his chest, and zapped into the water. The impact slammed Hushan face down, and he lay there, bobbing with the waves, streaks of red flowing out into the water and quickly disappearing.

*Ralph Hushan might have lived if he had not been 15 feet behind Camellion, if he had not turned around— and if he had been as fleet of foot as the Death Merchant. If—if—but Ralph Hushan was dead. . . .*

**The Death Merchant Series:**

#34 in the incredible adventures of the

# DEATH MERCHANT

## OPERATION MIND-MURDER

### by Joseph Rosenberger

PINNACLE BOOKS       LOS ANGELES

DEATH MERCHANT #34:
OPERATION MIND-MURDER

*Copyright © 1979 by Joseph Rosenburger*

An original Pinnacle Books edition, published for the first time anywhere.

First printing, June 1979

ISBN: 0-523-40477-8

Cover illustration by Dean Cate

*Printed in the United States of America*

PINNACLE BOOKS, INC.
2029 Century Park East
Los Angeles, California 90067

This book is dedicated to the men who lost their lives in a certain mission which we shall call "Operation Snowfall."

The American people will never know the true number of men and women who have died in the Silent War, in efforts to keep this nation free . . . men and women involved in operations that were a must.

*Richard J. Camellion*

# Chapter One

Oddly enough, Richard Camellion and the three Chinese-Americans with him in the cave didn't feel threatened, didn't feel in any way that they were sitting on a Russian time bomb that could explode in their faces at any moment. Psychologically it was always that way with men in Special Services. The "getting there" was always filled with free-floating anxiety. But by the time the participants were in enemy territory, the possibility of quick and violent death had been accepted emotionally, and fear had been replaced by a fierce determination to succeed.

It wasn't the same with the Death Merchant. He knew that the real difference between life and death was 99 percent superstition and 1 percent ignorance, that people are always terrified of what they don't understand.

Thomas Cholang, the security specialist, went about checking the acousti-sensor station while Dionysius Woo and Ralph Hushan sorted weapons and attended to the underwater gear, the latter, along with the Trass-III, the only link the four men had with *Tirante,* the nuclear submarine lying 46 miles north of the island.

On his knees on the rocky floor, the Death Merchant studied a map of Wrangel Island, or *Ostrov Vrangelya* as it was known in Russian. Technically the island was a Soviet Federated Socialist Republic. Administratively it was governed as an *Okrug,* a territory.

As far as Camellion and the men with him were concerned, Wrangel Island was a thousand miles past the end of the world and five thousand years behind time. On a world map the island was an insignificant blob at 71°00′N and 179°30′W. Considered an Alaskan island in the Arctic Ocean, Wrangel Island was only 160 miles west of Alaska and 80 miles off the coast of northwestern Siberia. The long, narrow island—79 miles at its widest point—was separated from the Siber-

1

ian mainland by *Proliv Longa*—Long Strait in English. To the southeast of the island was the Chukchi Sea. To the west, *Vostocno Sibirskoje More*—the East Siberian Sea. To the north was the Arctic Ocean.

Wearing a Russian-made, one-piece snowsuit over his Russian combat fatigues, Camellion told himself that they did have the season in their favor. Since it was summer, Wrangel Island was not hemmed in by an ice pack and the temperature seldom dropped below 20 degrees, even at night.

Tom Cholang got down on a knee next to the Death Merchant and looked at the map. Due to the briefing on the *Tirante,* he knew that they were 5 miles from the southwest shore and in the lower foothills of the *Mamontovvye Gory*— the Mammoth Mountains, which were large in name only.

Cholang stared at the red line Camellion had drawn on the map. The distance from the cave to Rodgers Harbor was 43 miles.

"Sir, this map was made from satellite photographs," Cholang said. "When you get to the nitty gritty of it, what assurance do we have that the map is accurate?"

"The cameras on WINKEYE II photographed what they saw," Camellion answered, "and don't use 'sir' to me. The same goes for 'Mister.' You know my name. Call me Camellion."

"I meant that the buildings at the south end might be dummies, and the three roads seem to go nowhere. The real target might be underground."

Cholang glanced speculatively at the tall, rugged man beside him and for the tenth time wondered about Richard Camellion. Colonel Gordon had introduced him only by name, with the comment that Camellion would be the CO of the recon operation. Camellion couldn't be Army since this was a Navy operation. A civilian expert? A spook from the CIA or from some other U.S. Government intelligence gathering apparatus? Probably. What else could he be? Anyhow, he was an expert at force recon[1] procedures and operations.

[1] Marine reconnaissance units are divided into two types: the force reconnaissance company—"force recon"—and division reconnaissance. Both force and division recons are tasked with reconnaissance of the landing area and terminal helicopter guidance. However, force recon teams are introduced clandestinely into the landing area prior to H-Hour, or prior to

The underwater trip from the *Tirante* had been made with the three young Chinese-Americans hoping that Camellion, driving the Trass-III SDV,[2] knew what he was doing. It became obvious that he did when they had arrived at a point three miles west of the coast. They had secured the Trass-III to the bottom of the ocean and had swum ashore with their equipment. Timing had been perfect: 03.00 hours. No moon. The night as black as obsidian. They had removed their closed-breathing swimsuits, worn over their snowsuits, and had moved inland, weighed down with equipment, using a special acousti-sensor to warn them of any approaching Russian patrol, the unit being able to sense the heat from a human body within a radius of 230 yards.

At length, the Death Merchant had chosen a cave in the foothills of the mountains. "One of the reasons we're here." Camellion said, picking up the map and starting to fold it, "is to find out what is real. We have three days in which to do the job." He stood erect, put the map into a small case on his belt, and turned to Dionysius Woo and Ralph Hushan.

"Everything in order?" Camellion asked, then bent down and picked up one of the Red Chinese Type-64 SMGs. Firing a 7.62mm x 25 R-Ball cartridge, the Type-64 was one of the few SMGs known to have been designed and built in Red China. The weapon, as well as its two companions, had a noise suppressor built around the barrel. The front third of the barrel was perforated to release propellant gases into a surrounding tube; this projected some 15 cm beyond the end of the barrel and carried a stack of dished-and-perforated baffles through which the bullet had to pass and which dissipated the energy of the emerging gases. They also prevented muzzle flash.

Hushan's round face broke out in a grin. "Everything's OK." He waved his hand toward the weapons and other ma-

---

D-Day. Operating in four-man teams, they provide intelligence information directly to the landing force commander. Division recon, following force recon ashore, may be introduced before or after H-Hour. Operating as platoons or companies, division recon gathers intelligence information for its own particular division or smaller task organization. UDT, Underwater Demolition Teams, are part and parcel of both force and division recons.

[2] Swimmer Delivery Vehicle.

teriel. "Weapons, ammo, L-rations, the works. The only thing I'm curious about is why we're dressed in Russian clothes and using Chinese and Czech weapons. I don't suppose you can tell me?"

"What makes you think I know?" Camellion put down the Chinese Type-64 submachine gun and picked up one of the three Czechoslovakian Model-61 submachine guns, better known as a "Skorpion." Only 20.55 inches long with the metal stock fixed and 10.62 inches with stock folded, the Skorpion could be called a machine pistol since it had been designed to be fired from one hand as well as from the shoulder. Like most experts in firearms, Camellion considered the Skorpion to be the Czech equivalent of the Soviet Stechkin machine pistol or the M1932 Mauser. The Skorpion had only one weakness: it used a relatively low-powered cartridge, the 7.65mm short.

Thomas Cholang, surveying the small cave, sounded annoyed. "If the brass wanted us to know what this is all about, they would have told us. You know that, Ralph."

"I'll tell you guys what we all know," Dionysius Woo inserted into the conversation. "We're pulling a fast one on the sickle-and-hammer boys. We're Chinese, except for Camellion, and he's fixed himself up to look Oriental." He laughed low and slyly. "The idea is that we're 'Red Chinese pretending to be Ruskies.' "

Hushan, who was in his middle twenties, as were Woo and Cholang, made a sad face. "Sure, and we'd have to be dead to fool the Russians," he said glumly. "None of us speak Chinese fluently—at least I don't—and anyhow, our diving suits are strictly 'Made in U.S.A.' "

"My grandparents were fluent in Cantonese," Woo said, sighing. "Mom and Pop didn't follow the old ways. They never forgave my parents for naming me Dionysius and my sister Rhea."

"I wouldn't forgive my parents either if they named me Dionysius," laughed Hushan. "What kind of a name is that for a Chinese boy?"

"Yeah, I know," admitted Woo. "But my father was nuts over the Greeks and that's the name I got stuck with—the name of an Olympian god, the 'giver of the grape and its wine.' I thought of changing my first name once, but then I decided that if I did, I wouldn't be me."

4

The Death Merchant pulled down the zipper of his snow-suit a foot and studied the cave, which was lighted by only the single small bulb of an electric lantern. The uneven ceiling was less than 8 feet at the highest point. The rest of the cave, as gloomy as an unkept graveyard, was about the size of a large closet. The entrance to the tunnel was not quite a yard in diameter. The tunnel itself was 10 feet in length, the same thickness as the lower part of the mountain wall.

Woo, the last of the four to enter the tunnel, had moved in backward on his hands and knees and had carefully blocked the entrance with loose rock and snow. They had been in luck. A light snow had been falling. The snow, coupled with the constantly blowing wind, had destroyed all traces of their footprints within a matter of minutes. The cave, however, was warm, made that way by a portable electric heater that operated on a cell no larger than a C-size flashlight battery.

The Death Merchant squatted down and looked at the acousti-sensor station which resembled a metal cigar box with a 5-foot telescoping antenna. There were two rows of red bulbs, eight bulbs in a row, the number under each bulb indicating the distance of an enemy from the station. In the upper right hand corner, a light glowing green indicated that the device was on and functioning.

"What range do you have it set on?" Camellion asked Cholang.

"Two hundred and thirty yards. That's the maximum." Cholang tapped the green light. "It's working at peak efficiency. But all it's good for is to let us know if others are around. We couldn't put up any kind of defense in here if they found us. I suppose though we could take some of them with us. That's not much consolation, is it?"

The Death Merchant didn't reply. Dying and death always involved an individual's private philosophy, and like killing, dying was a very private matter. You could drop dead in a crowd—but you always died *alone!*

"Hey, have any of you ever tried these L-rations?" called out Cholang, pulling the tab on a square packet that resembled an oversized TV dinner. "All you do is pull the tab, wait ten minutes while the tiny batteries heat the coil, then pull off the top. Then you have it—hot food. We have only twelve packs—a meal a day each for three days."

5

"It's enough," Camellion said positively. "On the fourth morning we'll return to the *Tirante*. When it's daylight, I'll go out and have a look around."

The men nodded. Camellion detected a worried look on Ralph Hushan's face.

"What's bothering you, Hushan? Put it on the line."

Tall for a Chinese but well muscled, Hushan came right to the point. "It's the feeling that the Russians are toying with us, that they know we're here. I don't mean here in this cave but on the island."

The Death Merchant's eyes narrowed ever so slightly. When a man was bothered with a problem, it was like having a pebble in his boot or a tack in his mind, and it interfered with his ability to stay alert.

Woo and Cholang, appearing puzzled, regarded Hushan with grave looks.

"Why?" Camellion asked.

"During the briefing, we were told that *Foxfire* was lying in a kind of trench eighty miles to the east of Wrangel," Hushan said. "We were told also that the Russian navy knows she's there and is keeping a watch on her."

"Affirmative," Camellion said. "It's a simple matter for the Ruskies to pick up another submarine with sonar and other modern detection devices. What's bothering you is why the Russians can't detect the *Tirante* by the same conventional means."

Woo spoke up. "We were also wondering why Russian sensing devices couldn't detect our SDV."

"I'll be honest about it," Hushan said. "I think you know the answer."

"I do and I don't." Camellion sat down, picked up one of the L-ration packages, pulled the tab, and glanced at his wristwatch. "The Russians don't know that the *Tirante* is out there because on board is a highly secret gismo that makes the sub invisible, as far as sound is concerned. The device is called an F-Unit. I haven't the slightest idea how it works. It's my impression that even the crew, including the captain, don't know how or why the unit works. They only know how to use it."

"So that's it! *Foxfire* is a decoy!" Hushan said quickly. "*Foxfire* doesn't have the unit or isn't using it. The Russians can't bother her because she's in international waters—but so's the *Tirante* for that matter."

6

"Then the SDV must also be equipped with the F-Unit," said Woo in guarded tones. "If you ask me, that's damned risky. The Russian scuba boys could accidentally find the Trass. What then?"

"It isn't likely that the Russians will discover the Trass vehicle," Camellion said. "But should they, and move it out of the water, it will explode. The F-Unit will go with it."

"An air-triggered destruct device," Cholang said. "You must have activated it after we left the sub and were in the water." Rather thin, Cholang had the annoying habit of rocking back and forth on his heels. "But suppose they find the Trass and just leave it? We could swim right into a trap."

"Either way, we'd never get back to the *Tirante*," Woo said dismally. "Sometimes I wish I had joined the Air Force."

"We wouldn't get back, but the Ruskies still wouldn't get the Trass or the unit," Camellion offered, thinking of the lie he had told the three Chinese-Americans. There was a secret device on board *Tirante* and on *Foxfire* as well. Only it was known as a Gf-Mechanism. The rest of what Camellion had told the men was the truth. He didn't know how the device worked. Furthermore, he didn't want to know.

Anything was possible. The Russians might capture the three Special Services men. They would talk; the KGB could make a statue talk. If that happened, the Soviets would learn about the ultra-secret unit on board the two nuclear submarines. The name of the device wasn't important. F-Unit, Gf-Mechanism, or XYZ-Device! The fact that the Russians could learn of such a device was the prime ingredient in a dangerous brew.

*But if I hadn't told them, they would have guessed that some sort of protective device was shielding the* Tirante.

Another factor had now entered the recon mission. Should the three Chinese-Americans be in danger of being captured —*I'll have to neutralize them.*

The Death Merchant wasn't concerned about the KGB ever learning anything from him. If worse became worst, he would simply terminate his own existence with either a bullet or a suicide pill.

*At least they think this recon job is the entire mission. If they knew the truth, they would have to try twice to believe it. . . .*

The L-rations were tasty, even though the "steak" and

"vegetables" were synthetic and made of seaweed. While the men ate and drank hot coffee, they discussed the plan for locating the main complex on Wrangel Island. No one said so, but there was automatic agreement on one point. There was no easy way to do it.

"We'll hole up here all day," Camellion said. "Tomorrow night—rather, early the next morning—three of us will swim out to the SDV. We'll use it for transportation. Any comments—other than that by using the Trass, we'll be cutting our overall transportation pretty thin?"

There was new concern in Ralph Hushan's deep-set eyes. "With the extra set of batteries, we shouldn't have any trouble getting back to the *Tirante*. It was forty-six nautical miles from the sub to the north side of the island. We came around from the north. That was another forty-four miles. That's a total of ninety miles. The round trip will be a hundred and eighty miles. It seems to me, the question now is"—he looked at the Death Merchant—"how far past Rodgers Harbor[3] do we go?"

The Death Merchant supplied the answer. "All the way around the southern end of the island, say another thirty miles. Back to Rodgers Harbor will be another thirty miles. The entire trip, from here to there and back . . . figure a hundred forty-six miles. OK, that makes the entire total three hundred twenty-six miles. Subtract that from three hundred thirty-five miles, the total range of the Trass, and that leaves us with nine miles to spare. But only theoretically. Even though the batteries are sealed in the SDV, the vehicle is still in four hundred feet of water. That means a cold temperature. Cold means an energy drain, very, very slight, but still a drain."

"Well, we sure can't do any surveillance by land." Woo's voice took on a sudden note of urgency. "Top submerged speed is forty knots. Let's see, figuring the total recon and the return trip to *Tirante*, I get two hundred thirty-six miles. That's more than eight hours of air that we'll need."

"The amount of air was calculated to the last cubic inch,"

[3] The island is named after F.P. Wrangel who investigated reports of its existence in 1824.

The harbor was named for the U.S.S. *John Rodgers*—the American ship which landed on Wrangel Island in August of 1881.

8

Camellion said. "We have more than enough air. Other than the four bottles here with us, there are eight more in the Trass and spare carbon dioxide absorption canisters. The greatest danger to us is the Russians—them and the possibility that we might have to swim the last twenty-five or thirty miles to *Tirante*. That's no big deal to big boys like us."

Cholang made a face as he stared into the collapsible aluminum cup he was holding in one hand. "Yeah, if we're lucky, we might still be alive by the time we reach *Tirante*."

"I'd like to know why only three of us are going on the recon. The man who stays behind won't have anything to do but count fly specks. We can't have radio contact!" Hushan, counting the cartridges in a box magazine he had taken from a Czech Vz pistol, leaned back against a wall of the cave and looked at Camellion, who was using a small slide rule to compute the GSD[4] of the air bottles.

"I want all the knots I can get," Camellion said, not letting the question or his reply interfere with his computations. "I'd do the job alone, but it requires a minimum of three to do the job. One on the camera, one to control the SDV, and one to act as a lookout. The three of you can decide among yourselves who stays here."

"I'll stay," offered Dionysius Woo. "It doesn't make me any never mind where I am." His gaze went from Hushan to Cholang. "Unless one of you guys would rather be here?"

Hushan shook his head, pushed the clip into the butt of the Czech pistol, and shoved the autoloader into its shoulder holster.

Tom Cholang said, "I'll take the water. Some action will take my mind off smoking." A chain-smoker, Cholang was miserable without cigarettes, and smoking in the cave was out of the question. Not only would the smoke foul the air, but the smell might be detected by a Russian Army patrol.

"Whatever happens, I think it's all cut and dried," Woo said thoughtfully. He had removed the hood from his snowsuit and, using it as a pillow, was stretched out on the floor

---

[4] Gas Supply Duration. A diver has to know the GSD in order to plan his dive, so that he does not run out of gas at a decompression stop or on the bottom. He will use 600 psi as a low-pressure safety limit. This safety limit allows for bypassing, purging, and setting up the rig.

on his back. "No matter who you are or what you do, this life is nothing more than a short training period for something much greater, for the life after so-called death. Why, the universe wouldn't have any reason to exist without man."

Cholang and Hushan exchanged sly glances. Woo was constantly reading books on metaphysics and the occult, and while his friends didn't laugh at his belief in a life after death, they often kidded him about some of his other convictions, such as reincarnation.

Hushan said with a laugh, "Tell you what, Di. When one of my dead relatives pops up and tells me there's a hereafter in some never-never land, I might believe it. Until then, I'm going to continue to believe that when the brain quits, the man does. That's it! Period! *Finis!* Oblivion!"

"That makes two of us," muttered Cholang. "With all the misery on earth, it seems to me that if the dead were 'alive' somewhere, they'd lend a helping hand and do something about it."

Woo wasn't at all at a loss for an answer. "Why should the dead be concerned about those who are still alive in this world? No matter what happens on earth, it's all meaningless. It's the next reality that matters."

Hushan gave a long, audible sigh. "Yeah? Then how come we're holed up in this cave? It won't be very 'meaningless' if the Ruskies find us."

"Yeah, I don't want to go to that next reality until I have to," Tom Cholang added. "The later the better, preferably a hundred years later. How about you, Camellion?"

"My opinion is that God helps those the most who help themselves the most. Right now we can help ourselves by getting some sleep."

"Good idea," Cholang said. "We'll need our strength; that's for sure. Carrying the deep-dive suits, the air bottles, and the other necessities from the beach pooped me out."

"We'll be several hundred pounds lighter tomorrow," Hushan said. "All we'll have to carry are the swimsuits and the air bottles."

"And the weapons," Camellion said.

"The weapons?" Woo sat up and looked at the Death Merchant.

Tom Cholang and Ralph Hushan were equally surprised.

"Two of us are going ashore," the Death Merchant said.

# Chapter Two

It was 15.00 hours in the afternoon when Camellion and the three other men were awakened by the *beep, beep, beep* of the acousti-sensor. Trained to sleep lightly and to be instantly alert the moment their eyes opened, the four men sat up and moved around the sensor. Camellion, the first to reach the station, switched off the beeper and looked at the flashing red light. Underneath the light, printed in black, was 230-Y—690 feet.

"A Russian patrol!" whispered Thomas Cholang in alarm.

"If they're carrying rock-penetrating metal detectors, we might as well write our wills," said Ralph Hushan, picking up one of the Czech Skorpions.

"I did that when I was selected for Special Services," complained Woo, "for all the good it will do me."

As they watched the panel, the next red bulb began to flash—220 yards. While the sensor didn't tell the direction in which the Russians were moving, the device did show that the patrol was moving toward the sensor, toward the cave.

"So what happens now?" said Woo. He then answered himself. "A stupid question. We sit here and wait. What else can we do?"

Hushan said, "They don't know we're here, or they wouldn't have waited until three in the afternoon to show up. They're just a passing patrol, that's all."

A puzzled expression clouded his face when the Death Merchant pulled up his hood and slipped on a pair of Servotex gloves. Cholang and Woo exchanged glances as Camellion picked up one of the Chinese Type-64 SMGs and readied the submachine gun for firing.

"Why are you going out there?" Woo's tone was slightly angry. "If we stay put, they'll go on by. Why borrow trouble?"

"Hushan has a point," Camellion explained. "The Russians could have metal detectors. We can't afford to take the

11

chance. Another thing is that we don't know how many of them are out there or where they are. We only know that they're within"—he glanced at the panel—"six hundred feet of us. There's a built-in flaw in the sensor. It's sensitive to only the greatest number of people within a certain radius."

"What are you driving at?" asked Cholang cautiously.

"I'm saying that there could be several men right outside and we wouldn't know it. They could use a satchel charge and blow us to that next life of Woo's and we'd never know it. It's a loose end and I'm going out and make sure the knot is tied."

"Hell, there could be a dozen of them out there!" protested Woo.

"Then the odds will be about even," Camellion said, sounding serious. "You men have never fought the ivans. By the time the average pig-farmer puts it together and decides what to do next, you can kill him three times over."

"Maybe so, but I think you're cutting off more than you're going to be able to swallow," said Woo. "You're not Superman—You'd look ridiculous in tights."

The Death Merchant's laugh was chilling. "Just think of me as one of the 'Sons of Light' fighting the 'Powers of Darkness.'"

With that he turned and crawled into the inner mouth of the tunnel, taking the Red Chinese SMG with him.

The three Special Services men watched him disappear into the tunnel, Ralph Hushan muttering, "I have the feeling that every day he remains alive, he considers it pure profit."

Very carefully, Camellion unblocked the outside opening of the tunnel, taking out one rock at a time. It took only a few minutes for him to clear away the rocks, crawl through the opening, and stand up. With the wind blowing furiously, it was difficult to tell whether the snow was coming from the low, gray sky or being whipped up from the ground.

There wasn't any danger of his being spotted by the Russian patrol. They hadn't had time to climb the notrheast side of the rise. The cave was at the bottom of the southwest side of the hillock. More hills, covered with rocks, snow, and tiny bushes, were to the northwest and the southeast. To the southwest was a large plain of rocks and boulders, some the size of a football, others as huge as a pickup truck, the closest only eight feet away from Camellion. All of Wrangel

Island was part of the region of Arctic tundra, much of it low-lying lichen. There were no glaciers, although the highest part of the island reached 3,596 feet—this was Sovetskaya Mountain.

The Death Merchant didn't expect any real trouble. He would go to the top of the rise and see how many Russians there were and what they were up to. He didn't get what he had anticipated. He was about to start up the rough incline when a Russian trooper, in fur hat and white parka, stepped out from behind the nearest boulder, 8 to 9 feet away.

In that bare blink of time, it became obvious to the Death Merchant that the Russian and his two companions—the two troopers who had stepped out behind him—had not been lying in wait but had been moving on a northwest route, one perpendicular to the boulder. The large rock was in their way and they had merely stepped around it.

Private Dmitri Baronov was twice as stunned as the Death Merchant, who went through life primed for trouble. For the moment, all Baronov and Pvts. Yakatoff and Veradsky could do was stare at Camellion in complete astonishment as though he were an alien from another planet.

Certain survival instincts are based on previous experience, intuitive reaction which speeds through the neurons too quickly to reach the surface of consciousness. It was this kind of lightning instinct that made Camellion know automatically that it would be a huge risk to try to terminate the three Russian soldiers with the Red Chinese SMG. The 7.62mm cartridges were not powerful enough to send slugs all the way through the heavily clothed body of the first Russian. Camellion could kill two of the troopers with a single burst from his SMG, but if the projectiles didn't bore all the way through the first man and X-out the pig-farmer behind him, the soldier would have time to duck behind the boulder. Should that happen and the man get off a single shot, the sharp report would warn the other Russians coming up the northeast rise.

Camellion leaped three feet off the ground and, using a *tae kwon do* double-piston kick, propelled himself at the first Russian soldier.

"*Dov na padmon*—!" Dmitri Baronov spat out and started to bring up his Kalashnikov automatic rifle. He was too late. The Death Merchant's feet crashed into his chest, pitching him backward into Viktor Yakatoff. Both Russians went down in a tangle of arms and legs, Baronov dropping his AK-47 and crying out in pain.

Pytor Veradsky, the third Russian trooper, jumped to his left and attempted to swing his AK-47 at the *rovoiny v likoi*,[1] who was also going down. Cam*e*llion, however, had planned his move with split-second timing. Even as he was falling, he turned the Chinese SMG and squeezed the trigger, the weapon making a loud, buzzing sound. Five bullet holes appeared in Veradsky's chest. The AK-47 fell from his hands. A long sigh, along with blood, slid from his mouth and his corpse dropped to the ground.

The Death Merchant hit the ground on his right side, breaking the fall with his elbow. On top of Yakatoff, Baronov had a fractured breastbone, was in pain, and in no condition to move rapidly. Yakatoff struggled desperately to free himself from Baronov's weight and at the same time pick up his AK-47. If he couldn't kill the man—he had to be an *Amerikanski*—he might be able to warn the rest of the patrol. His groping fingers reached the stock of the AK-47— the last act of his life.

Camellion fired from the ground and 7.62mm projectiles rained all over Yakatoff and Baronov, the slugs ripping through cloth and flesh and killing the two Red Army soldiers instantly.

The Death Merchant jumped to his feet, picked up Pytor Veradsky's AK-47, saw that it was fully loaded and on Safe, then spun and started up the incline, carrying both the AK-47 and the Chinese SMG. The fierce wind whipped snow in his face, and at times he almost slipped on stones as his booted feet crushed through the foot of snow. It was hard times, warm beer, and cold women all the way up, with Camellion knowing that if the other pig-farmers got there first, his life expectancy would be cut by 99 percent.

He flopped to the ground 8 feet from the top, wriggled the rest of the way on his belly, stopped by the side of a bush which was the support of a small mound of snow, and looked down over the other side of the hill. Seven Russians, spread out in no specific pattern, were plodding up the hillside, their heads bent down against the wind and swirling snow.

*You pig-farmers aren't going to get my Christmas card*

[1] Foreign invader.

*business this year!* Camellion watched the Russian soldiers for a few seconds, then opened fire with the SMG. Three of the troopers were riddled and falling backward by the time the other four realized that they were attending their own executions. By the time they caught on that they were under fire, 7.62mm projectiles were ripping into their bodies and tearing away their lives.

All except one Russian!

Tht firing pin of Camellion's SMG hit empty air in the firing chamber. The Red Chinese submachine gun was empty.

The Russian threw himself down in the snow on his belly while Camellion snatched up the AK-47 he had taken from one of the Russians on the other side of the hill. The Russian, who had unslung his own automatic rifle was unnerved by having seen his comrades cut down by an assassin using a noise suppressor. He hesitated, trying to decide where to aim. Rearing up slightly, he had just about made up his mind to rake the entire rim when Camellion cut loose, the AK-47 roaring out a stream of high-velocity 7.62 X 39mm slugs. The Russian's face vanished in a spray of flesh and bone and blood, and his skull exploded. Two more slugs ripped into his throat and tore out his Adam's apple; three more slammed into his upper chest.

*"Dosvidanya*[2] you commie piece of trash," Camellion muttered. He surveyed his handiwork. The seven Russians lay with the wind blowing snow against them.

The sound of snow being crunched behind him made the Death Merchant shift around and throw up the AK-47.

"Don't fire, dammit! It's me!" Dionysius Woo called out.

Camellion waved him forward. Presently Woo was down beside Camellion, staring at the dead Red Army troopers.

"Holy Smoke! With the three on the other side, that makes ten!" Woo said with a kind of awe. "The way this wind's blowing, they'll be buried within fifteen minutes. But there'll be hell to pay when they're missed at their headquarters."

"Why did you leave the cave," Camellion demanded, his keen blue eyes surveying the surrounding hills through the snow and the gloom.

"We talked it over and it didn't seem right that you should have all the fun. I came to lend a shooting hand. Now what?"

[2] "Goodbye."

15

"Intelligence found out that the Ruskies use three kinds of patrols on Wrangel," Camellon said. "Aircraft and land patrols. One kind of land patrol uses snowmobiles. Those patrols return to their base each day. Other patrols are on foot and stay out for as long as a week."

Woo tightened the strings of his hood against the biting wind. "There aren't any snowmobiles out there, and look at the size of the packs on those dead guys. You whacked out a foot patrol. They won't be missed until they don't report in by radio."

"Get Hushan and Cholang," Camellion ordered, satisfied that he had killed the entire patrol and that there weren't any stragglers. "We'll search the bodies. We might find something of importance."

Woo gave Camellion an odd glance. The Death Merchant's no-cause-for-alarm manner worried him.

"We're going to have to change our plans," he said pensively.

"Get the others." This time Camellion's voice was sharp. His mouth tight, Woo went down the hillside.

A quick search of the Russian corpses was found to be a lesson in futility. They did find proof that Camellion had been wise in going out to investigate. Two of the corpses carried metal detectors, the kind that could be used while leaving one's hands free. The main unit was worn on the back; the sensitivity probes were attached to the wearer's legs, close to the ankles. An examination of the devices revealed that they operated on a max of 400 to 900 ohms, more than enough power to penetrate 10 feet of rock. There wasn't anything else of importance. Other than arms and ammo and camping equipment the Russians carried paybooks, letters from home, cheap *mahorjka* cigarettes, and other personal items.

One man, a sergeant, carried a two-way radio similar to a U.S. PRC-8. The sergeant and another man, perhaps an officer, also had Stechkin machine pistols in holsters and spare magazines in belt pouches. Camellion and his men took the two Stechkins and three AK-47s, returned to the cave, and resealed the outside tunnel entrance.

Camellion didn't waste any time in outlining his new plan to the men. As soon as it was dark, he and another man would go to the shore, swim out to the SDV, and steer it to Rodgers Harbor. Camellion would go ashore and take all the photographs he could. He would then return to Trass-III—"We'll come back here, pick up the other three and head back toward the *Tirante*. We should be able to get back here by dawn."

The three men stared at the Death Merchant in disbelief. He was telling them that he was going to accompiish the impossible.

"It can't be done," Tom Cholang said stubbornly. "Earlier we figured that the round trip would be a hundred and forty-six miles. How can you cover that distance by dawn—and go ashore at Rodgers Harbor to boot?"

"Cut the round trip to eighty-six miles," the Death Merchant said. "It's only forty-three miles to Rodgers Harbor. We'll have to nix going around the south end. We don't have the time."

"In short, we do half a recon," Dionysius Woo said dully. "Colonel Gordon won't like that."

"He'd like it even less if we got killed," Camellion said roughly. "He'd end up with nothing, and certain people would have to start all over. Now, who wants to go with me?"

# Chapter Three

20.00 hours. The office was modestly furnished but comfortable. There was a steel desk, its top bare except for a model of a Mikoyan Mig-19 Air Force fighter; a row of wooden filing cabinets, a long leather couch, and numerous padded easy chairs. A table held nine telephones and a portable transceiver. On the wall were two large photographs in plain wooden frames. One was of Leonid I. Brezhnev, the Soviet Communist Party boss; the other of Yuri Andropov, the chairman of the *Komitet Gosudarstvennoy Bezopasnosti*, the KGB. The Persian rug on the floor looked new and was very clean.

General Walter Vatutin flicked ash from his cigarette, leaned back in the easy chair, and looked expectantly at Major Konstantin Rinchino, who had just entered the room. "Well, Major?"

"Sir, we still have not received word from Lieutenant Putyatin and his patrol," replied Major Rinchino uneasily. "We have been sending radio signals since six-thirty, but there has been no reply. The two planes we sent up have not seen any fires or distress flares."

Rinchino wanted to add that, in his opinion, Putyatin and his men had met with disaster of some sort, but he didn't dare. General Vatutin didn't want the officers under his command to form conclusions for him. Rinchino maintained an attentive silence, then sat down when Vatutin waved him to a chair. The General then turned to Colonel Josef Milovanov, who, sitting to his left, was the chief of security on Wrangel Island.

"Josef, I want your opinion," Vatutin said crisply. "Either we have a situation that is extremely serious, or else there's some simple explanation. There's a reason why Lieutenant Putyatin hasn't reported and I want to know it."

Colonel Milovanov cleared his throat and shifted somewhat in his chair. "I have no idea why the Lieutenant hasn't reported. Should the radio give out, procedure is to send up flares every six minutes. The aircraft hasn't spotted any. On such evidence, it is safe to assume that for some reason, Lieutenant Putyatin and his men have not been able to shoot off flares."

For a moment, General Vatutin stared at Milovanov, who was solidly built, of medium height, with thinning dark brown hair. His eyes seemed to have a perpetual squint, as though he had spent too much time in the bright sun.

"Colonel, you're repeating what we already know." Vatutin's tone was heavy with annoyance and impatience. "I want to know why he hasn't reported. When we know the 'why,' we'll know what happened to him and his men."

"Let's start by listing what could not have happened," Milovanov said heartily. "First of all, we can eliminate as suspects the American submarine a hundred and twenty-nine kilometers east of us. The Americans have us under surveillance, but we are also keeping a watch on them. We have television cameras monitoring all sides of the sub, from a distance of eight kilometers. Divers could not leave the submarine without our knowing it. *Nyet,* General. It is not the Americans who have harmed our patrol."

"Colonel Milovanov, I'm curious about something," spoke up Major Rinchino. "Why is it necessary to monitor the *Amerikanski* submarine with television cameras when we have the entire island ringed with automatic detection sensors? An enemy couldn't row to shore in a rowboat without our knowing it!"

"It is no secret that the Americans watch us at various places," Milovanov said. "Our submarines watch the Americans. We have subs off both American coasts. The Americans know it, just like we know their nuclear sub is out there. We're monitoring that submarine to let them know we're not stupid, to let them know we know they're there. They're in international waters. They know we can't do anything about their being there. They've floated up an antenna and are recording messages from us to the mainland and vice versa. That submarine is on a routine snooping mission. That's all it is."

"Which still doesn't explain what might have happened to the patrol," General Vatutin said acidly.

19

"I see two possibilities," Milovanov said quickly. "Polar bears and landslides, or cave-ins."

Vatutin blinked in surprise. "Ridiculous!" he snapped. Folding his arms, he looked despairingly at Milovanov. "Josef, I want you to explain how it would be possible for a polar bear, or several if you like, to kill ten well-trained, well-armed men?"

"General, we know that during the summer months, this island teems with fox, lemmings, and polar bears," Milovanov said. "Bears are especially thick on the coasts. Lieutenant Putyatin and his patrol were to patrol the north coast, turn and take a route through the Mamontovvye Gory, then come home along the south coast. It was a nine-day patrol."

"What about the bears?" The General's face wore a faint smile.

"We know the bears couldn't have attacked the patrol last night," Milovanov said studiously, folding his hands in his lap. "Putyatin reported in this morning. But a pack of polar bears could have come up behind the men sometime during the day. Those animals are very vicious and move with tremendous speed."

Major Konstantin Rinchino kept his expression carefully neutral. After all, Josef Milovanov outranked him. Let him and General Vatutin thrash it out. To insult Milovanov might incur the eventual wrath of Vatutin. Both men had reputations of being ruthless.

General Vatutin sighed. "Josef, I think your polar bear theory is preposterous. Bears might get one man or two, but all ten? Ridiculous. The other men would cut them to pieces with AKs. I think we can forget your bear theory."

Milovanov cracked his long bony fingers—a sure sign that he was annoyed. "I said the bears were a possibiilty. The other likelihood is a landslide. This time of the year the ice partially thaws. Water loosens the rock and landslides are common. The patrol could have been caught in a gully by such a slide. Those mountains, too, are riddled with caves. They might have gone in to inspect one and have been caught in a rock fall. We lost two men last year that way."

General Vatutin's eyes lingered for a moment on Milovanov, then moved calculatingly to Rinchino. "I'm sure you have an opinion, Major?"

"I am inclined to think that some natural calamity befell the patrol." Rinchino formed his words carefully. "There

20

isn't any other explanation. A snowslide is the most likely explanation."

Vatutin's face did not change expression. Milovanov nodded vigorously in agreement. "We might not find their bodies for weeks, the way the wind is blowing the loose snow. It might take even longer if we get a sudden freeze. All we can do is send out search patrols in the morning." He turned and looked at General Vatutin, who was lost in thought. "General, do you have any specific orders regarding Lieutenant Putyatin and his men?"

Vatutin shook his head. *"Nyet.* Search patrols will be sufficient." His face clouded, and Rinchino and Milovanov could see that he was not satisfied, that something was troubling him.

Walter Vatutin was a hardheaded, pragmatic planner. In his late forties, he was built like a barroom bouncer, with piercing eyes that looked as if they had seen it all—and they had, lots and lots of misery, suffering, and death. Like Major Rinchino and Colonel Milovanov, he wore the blue uniform of the KGB's Political Security Service, for it was the KGB that operated Wrangel Island and directed the 350 Red Army soldiers stationed there. However, KGB *Sluzhba*[1] guards ran the prison and were stationed in the medical laboratories.

General Vatutin walked over to the side of the room whose wall was covered with an enormous map of Wrangel Island. Exchanging glances, Rinchino and Milovanov got up and followed, taking positions on either side of him. They too stared at the colored map of the island.

Everything was there, each sensor placed four miles offshore, each elevation of land, each tiny place where any enemy could possibly come ashore. To the northwest were the Mamontovvye Gory. In the center of the map, drawn to scale, was the airfield, the runways so long that jumbo cargo jets could land and take off with ease.

The south end of the island contained the various buildings of the military installation. There in blue were the barracks, the kitchen, the mess, the storage areas, and the hospital for personnel. East of the barracks were the officers' quarters, the radio station, and the administration building.

---

[1] A Russian acronym for the Political Security Service. It means "The Service."

South of the officers' quarters was the stress evaluation center and the two large laboratories where various kinds of testing were carried out, day and night, in search for new methods by which a human being's memory and system of ethics could be erased and the mind reshaped and reconditioned to new thoughts and new morals acceptable to the Soviet Union.

To the west were the prison, the garage, the generating station, and the monitoring building.

Major Rinchino and Colonel Milovanov pretended patience while waiting impatiently for General Vatutin to speak. He finally did, a few minutes later.

"I want extra guards posted at the prison and the research centers," he said, turning from the map. "I also want extra men stationed at vital points around the harbor. I want it done immediately."

"May I ask why, sir?" inquired Colonel Milovanov politely.

"I don't like that American submarine out there," Vatutin said. "It's been there for almost a week. Now I ask you: suppose that submarine is a decoy? Suppose there's another sub in the area and that vessel put men ashore? Is that not possible?"

"*Nyet*, it is not!" responded Colonel Milovanov quickly. "A single swimmer could not come ashore without being detected. Our monitoring station knows instantly the difference between the sounds made by fish and whales and human swimmers. *Nyet*, General. It is impossible for any enemy to come ashore."

Major Konstantin Rinchino chuckled. "I wouldn't worry too much about the Americans, sir. Their fighting forces are sick with lack of discipline and hard training."

"Don't underestimate the Americans," snapped Vatutin. "they have an amazing vitality and know-how. That is exactly why I am concerned about that sub out there. . . ."

# Chapter Four

A womb! An all-compressing dark world, a world of watery life. Any time the Death Merchant was underneath the surface of an ocean, he had the feeling that he was in the matrix of all creation. He felt that way now as the Trass-III made its way through the water toward Rodgers Harbor; and he recalled the words of old Joe Black Rock, a Papago medicine man who lived on the Papago Indian Reservation in southern Arizona—*It is Mind or Consciousness that creates all that can be felt and observed. Man himself is a necessary expression of God, and the Universe could not exist without man.* Another time when Camellion had visited Black Rock, the old Indian had said, *The Universe is vast beyond human conception. It contains many, many worlds, and over each there is a ruler delegated by the Supreme One. Creation has been going on forever and will continue forever. There is work for all who are advancing to do. . . .*

Camellion chuckled softly to himself. *Work for all to do? Well, surely I was cut out to do something better than this! Great Spirit of the Universe, you have goofed! You should reprogram your computer!*

Steering the SDV to the harbor was not a problem. One merely had to have the right fix, then steer in by compass. Made of reinforced fiberglass, the Trass-III was 23 feet long and 3 feet 5 inches at the beam. Completely open, the little vessel contained three watertight chambers: the forward sphere, which was a permanent buoyancy tank, the battery case in the center, and the motor case in the stern. Power to drive the single screw, or propeller, was supplied by a 15.8 HP electric motor, the source being six thirty-cell, 82-volt lead-acid batteries. But because this Trass had to make such a long trip, it carried twelve batteries, six of which were extra.

Operation of the craft was similar to that of an airplane:

movement forward on the control wheel would dive the SDV. Movement to the rear would raise it. Turn the wheel to the right and the Trass would move to the right; to the left, and the vehicle would move to the left. The motor switch had five positions: two speeds forward, two speeds reverse, and neutral. However, one could not switch from forward to reverse or vice-versa until the screw stopped turning; otherwise, there was the danger of burning out a fuse strip in the switch. Other than the motor, the trim tank was the most important feature on the vehicle.

In the cockpit, the two left-hand levers operated the trim tank. A half-forward movement of the inboard lever opened the bottom flood valve; full forward movement also opened the high-pressure airline into the tank, thus expelling water out the bottom flood valve and causing the SDV to ascend. Forward movement of the outboard lever opened the trim tank vent valve; this allowed water to come into the tank and cause the SDV to descend.

Camellion looked at the dials, glowing a soft green, on the control panel. The depth gauge read 20 fathoms. *Not bad. A hundred and twenty feet is just about right since we're only a mile from the shore.* He glanced at the heading figures he had written on the underwater scrawl-board, then at the compass. Right on course. The speed needle rested solidly on 40-K, tht highest figure on the dial. Camellion knew the Trass was going faster than 40 knots since it did not have a full complement of four on board. The voltmeter showed 58 volts and 41 amps; the mileage clock, 34 nautical miles.

From the rear of Camellion's helmet to the back of Woo's was the plugged-in communications cord. Woo sat in back of the Death Merchant, and now his voice floated to Camellion's ears through the tiny speakers on either side of the helmet.

"How close are we to the center of the harbor," Camellion replied. "We're going to a point a mile north of the harbor. We'll surface a few miles out and raise the portable periscope for a lookover before we head toward shore. How is everything back there?"

"I've an itch on my back I can't scratch," Woo said, "and I think I've got a slight toothache, but it's nothing to worry about."

"Are you sure?"

"Positive."

Camellion steered slightly to the left, to the southeast. Several times he and Woo had heard the racket of screws overhead on the surface, and knew that patrol boats were in the area.

Smiling within the blackness of his helmet, Camellion thought of how surprised the three Chinese-Americans had been when, back in the cave, he had taken two very special weapons from the plastic watertight cylinder. One handgun had been a Webber-4B dart pistol, a nasty device that had been invented by Company research specialists. Resembling a broomhandle Mauser, the W-4B contained twenty-six steel darts, each one the size of an average sewing needle. But the needles weren't used for sewing. Each hollow needle contained a modicum of poison from *Pelamis platuri*, the very deadly Pacific Ocean sea snakes whose poison is ten times more venomous than the venom of the king cobra. The W-4B could drive a needle-dart into a target's body with the force of a .22 slug. Once the target was as much as scratched by the needle-dart, he had only four seconds of life left, for the poison had been refined and made more deadly and swift-acting by traces of saxitoxin from the sex organs of the puffer, or globe fish.

The second weapon was a Lee E. Jurras Model 200/International .357 Auto Mag, to which had been attached a noise suppressor, an M8-7X Leupold scope, and a stainless steel shoulder stock. In the butt was a special twenty-round magazine.

"Hell, Camellion, you must think we're up against supermen?" Ralph Hushan had commented.

"No, not supermen," Camellion had growled. "Only super-liars, super-hypocrites, and super-trash. The only secure peace we'll ever have with the Soviet Union is a Carthaginian peace."[1]

Camellion wished he could have told the three men the truth about Wrangel Island. But they didn't have the clearance for a need-to-know, or he could have told them a story so bizarre that it defied belief—but not preposterous

---

[1] Ancient Carthage was a constant source of trouble for Rome. The Romans finally defeated the Carthaginians in the battle of Zama, 146 B.C. The city was utterly destroyed and every Carthaginian killed.

to the Death Merchant, who knew that the Russians were capable of anything.

On Wrangel Island, the Soviets were doing many things. The KGB had a brainwashing laboratory in which experiments in mind-murdering were being conducted constantly. Connected to this lab was a vast torture complex, laughingly referred to by the Russians as "The Palace of Laughter." In this hideous place, prisoners were tortured in various ways. There were tiny cubicles, smaller than telephone booths, where prisoners were locked up with their hands and feet tied. There was the "submarine," in which a man or a woman, bound hand and foot, was lowered into a drum of urine, sewage water, and petroleum, thereby provoking temporary asphyxiation. There was the "pigeonhole," where the victim was given a series of electric shocks. Programmed beating in one part of the body to cause insanity was another method, the constant beating of the feet, groin, armpits, head, etc. There were sexual outrages committed against women subjects, including rape and the use of animals specially trained for sexual assault. Prisoners were hung in chains and their bodies slowly turned so that electric shocks or blowtorch flames could be applied to mouth or genitals or any other part of the body. Special instruments were used to break bones—all this as part of studies in "stress evaluation." Acid was used to burn the eyes, the feet, the testicles, the vaginas, and the breasts. The list of tortures was almost endless—cold-blooded extraction of teeth, very, very slowly; the drilling of teeth to expose the nerves; the pulling of nails from toes and fingers.

Prisoners were seldom interrogated since the purpose of the tests was to evaluate limits of resistance to different methods of torture, to experiments designed to drive detainees insane through administration of drugs, and to prolonged periods of isolation. Prisoners would hear nothing from their KGB captors other than orders for torture. Many subjects were kept in underground cells that were completely soundproof. Leather hoods were placed over their heads and stuck to their faces with chemical adhesives. In these special cells, the KGB sadists carried out mock questioning over a closed-circuit radio system, with the helpless victims stark naked and tied to their bunks while electric shocks were applied.

There was a second medical lab in which Russian scientists carried out other experiments on prisoners, such things as endurance thresholds of the human organism, how the body responds to an insufficient supply of oxygen . . . to motion . . . to weightlessness.

None of this was speculation or rumor. Camellion wished it had been. There was an eyewitness—Avraham Shifrin, an internationally recognized authority on Russian prisons and a survivor of ten years hard labor, had been an inmate of the infamous complex on Wrangel Island. In sworn testimony before the U.S. Senate Internal Security Subcomimittee investigating Soviet labor camps, Shifrin exposed the carefully concealed prison island to Congress in 1973.[2] Not only had Shifrin been a prisoner on Wrangel Island, but he had talked to another eyewitness who had been on Wrangel.

Explained Shifrin: "In Israel I met with one man in 1971 and he explained to me, this man, that he was also in Wrangel Island in 1962, and he has seen the prison that holds almost two thousand men and some women who were prisoners of war, and this man, he said to me, that the KGB has an atomic reactor and that they make experiments on live prisoners with radiation.

"In another large place, some kind of laboratory, they have many doctors who experiment with live people under water. And it is a big secret, and this man I met and talked to in Israel, he was there in the groups of prisoners and he gave the prisoners food."

Another account of the human experimentation going on at Wrangel Island was given to the stunned senators by an Israeli known only as "Koslov." His true identity had been carefully guarded to protect his close relatives still living in the U.S.S.R.

Koslov had been in a position to have access to prison records, and he was able to name some of the high-ranking POWs on Wrangel. An Italian committee, interested in tracing missing Italian POWs believed still held in the Soviet Union, had been able to identify some of the names Koslov found in the prison records.

Testified Koslov: "At the prison I made the acquaintance of many Germans and Italians and other nationalities, who had long been declared dead, but who are actually living on Wrangel."

[2] This is fact, not fiction. The Washington *Spotlight* reported on Wrangel Island in its Feb. 20, 1978 issue.

The U.S. Defense Mapping Agency did prepare an accurate map of Wrangel Island from satellite photos (Series 1505-NR 1, 2-1).

The Central Intelligence Agency had decided to do something about Koslov and Shifrin's testimony, but the venture required years of meticulous planning and information gathering—especially so since the information had to be kept secret.

More and better satellite maps of Wrangel were made, in preparation for the time when a small but highly trained American force would invade the island, kill every Russian in sight, and, if possible, learn the island's secrets.

*That time is now!* The Death Merchant looked at the mileage clock. *Forty miles. Three miles to the center of Rodgers Harbor.*

The Death Merchant turned the Trass to the right and said to Dionysius Woo. "I'm going to take her out several miles; then we'll surface and have a look at the pigpens."

Woo's laugh was light and cheerful, but low. "I know people who would call you a racist."

"Let 'em get in line with the liberals who would call me a warmonger, and the others who have conned themselves into thinking that we can live in peace with international gangsters."

The Death Merchant's hands were steady on the wheel. He kept his eyes on the mileage clock, watching the feet flow into yards and the yards pile up. Six minutes later he shut off the electric engine. They had come a distance of 3.218 kilometers, an even two miles.

"Hang on, I'm going to blow the surfacing air chamber," he said, moving his line of vision to the depth gauge. "We'll go up until we're about ten feet from the surface, then run up the scope."

"Be damned careful," warned Woo, a nervous quality to his voice. "You said yourself that if this tub leaves the water it will go off with a big bang."

"But only if it's completely out of water. Not to worry, old buddy. I'm not going to let our bodies be scattered all over these pig-farmer waters."

"The hell with that noise," retorted Woo. "I don't want parts of my carcass scattered over anybody's waters. I want to live to be ninety-five, then get knocked off by a jealous husband; then they'll cremate me and scatter my ashes over a tub of beer. Come to think of it, where is the explosive stuff and the F-Unit?"

Camellion put his hand on the lever that would blow the water from the main tank; he hesitated, thinking things over as he said, "The Unit's in the nose. Six flat packs of RDX are between the center tank and the inside bottom of the hull."

He heard Woo's quick inhalation of surprise. "Screw a cross-eyed goony bird! We're sitting on six pounds of cyclonite! That's one Excedrin headache Number Twenty-Two! With the five M-mines we're carrying, that thirty pounds of high stuff we have."

"Thirty-six pounds," corrected Camellion. "Each pack of RDX is a two-pound pancake. But listen! I've changed my mind about surfacing this baby. I can go up there in a lot shorter time."

"I was going to suggest that you do just that." Woo sounded relieved. "I'll take over the controls when you get out. But I don't think she'll rise more than five feet with your weight gone. I'm ready."

"I will be in a moment." Camellion removed his hand from the air-lever, unfastened the rubber seat belt, and carefully eased himself from the seat. When his body was free from the open confines of the SDV, he pushed out with his feet and moved upward through the dark water. Holding the depth gauge, fastened to his left wrist close to his face, and counting every meter, he stopped every ten feet to allow for proper decompression, to make sure that the air within his body did not come out of solution within the tissues and joints, and form bubbles.

After ten minutes his body broke the surface, giving him the feeling that he had popped up through the opening of a fishbowl. He didn't have any trouble staying afloat. His hermetically sealed dry suit was full of air. The suit had also been literaly tailored to fit his height and weight and the thick snowsuit which he wore underneath it. There was a distinct disadvantage to wearing the dry suit over the snowsuit: the very bulk made movement on land cumbersome and greatly reduced speed.

He couldn't see clearly because of the water running down the outside of his faceplate. He unloosened the main set screw, raised the plate, and looked around. No moon. All around him was total blackness. There wasn't even skyshine since thick clouds formed a solid ceiling. The air was cold and smelled clean, with just a faint trace of rubber and perspiration.

To the southeast there were numerous pinpoints of light poking holes in the velvet night. Radiating outward from these lights, toward the west, sweeping shafts of brightness moved back and forth, from side to side, then leaping ahead or drawing back—searchlights from the wharves at Rodgers Harbor. There were two series of lights toward the west, each red and green group far removed from each other. These lights came from the L7 patrol boats, crafts that resembled an American PT boat of WW II days, only larger and not quite as fast.

Camellion could not be sure; yet, judging from the angle of the lights from Rodgers Harbor and the Russian base to the east of the harbor, he calculated that by going east, the Trass would take him and Woo to a point that was slightly less than a mile north of the harbor.

After pulling down the faceplate of his helmet and fastening the set screw, Camellion went back under water and swam to the swimmer delivery vehicle. He eased himself into the seat behind Woo, pulled in the floating communications wire, and plugged it into the rear of Woo's helmet.

"Steer us straight east," he said, "and keep an eye on the mileage dial. I don't want you to go more than half a kilometer."

Woo switched on the electric motor and once more there was a soft humming sound and the louder swishing as the small propeller of the craft churned the water. "I'm wondering how you're going to get out of your dry suit," Woo said, turning the wheel. "It seems to me there should be a better way than taking it off on shore."

"There isn't," Camellion said, "not without my taking a bath in the process. In these icy waters, I don't think that would be very advisable."

Woo guided the SDV in a large semicircle and headed the craft straight east by the compass.

"What's our present depth?" Camellion inquired.

"Twenty-two fathoms."

"When we're at the half-mile mark, I want us to be on the bottom. Better glide her in."

30

"Affirmative." Woo pushed in on the outboard lever, but only very slightly, so that the trim tank would flood very slowly. The Trass moved forward at a downward angle, but the vehicle never reached the designated 2,640 feet. The rounded hull of the SDV struck the bottom at 1,850 feet, Woo calling out the mark in disgust.

"Don't let your hair turn gray over it," said Camellion. "We're close enough." Leaning over to the right, he began unfastening the metal straps securing a plastic waterproof container that was 26 inches long and 13½ inches in diameter. "What's our depth?"

"We're at two hundred and ten feet," Woo answered, sounding as if he were beginning to regret the whole businss. "I hope the F-Unit doesn't go on the bum. We're totally defenseless against Scuba men."

"We're safe enough," Camellion reassured him. He released the last strap holding the cylinder, then prevented the cylinder from floating to the surface by slipping the end of the loop line over his left wrist. "The Russians would have to detect us by sonar to know we're here. They can't do that because of the F-Unit. As far as they're concerned their waters are free of foreign intruders. You know what to do?"

"I sit here at the bottom like a bump on a log for two hours," Woo said heavily. "If you're not back in two hours, I consider you scratched. I return to our original point of departure, pick up Ralph and Tom, and the three of us go back to the *Tirante*."

Camellion looked at the diver's watch attached to his wrist above the compass. "Time check."

"Twenty-one hundred hours."

"We're together on it; I'm going to disconnect now. Any questions?"

"Luck. . . ."

Camellion pulled the communications wire from the back of Woo's helmet, then disconnected the other end from the rear of his own headpiece. He made the wire into a loop and clipped it to a ring on the left inner side of the vehicle—
*Time to do it!* He unfastened the seatbelt, pushed himself upward, and began to swim east, pulling the cylinder behind him.

Ahead lay success or failure.

Life or death. . . .

31

# Chapter Five

To hasten his journey and so that he would not have to pause periodically for proper decompression, Camellion pulled himself through the water at a slight upward angle, constantly checking his depth gauge to make sure he did not move toward the surface at too steep a pitch

He was only 150 feet from the shore. Ahead he could hear the surf breaking over the sand and rocks, although he could tell from the sound that the waves were not large. There was no roar of water smashing itself against rocks, and he knew that the breakers would not offer any resistance.

He swam to shallow water, stood up, and waded ashore, the surf scattering itself around his legs. The sand and gravel, constantly being washed by water, was bare and as clean as a virgin's heart. Farther back, past the high tide mark, the shore was covered with patches of snow, much of the ground weirdly shaped with small rises and depressions, as well as very tiny pinnacles, where the snow had partially melted under the daytime sun and then had refrozen at night. In this area the rocks were tumbled about like carelessly tossed dice but much larger, some together in clumps, others in pairs or protruding singly from the ground. All of it some of the most useless and inhospitable real estate in the world. In the old days, even seal hunters, who would stop at nothing to slaughter a seal, avoided Wrangel Island. Until 1910, the island had remained isolated from human beings; then 107 Americans had settled on the desolate island; twenty-seven Americans were on the island when, in 1924, a Soviet gunboat had landed. The Americans had simply vanished—so the Russian government claimed.

Carrying the cylinder over one shoulder, Camellion moved across the beach, every now and then half-closing his eyes, then opening them quickly in order to adjust his vision to the darkness. Presently he found a place that was ideal. A hundred and fifty feet east of the beach were masses of larger rocks, some almost five feet high.

Once he had moved into the tallest group, he unfastened one front section of his deep-dive suit, reached inside the snowsuit underneath, and turned on the thermal batteries that would heat the strips of Seltex-foil. There would be a sudden loss of heat when he removed the D-D swimsuit; a five minute warming of the snowsuit would compensate for this loss in a temperature that was 17 degrees above zero.

First he opened one end of the watertight cylinder and took out a folded bag of thin but very tough plastic. He then proceeded to take off the swimsuit, starting with the two gas tanks and the helmet and finishing with the rubberized-citrex suit which had been designed around the central theme of underwater physiology—metabolism, respiration, circulation, blood, heart, and lungs.

The primary advantages of the closed-breathing system were that it was quiet, could be utilized on very long and deep swims, could not be detected by gas bubbles rising to the surface, was economical of gas, and was comfortable to wear. However, the suit system did have some disadvantages, the main one of which was depth limitation. Four hundred and fifty feet was the absolute maximum. Oxygen becomes extremely toxic at two atmospheres. Should any part of the breathing regulator—0-ring, diaphragm cap, spring button, etc.—become defective while the diver was under water, he would face the deadly problem of CO build-up.[1]

Camellion put the D-D suit and air tanks into the bag, sealed the end by folding the flap and then zipping it shut. He pulled a carryall bag from the cylinder, slipped it over his shoulder, and took out the special movie camera and a Model-1000 Starlight Viewer and placed them in the bag. The Webber-4B dart pistol and Auto Mag were next. He put the W-4B dart gun in the right flap pocket of the snowsuit and slung the AMP over his shoulder by its leather sling

---

[1] Nitrogen narcosis: the exact mechanism for the cause is unknown. Indications are that excessive partial pressure of nitrogen produces an anesthetic or intoxicating effect, especially when combined with any $CO_2$ buildup.

strap attached from underneath the barrel to the metal stock. Two thermite grenades and two fragmentation grenades went into the left flap pocket. The last item he removed from the container was a belted ammo pouch containing ten spare magazines for the Auto Mag. He put the belt around his waist, belted it, and screwed the large, round cap onto the end of the cylinder, which he placed next to the bagged D-D suit. He next took a dozen large rocks and placed them, in no certain pattern, around the bag and the cylinder, after which he scooped up snow with his gloved hands and scattered it over the mound.

Footprints were his most vital problem. He didn't have to worry about them on the beach. They were already gone, washed away by the surf. Beyond the high-water mark was another matter. In some places he had left tracks in the snow. These would remain until more snow fell or until the snow melted. He had been fortunate in that he had been able to step on bare rocks for the last sixty feet. So what? Should the Ruskies suspect that he was in the general area, an intensive search would quickly reveal where he had stashed his vital gear, his lifeline from the shore to Trass-III. Should anything happen to the deep-dive suit—*I'll be trapped in the center of a nightmare. The only way out will be either suicide or capture by the pig-farmers. The first is preferable to the second.*

With a sigh of boredom, Camellion took the Starlight Viewer from the carryall bag and adjusted the brightness control to maximum. The device, utilizing a 25mm three-stage intensifier and a high-speed objective lens, intensified the received light 35,000 to 50,000 times and had equivalent background input of 2 X 10-lumen/cm$^2$, that is, about 1/1000 times the mean starlight level 3 X 10-lumen/cm$^2$.

He held the device to his face and looked through the screen. Instant miracle! Worked by the magic of the infrared light source! The entire area now appeared as though the time of day were early twilight. There were very low hills, many thick with dwarf willow, and stretches of rough plains covered with thick tundra grass. And among the rocks were purple saxifrage, the first flowers to bloom in the arctic spring, and a sprinkling of chamomile, the daisy of the north.

Camellion could see that many of the rocks—where the snow had melted—were covered with lichens shining vivid, nearly fluorescent green. Although tiny, these lichens were extremely old.[2] But not all the lichens were small. Large, black foliose lichens encrusted many of the tundra boulders with their splayed and leathery growth. These were the rock-tripe lichens,[3] bloated visibly with water.

Another bit of concern was polar bears. These high-rumped, low-shouldered animals are massive, immensely powerful, and very dangerous. They shuffle across the ice in a slow, smooth, rolling gait, testing the breeze with their large black noses. Their eyesight is poor; their hearing average; but their sense of smell is incredibly acute. Polar bears live in a world of smells, with each slight shift of the breeze bringing them new messages.

*And they are utterly fearless,* Camellion thought. *If one of them sees me, he will come to investigate. How am I supposed to know if he's hungry?*

With the Auto Mag in a position by which he could use it very quickly, the Death Merchant moved out from the rocks, doing his best to step on rocks or ground that were not covered with snow. Every now and then he paused to peer through the Starlight Viewer, looking not only for a Russian patrol but for that part of the terrain that would be high enough to enable him to photograph the Soviet base 3 miles northeast of Rodgers Harbor.

Each time, all he saw was desolation—chopped up hills and uneven stretches of land partially covered with rocks and snow.

Until he saw the polar bear! A few hundred yards to his east, the big, shaggy animal had not seen him, but Camellion could tell, from the way the bear was acting, that it

2 Many of these lichens, only a few inches in diameter, are thousands of years old. They are, perhaps, the oldest things on earth—and extremely hardy. The French scientist Becquerel once subjected the lichen xanthoria parietina to temperatures that were close to absolute zero—459.6 F. Some of these lichens had been under vacuum for eight years and had been for two weeks in liquid air. But they survived; they lived.

3 "Tripe de roche" the voyagers used to call them. They were the food of starving explorers. The nutritive substance in lichens is lichenin, a carbohydrate akin to starch. However, lichens taste terrible and contain acids that tear apart the human digestive system.

had caught his scent and was letting his keen nose lead him to the source of that scent.

*Damn!* Camellion pulled the Auto Mag from his shoulder and again looked at the polar bear through the Starlight Viewer. The animal had put on speed and was coming in his direction. At 50 yards, the animal began to run. No doubt about it. The bear had located him.

Camellion raised the Auto Mag, put the end of the metal stock against his shoulder, and, holding the Starlight Viewer a few inches to the rear of the AMP, looked through both the Viewer and the Leupold scope and sighted in on the bear that now was coming at him like a juggernaut. Camellion pulled the trigger when the animal was 18 to 20 yards away. The noise suppressor coughed slightly. The bear roared and went down, its left shoulder broken. Camellion aimed again and pulled the trigger twice. The first bullet, missing the mark, hit the animal in its right side. The second projectile bored into the right side of its head and silenced the bear forever.

*Damn! Damn! Damn!* A dead bear was all he needed! *I might as well stick out a sign that reads, HEY GUYS! I'M HERE!* Should a Russian patrol stumble across the dead animal, the enemy would know there was a *rovoiny v likoi* loose on Wrangel Island.

The Death Merchant increased his efforts, his feet searching for rocks and ground not covered by snow. At times he was successful. Other times he found it impossible not to leave two lines of footprints. At one place, the ground was almost level and entirely covered with snow that had not had a chance to melt because of shade provided by tall scotch pines on a hillside, a long mound that, sloping on each end, reminded Camellion of a loaf of Italian bread. For a quarter of a mile he was forced to leave tracks.

He came to a stream that meandered crookedly along, its source being a distant range of hills. Some parts of the stream were ice covered and Camellion could hear water underneath the ice as he stone-stepped across the twisting ribbon of water.

He paused and scouted the area through the Starlight Viewer. The only sign of life he saw was an arctic hare, fifty feet to his right. As big as a Western U.S. jackrabbit, the hare was all white, with only the tips of the ears ink black. This hare and all its fellows liked the boulder fields;

there, they could find shelter from the icy wind, and add to their meager fare by eating moss and lichens.

The Death Merchant was about to continue when he heard the faint sound, the distinct grinding noise of a motorized patrol sled.

*It's a few miles to the northeast and seems to be moving northwest. That's one of the troubles with fighting pig-farmers. You kill one and the rest are like mosquitoes! A million show up to take its place.*

Camellion moved on. At length, with the aid of the Starlight Viewer, he found a hill that was ideal for his purpose, a tall boulder-covered hill whose peak was devoid of trees. He hurried up the hillside, got down between two large granites, and, with the Viewer, searched the southeast, the south, and the southwest.

The Soviet base lay two miles to the south and the southeast. And it was big, more than a mile square. The prison was obvious. It was an enormous four-story building surrounded by two chain-linked fences, each topped with barbed wire strung out concertina style, a 30-foot space between the inside of the two fences. To the right was a much smaller building, one side of which had huge conduits leading out of it, the wires in the closed channels stretching out to crossarms of steel electric poles.

*The generator station. We'll blow it the same time we destroy the communications building and the sensor-watch station.*

To the right was another large building, several floors high and 200 feet long. Pipes led from its south side, moved along the ground, and continued on—presumably to Rodgers Harbor. It was one of the laboratories, like the building next to it. *That other building—yeah, there's the flag. It's the administration building. Uh huh. There's the barracks.*

He sized up each building through the viewer, including the radio station with its red lights flashing on and off on the triangular, three-girder tower.

Camellion took the movie camera from the carryall bag and let the special camera do the job for which it had been designed. The camera had a macro power-zoom 9.5x, f/2.3 lens which gave complete flexibility for all filming conditions. The electric eye was CdS; 22fps filming speeds; dichroic reflex housing; 1.3 inches to infinity. In front of the lens was the infrared adapter.

For two and a half minutes Camellion operated the camera, photographing everything ahead of him, at all angles, and to his left and his right. And when he was finished, he had shot more than 200 feet of 8mm film.

The job was done. He returned the camera to the bag, zipped the cover of the carryall, and moved down the hillside. Now he had only two goals: back to where he had hidden the deep-dive suit and then the SDV.

He estimated that he had covered half the distance to the suit when again he heard the motorized snow-sled, but this time its engine wasn't fading in the distance. The roaring—now in front of him—was becoming louder. The Russian patrol was coming at him.

It had been a bad day all week for Camellion. He now had the feeling that he was about to be in for trouble of the worst kind. The Russians were in front of him. Could they have discovered any of his footprints? Worse—*Could they have found my swimsuit? Will they go on by?* Camellion sighed deeply. *Does a mermaid wear pantyhose?*

Camellion moved to the left, over ground where the snow lay in patches, his objective a good-sized area of boulders of various sizes. All of them were large enough to hide a man.

By this time the sound of the engine on the sled was almost a roar. Then he saw the vehicle, which appeared to be a cross between an airboat and a long toboggan with wheels. The powerful gasoline engine was mounted in the rear. It turned a 5-foot-long propeller encased in a round, wire cage to the rear of the motor. This prop could move the fully loaded—fifteen men—sled 30 mph on its big runners. The sled was also equipped with double dig-in tracks, like a conventional snowmobile, the same engine furnishing the power. On uneven ground partially covered with snow, the four wheels with the wide tires were geared into position and th prop throttled back one-fourth.

Through the Viewer, Camellion saw the sled arrive, the twin beams of its two front lights poking two bright yellow tunnels in the darkness, 100 feet in front of him. The driver stopped the engine and gently applied the brakes to the four wheels. The vehicle came to a stop.

Dressed in high snow boots and gray parka and carrying AK-47 assault rifles, the Russians piled off the sled and an officer barked orders, his words carrying faintly to the Death

Merchant, *"Zhizn otchet po y delu sudebnyi ovaya voina, venza, venza!"*

The Death Merchant knew he was in for it, for the Russian officer had told his men to try to pick up the trail of footprints and to hurry up and get with it.

The Russians spread out and, using flashlights, began searching the ground. Camellion unzipped the carryall bag and took out the Webber-4B dart gun. He thumbed off the safety of the Auto Mag and did the only thing he could do: he waited, very much aware that he wouldn't be able to remain passive for more than a few minutes. All too soon the Russian soldiers would find his first set of footprints. Ten to fifteen feet later, they would find the second set. The hell with the second set. It was the first set that counted. Every footprint was like an arrow. Every footprint pointed west, pointed toward the rocks where he was hiding. The only thing in his favor—as tiny as it was—was that the ground was frozen. The Russians had no way of knowing when the prints had been made in the snow. Two hours ago? An hour? Or fifteen minutes? The biggest black mark of disadvantage was that an AK-47, on full automatic, had a cyclic rate of six hundred rounds per minute.

*If as many as ten of those pig-farmers get wind of my location and start firing, all I'll have time for is one last breath!*

To entangle the slim threat dangling him between life and death, between success and failure, was the darkness. Without the help of the Starlight Viewer, he couldn't see the pig-farmers rooting around in front of him. All he could see were the shafts of yellow lights from their flashlights, the bright beams crossing back and forth on the ground.

Co-consciously, while watching the Russians through the Starlight Viewer, Camellion took out a thermite grenade and a demolition grenade and placed them on the ground next to him.

The moment arrived. The Russians discovered his first set of footprints. As several soldiers bent down and examined the prints with their flashlights, a third one called back to the two officers at the sled, *"Za bitva'lu terialov tu zhizn po mstiteli odnyie!"*

The Death Merchant's face remained without emotion. The Russian soldier had told the two officers that they had found footprints that led west.

39

One officer pulled up the antenna of a walkie-talkie and began to talk into the mouthpiece. *Damn him! He's reporting to the main base!*

The second officer yelled back, *"Uvshem v otechvennoi tsifrakh lyudi, zenovyoli po yatuie trevoge. Venza!"* ("Follow them but be very careful. Hurry!")

The Death Merchant took one last look through the Starlight Viewer. Other than the two pieces of trash standing by the sled, the other Russians were directly ahead of Camellion, six of them waiting and watching, the remaining seven advancing, the beams of their flashlights raking the snow ahead of them.

Camellion mentally measured the distance, then put down the Starlight Viewer and picked up the thermite grenade, which was actually a TH3 bomb since it was a mixture of thermite—powdered aluminum and powdered iron oxide—barium nitrate and sulfur. This was thermate.

*By the time I throw it and it lands, the pack of pigs should be twenty feet closer. Here we go!*

He pulled the pin of the canister, stood up, and threw the firebomb. He then dropped down behind the boulder, picked up the demolition grenade, pulled the pin, held down on the safety lever, and waited.

The canister fell a few feet short of the first group of advancing Russians and burst with a loud *whooshhhhhhh*. One moment there was darkness, the next, an intense burst of white light, a giant flower of pure flame that opened instantly, and a lot of high shrieks and screaming as burning thermate, turned into white-hot molten iron, splashed over the seven Russians. Burning at a temperature of 4,000° F., it required only a particle to burn through clothing, skin, and bone.

To the loud music of shrieks of agony, the Death Merchant reared up and threw the grenade as hard as he could, during that flash of a few seconds seeing the destruction he had caused. Three of the pig-farmers, their parkas and uniforms blazing, were running back and forth like torches with burning legs. The other four were rolling on the ground, kicking and screaming hideously at the top of their lungs, legs kicking, arms flailing the frozen earth that was rapidly thawing from the intense heat.

The other Red Army soldiers were like blocks of limestone, the horror of what was happening having stunned them into a conscious intellectual lethargy. By the time they snapped into action, the demolition grenade exploded. There was a flash of flame, a big roar, and some screams.

Shrapnel killed outright one of the group that had stood back. Two others were peppered with steel to the extent that they fell to the ground, blood streaming down their faces.

The smoke of burnt TNT had not yet begun to dissipate into nothingness when Camellion reared up, leaned over a boulder to brace his elbow, and began to fire the silenced Auto Mag. His first three slugs took out the last three Russians of the group that had hung back, the impact of the .357 magnum projectiles doing far more than knocking them to the ground as though they had been knocked in the head with a fifty-pound sledgehammer. There had been a loud popping sound each time one of the men had been hit.

Camellion was using cartridges whose flat-nosed projectiles contained a recessed impact fuse; underneath the fuse was a small explosive charge—1.6 grains of PETN. When dropped or stepped on or thrown by hand, none of the cartridges would detonate. But when fired, the impact was sufficient to explode the tiny charge.[4] The three Red Army soldiers had hit the ground with half a pound of flesh torn from their bodies.

Lieutenant Gorlin Tiraspol and Captain Alexei Uritsk, the two Russian army officers by the motorized sled, knew what to do, but they had taken ten seconds too long to make up their minds. The soldiers who had been splashed with thermate were dead, their charred bones exposed to the wind. The stink was loathsome to the extreme, the fetid stench of burnt cloth and leather, flesh and metal; the popping of cartridges in ammo packs.

The other Russians were dead, except for the two whose faces had been ripped by the grenade and who lay moaning on the ground. There wasn't any way that Tiraspol and Uritsk could rescue them—and still remain alive.

"*Chort vozmi!*" cursed Captain Uritsk. "*Yu dnom s estuyu!*" He turned and ran for the sled six feet behind him. Lieutenant Tiraspol also rushed toward the vehicle.

Uritsk, a deep dread stabbing at his brain, was climbing

---

[4] To give the reader an example of the size of this kind of explosion, let us explain that an electric blasting cap consists of 13.5 grains of PETN.

into the driver's seat when a .357 AMP struck his right side and exploded, the *bang* tossing out pieces of parka, padding, uniform, pieces of flesh, and chips of rib bone. Dead, Uritsk fell off the seat to the left.

There was another firecracker bang from the center of Lieutenant Tiraspol's back—and another tiny cloud of cloth and flesh and bone. Tiraspol fell forward over the side of the center seat, as dead as any human being could possibly get.

Without any emotion, the Death Merchant observed the results of his handiwork. Death was never a thing of beauty, but only because human beings are so obsessed with mortality. Death is always neutral and without friends.

Camellion returned the Webber-4B dart gun to the carry-all bag. The range had been too great for him to use it. He zipped the bag, picked up the silenced Auto Mag, and ended the suffering of the last two pig-farmers alive by putting slugs into their bodies.

He looked at the motorized sled. There it was, all ready for his use. *If I took the sled I could get to the D-D suit in ten minutes. But the roar would advertise my position. One piggy boy reported my presence. The hotshots at the main base to the south know I'm here. Soon they'll be out in force. Damn it.*

Auto Mag in his right hand, Camellion moved out from behind the boulder toward the dead Ruskies, his way partially illuminated by the still burning thermate that was throwing out a nightmare of flickering, dancing shadows. *Yeah, yeah, yeah! Halloween in July!*

He moved to one of the Red rubes he had eliminated, unbuckled the man's ammo pouch, and pulled the belt from the corpse. He strapped the spare magazines around his own waist, and picked up the man's AK-47, as well as an AK-47 dropped by another dead Russian. The automatic rifles might come in handy. He put the two straps over one shoulder and began moving to the northwest, staying on a course that would keep him close to the chain of larger rocks. A hundred feet from the sled, he turned, raised the Auto Mag, and put an explosive .357 projectile into the gas tank mounted on top of the engine. With a loud roar the gasoline exploded. The entire shed jumped 4 feet off the ground, the force of the explosion sending parts of the blazing engine flying high into the air. The propeller and the wire enclosure fell to the ground and so did the corpses of Captain Uritsk and Lieutenant Triaspol. The sled burned with flames licking upward, fire that mingled with oily, black smoke, flames that made the surrounding area glow and flicker with a red-orange light.

*A good marker,* thought the Death Merchant. *Any other patrol will head straight here.*

He moved as rapidly as he could, stepping down on snow only when he was forced to. Despite his highly vulnerable situation, he found himself admiring the landscape—what he could see of it through the Starlight Viewer. The leesides of hills and mounds were buried by drifts, but where the snow had vanished, the ground was covered with a profusion of flowers. The tiny bells of arctic white heather moved back and forth in the wind. There was Lapland rhododendron; and the delicate, feathery blossoms of Labrador tea. And death! For the Arctic is totally without mercy. Like the Cosmic Lord of Death, the land beyond the Arctic circle is utterly ruthless.

The Death Merchant brought himself back to the Now. There was only the silent cold, the stiff breeze, the darkness, and the rough landscape. At one point, just before he moved between two low mounds, he turned and looked behind him. There was a flickering glow a mile away. The sled was still burning. He looked at his wristwatch and consulted the compass strapped above the Heuer Chronosplit. He judged that he was less than 80 meters from the rocks where he had stashed the deep-dive suit and the plastic cylinder.

There were several problems—the two motorized sleds he could hear in the distance. One was coming from the south —*No doubt from the main base.* The second sled was moving from the northeast and sounded as though it might be twice as far away as the first sled.

Camellion shifted mental gears. He was about 275 feet southwest of the rocks where his D-D suit was hidden. Once he reached the rocks and slipped into the diving suit, he could head west toward the beach with some slight measure of safety. Numerous boulders would be between him and the two Russian patrols, provided the sleds did not go straight to the one that was burning. They wouldn't. The patrol from the south wouldn't bother to stop to investigate the sled that was burning. They would want the man responsible; and since the patrols were in contact with each other by radio, the sled coming in from the northeast would probably link up with the patrol from the main base. Once the Russians started looking, it wouldn't take them long to find his tracks.

With the aid of the Starlight Viewer, he hurried toward his suit, hating the darkness. *Maybe I should have eaten ten dozen raw carrots last week. They wouldn't have given me more strength and I wouldn't be able to see any better in the dark.* He chuckled to himself. *But on a clear day I'd be able to see forever!* What made him feel uncomfortable was the idea that the Russians had the advantage. They could use flashlights. He couldn't.

Now the landscape was becoming familiar. He looked again through the Viewer and saw that he was 150 feet southwest of his D-D suit. Presently he found what he wanted: the proper sized rocks he could use for wedging one of the AK-47 automatic rifles. He placed the AK A-R between the two rocks with the muzzle pointing south, reached into one of the top pockets of his snowsuit, and took out a length of thin but very strong Limmix cord. With a small folding knife he cut off two lengths of cord and tied the AK to the rocks. He next tied one end of the main cord around the trigger of the weapon, then pushed the selector switch to a four-round burst and shoved the safety catch to FIRE. All the while he listened to the engines of the two sleds; with each second they became louder.

Carfully playing out the line, he moved toward the granite boulders hiding his swimsuit. There were those times when he was forced to leave deep footprints in the snow; at other times he was able to move on rocks coated only with ice or lichen.

*At last! In another fifteen minutes I can be in the water.*

Happy that for the last 50 feet he could move over rocks not covered by snow, he hurried toward the mass of 5-foot-high rocks, being very cautious as he played out the line. Soon he was inside the rocks and bending down. Working faster than a beaver tearing off birch bark, he scooped snow off the mound, lifted the plastic bag and the cylinder from the smaller rocks, opened the bag, and pulled out the rubberized-citrex swimsuit, the helmet and the air tanks.

He cut the Limmix line and tied the end that ran from the AK around a small rock. With even greater speed, he took off the other AK-47, the carryall bag, and the ammo-pouch belt he had taken from one of the dead ruskies. After taking the second thermate grenade and the second demolition grenade from the carryall bag and placing them on the ground next to the AK-47 and the Starlight Viewer, he stuffed the bag containing the W-4B dart gun and the movie camera into the underwater cylinder. The last item to go into the container was the Auto Mag. He braced the AMP against the bag, then screwed on tightly the large, round cap.

Camellion had struggled into the deep-dive suit and was zipping it up when the motorized sled from the south roared into the area and the driver switched off the engine. The sled had stopped, not because the Russians suspected that Camellion was in the rocks, but because of the harshness of the region. The rocks were too large for even the wide-track wheels of the sled.

The Death Merchant didn't screw on the helmet of the D-D suit. Concerned about the time factor—the sled from the northeast could not be more than half a mile away—Camellion picked up the Starlight Viewer and looked out at the Russian soldiers who had gotten out of the sled and were probing the area with hand-held glare-free quartz spotlights.

*Damned pig-farmers! "Renaissance men of the Atomic Era"—with Neanderthal minds!* Camellion ducked in the nick of time, a split second before a beam of bright white light stabbed over the boulder in front of him. Then a second and a third shaft of light knifed out over him.

Down on his knees, the Death Merchant placed the Starlight Viewer on the ground, picked up the AK-47, and looked around the side of the boulder. The ivans were being cautious. Three of them were still on the motorized sled—the driver, one man sitting in the middle seat, and a third goof in back. The third man was in front and slightly underneath the high-mounted engine, leaning over a Degtyarev light machine gun mounted on a central axis that rose up from the floor of the sled. The DLMg was pointed in Camellion's direction. Other Red Army morons were probing the area with spotlights, while next to them their comrades stood ready with AK-47s and 43-PPS submachine guns. All the Russians were advancing and slowing spreading out in a large semicircle. Very soon they would be spread out too far for him to neutralize with one long burst.

Camellion picked up the rock around which he had tied the end of the Limmix cord and once more looked around the side of the boulder. It was now or—*forget it!* He gave the line a steady second's pull and the AK-47, tied to the rocks 150 feet to the southwest, roared out a five-round burst.

The reaction of the Russians was typical and automatic. To a man they spun toward the southwest, including the soldier sitting behind the Degtyarev light machine gun. He swung the weapon toward the southwest at the same time that the Death Merchant reared up, used the quartz lights of the Russians for illumination, and cut loose with the AK-47. first scratching out the trooper behind the Degtyarev light machine gun, and the other two commie creeps in the sled.

The only thing dumber than an average Russian is two average Russians. But even if the soldiers had had the intellect of an Einstein, they still would not have been able to save themselves. Not even Richard Camellion could outrun a bullet. Neither could the Red Army soldiers. Before they had time to fully react, a storm of 7.62mm projectiles was chopping into them, the hail of spitzer-shaped slugs slamming them to the ground.

A few of the soldiers did make a brave effort to flop down and get their own weapons into action. One soldier was throwing himself to the ground when a 7.62mm projectile tore off his lower jaw and a second bullet ripped through his throat and buried itself in the stomach of the trooper next to him. The second Red private caught slugs in the chest as he tried to swing his submachine gun in Camellion's direction. Another slug zipped into his left eye, bored through his brain, and tore out through the back of his head.

The massacre ended as quickly as it had begun. Thirteen seconds of sporadic firing! Fifteen dead men! Camellion didn't know how many rounds he had left in the banana-shaped magazine of the AK, but he now found out—three projectiles which he put into the gas tank of the sled's engine.

*Woommmmmmm!* A bright flash of fire and parts of engine and sled went flying to the sky, the sound of the explosion losing itself in the roar of the other patrol's sled which was pulling into the region, although Camellion could not see the odd-looking vehicle. The driver parked it behind a hill, several hundred feet to the east.

Camellion pulled a full magazine from the AK's ammo bag, reloaded the automatic rifle, and slung it over his shoulder. He put on the helmet of the deep-dive suit, strapped on the air tanks, and secured the breathing connection. *Time to get the hell out!* He picked up the cylinder and the Star-light Viewer, then leaned down and placed the Viewer on the ground when he remembered the thermate canister and the grenade, which he picked up and put into the sea-pocket of the swimsuit. Again he picked up the Viewer, after which he stepped out from the rocks and began to head straight west, this time not caring if he left footprints in the snow. He was taking an enormous gamble, but the choice was not his to make. He had to play the game. It was the only one in town.

The ivans were several hundred feet to his east while he was much more than 175 feet from the beach. Seeing the burning sled, this new Russian patrol would creep in very slowly. Camellion hoped that by the time they added up the total column and came to a halfway intelligent conclusion, he would be in the water.

As fast as he could move in the bulky swimsuit, he headed for the beach, taking the shortest route and keeping the larger boulders between himself and the approaching Russians. Panting from exertion and sweating like an Israeli spy at a PLO meeting, he reached the beach, hurried over to one of the largest boulders, dropped the Starlight Viewer and the watertight cylinder, and pulled the demolition grenade and the thermite canister from the D-D suit's swim-pocket. He heard shouts to the east. The Russians were only a hundred feet away.

He pulled the pin and threw the grenade as hard as he could, aiming it at the voices he had heard. As quickly as he could, he pulled the tab from the thermate canister. He was throwing the canister when the grenade went off with a roar. The canister became a blinding white flash a few seconds later.

Camellion pulled down the faceplate of the helmet, tight-ened the set-screw, and opened the air valve. Hearing the gas hiss into the helmet, he tossed aside the AK-47, shoul-dered the watertight cylinder, and, with the Starlight Viewer in one hand, moved across the wet sands of the beach. Thirty feet in front of him were the waters of the *Vostocno Sibirs-koje More,* the East Siberian Sea, the waves breaking over the rocks and sand. Several more minutes and the Death Merchant was in water up to his knees, then his hips.

47

Behind him a voice shouted in Russian, *"Zemnoi, y dneui dorogoi bor'by po deidtvuyet!"*

"You'd better believe I'm in the water!" Camellion muttered in grim satisfaction. He was submerging himself when the Russians, some of whom had climbed low hills, began to fire.

*Zip! Zip! Zip!* Slugs started to dig tunnels in the water all around him. He felt the cylinder jerk slightly at the end of the line looped around his left wrist. The thought was hideous. If a bullet had pierced the plastic and water flowed into the cylinder and reached the camera, the film would be totally ruined. *Zip! Zip! Zip!* He could not be sure, but had a slug scraped the swimsuit over his right shoulder? Yet there wasn't any leakage. If a projectile had raked the material, it had not penetrated the inch-thick rubber. He dropped the Starlight Viewer and for a moment watched it as it zigzagged down in the darkness—*The Russians will never get their hands on it.* The device had been ruined by the water since it was not meant to be used below the surface of the sea.

The Death Merchant, now 20 feet down, was safe from the Russian soldiers. But the secret was out of the bag. The KGB, knowing that invaders were on Wrangel Island, would make every effort to find him. The KGB would think of the mountains, of the Mamontovvye Gory, and of how the foothills were riddled with networks of caves. The conclusion was inescapable: *The KGB can send troops by helicopter to the foothills before Woo and I can get back. The odds for our escaping to the* Tirante *are definitely against us.*

A half-mile to go! Camellion swam steadily toward the Trass SDV, not too certain of its location. Time to activate the Harmonica Box.

Built into the swimsuit at the waist, the H-Box was a miniature transmitter and amplifier whose twin was part of Dionysius Woo's swimsuit. Each box had a single button.

Camellion found the button underneath the rubber and began pressing it. With each press of the button a signal was sent out on an audio frequency of 440 Hz—a C note on a harmonica—and transmitted to the H-Box in Woo's suit. He in turn would return the signal. The louder the signal in the Death Merchant's helmet, the closer he would be to the SDV. In short, each H-Box acted as a homing device.

Seconds later, Camellion heard the return *beep, beep,*

*beep* coming through the built-in headphones of his helmet. He moved with confidence through the icy and black water, hoping that there weren't any patrol boats in the immediate vicinity, for each time Woo sent a signal, the Gf-Mechanism automatically clicked off.

Camellion swam steadily downward, pulling the cylinder behind him. From now on it would be more than instinct and experience that would keep him and the three Chinese-Americans alive.

*Fate will have to lend us a hand.* . . .

# Chapter Six

Upon reaching the Trass, the Death Merchant struggled into the seat behind Dionysius Woo, fastened the safety belt across his middle, and started pulling in the line attached to the plastic cylinder. Woo turned around in the front seat and pointed at the communication wire, motioning that he wanted to talk. Camellion nodded and continued to pull in the line, finally getting his hands on the cylinder which he strapped to the upper right side of the SDV's hull, taking extra pains to make sure the three metal straps were locked within the grooves of the rounded plastic. On one side of the cylinder he noticed a deep groove several inches long, like a wide cut. He ran his gloved finger over the eighth-of-an-inch-deep slash. Yes, a bullet had struck the container.

No longer concerned, now that the cylinder was secure, Camellion picked up the communications wire and plugged the end into the back of his helmet. Instantly, Woo's nervous voice floated through the headphones.

"How did it go?"

"Get us out of here and fast," Camellion said. He quickly explained what had happened, telling Woo how he had terminated thirty men of the two patrols and finishing with, "Right now it's a race against time. All we can do is get back, pick up Tom and Ralph, and head for the sub. Keep a sharp eye on your compass heading."

"Man, oh man, oh man," sighed Woo. "We have troubles." He turned on the craft's electric motor and, with it humming softly, he blew water from the main tank. The Trass began to rise. After it had risen some 25 feet from the bottom, Woo shut off the air, geared in the propeller, and turned the rudder, behind the prop, to port. He pushed in the throttle to maximum, and the SDV moved ahead through the water, picking up speed until the needle was at 40-K. Fortunately for Camellion and Woo, their electrolungs were working perfectly and the gas mixture of helium and oxygen flowed at an even rate.

The blue-black water was astonishingly clear and free of sediment and organic growth; yet, because of the depth, vision was very limited and steering had to be done by magnetic compass. It was a total water environment that was strangely beautiful but extremely deadly—and the Death Merchant and Woo knew it. They were calm because they were experienced, because they had learned to handle the hazards of diving in the Arctic—not only mechanical failures and physical stress, but the psychological pressure: the darkness that can swallow an unwary diver within seconds . . . the fear of being trapped under an icy expanse.

In some respects, it was much worse for Camellion and Woo, both of whom were now faced with the possibility that L7 patrol boats might depth charge the area or use sound- or heat-seeking rocket torpedoes. Camellion and Woo had space and distance on their side, mainly because of the cloaking Gf-Mechanism which had the SDV draped with a kind of force field, an electromagnetic shield that could not be penetrated by Russian sonar. As long as the Gf-Mechanism functioned, the sound of the electrically driven engine could not be detected and, practically speaking, Trass would remain "invisible." At the same time, while sound could not pass outward beyond the shield, noise could filter inward.

Camellion and Woo heard the *chug-chug-chug* of the screw—an L7 patrol boat.

"They can't know our exact location," Woo said, his tone indicating doubt.

"They saw me go into the water," the Death Merchant said. "All they know is that we have some kind of submersible. The corollary to this is that they know we're off the west coast of Wrangel. That's all they do know. How far have we come from our original position?"

Woo checked the panel in front of him. "Slightly more than four kilometers."

"Good. Three miles widens our chances for survival. From the sound of the screw, the L7 is moving southeast. We're headed northwest. Listen."

As the SDV moved northwest and the Soviet patrol boat cut through the southeast waters, the distance between the two crafts widened steadily. The *chug-chug-chug-chug* of the L7's screw became fainter. Four miles and seven minutes

51

later, the Russian boat began dropping depth charges, the first big *Blammmmmmm* sounding to Camellion and Woo as though it were only a few hundred feet away. Sound is conducted very rapidly through water. Being in an open vessel, Camellion and Woo were very susceptible to water concussion. Dropped within 300 feet of their center position, the concussion from a depth charge would kill them. The intense pressure would induce hemorrhage of the brain.

*Blammmmm! Blammmmm! Blammmmm!* But the Trass did not rock from the underwater explosions; the tiny craft was too far from the source of the explosions.

"See what I mean?" Camellion asked slyly. "The Russians are guessing. Since they have no way of knowing about our protective shield, they're assuming that we don't dare start our motor for fear of being detected by sonar. They think we're lying quietly on the bottom off shore."

"Let's hope they keep thinking that way," Woo said.

There were six more *Blammmmmms* in quick succession, each explosion a reminder to Woo and Camellion of their vulnerability.

The sound of the second propeller did not come as a total surprise. A *chug, chug, chug* could be heard very faintly. 500 to 600 feet in front of the SDV.

"I don't think we're hearing Santa Claus' sleigh bells!" cracked Woo. "Should I turn to the west?"

"We don't have time to play games," Camellion said, "and we can't risk his dropping depth charges. Turn us around and head south. I'm going to give him a mine."

Camellion reached down to the left, opened the lid of the compartment and took out one of the five magnetic M-mines. Symmetrical, its rounded surface covered with small bumps, the Nichrome mine is a very simple device. Selenium sensors in the bumps sought the largest source of heat within a 380-meter radius; a selenide photoconductive cell did the rest, guiding the deadly mine to that largest source of heat, the metal of the target, acting as a giant magnet, furnishing the propulsion. Once the mine made contact with the metal of the target, it exploded.

As Woo turned the Trass, the Death Merchant turned the activating knob and pushed the mine upward. The mine shot up at an angle and soon had disappeared in the water.

By now the sound of the enemy propeller was louder, Camellion estimating the distance of the patrol boat at 125 meters, more than 400 feet. Half a minute later, the mine struck the patrol boat and exploded with an ear-pounding roar.

A blink of an eye and the concussion reached Woo and Camellion. They felt an instant's crashing and pounding in the center of their brains and for a fraction of time, blackness folded over their consciousness. The water churned violently, rocking the SDV from port to starboard, from bow to stern. Just as quickly, the pressure was past and the SDV righted itself.

"Turn and head straight west," Camellion told Woo. "Once we're past the sensors we'll be in the open sea and you can take us straight north and one degree east. Out there we'll have a faster current for push."

Behind them, the Soviet patrol boat plunged to the bottom, prow first, while men trapped belowdecks struggled to keep from drowning in rapidly flooding compartments.

02.00 hours. At a depth of 41 fathoms, the Trass-III headed north by east, the electric motor purring faintly, the small prop cutting into the dark water. Since there weren't any sounds of enemy screws and since their own sonar revealed that the SDV was alone in the water, Woo now and then turned on the sealed spotlight in the bow, to make sure the craft would not rake itself on the bottom. At times they saw very large, round boulders that seemed to be out of place. Camellion explained to Woo that these stones were glacial erratics. "During the last Ice Age—some 12,000 years ago—huge glaciers bulldozed the land, scouring the earth and picking up rocks and other material. The powerful grinding action of the glaciers gradually smoothed and rounded the rocks, and carried them eventually to sea."

"It seems impossible," Woo said.

"Not really. What happened is that great icebergs broke off from the glaciers—just as they do now in Greenland and Antarctica—and drifted on the surface. Eventually they melted and dropped their load of boulders. Those are the erratics now on the bottom."

"Shouldn't we be sending the signal to Tirante?" Woo asked.

"We'll wait until we're gack at the place offshore from the Mammoth Mountains," Camellion said. "I don't want to take the time to stop and send up the antenna here."

"I estimate we're another hour from 'home,'" Woo said, pride in his voice. "Personally I'll feel a lot better when the four of us are headed back toward the sub."

*We're a long way from that mark!* But Camellion only said, "Yeah, so will I. I'd rather fight the pig-farmers on land."

05.00 hours—five o'clock in the morning. Very slowly, Woo guided Trass-III toward the craterlike depression, his left hand steady on the control wheel, his right hand on the handle that moved the spotlight in the bow. Forty feet from the depression, Woo shut off the electric engine and began to coast the rest of the way on glide. Halfway in, he switched off the spotlight and opened the vent valves of the trim tank. Gently, as water rushed into the tank, the SDV settled to the bottom of the crater. They had arrived. They were "home."

"How do you want to do it?" Woo's voice sounded hollow. At the same time it was harsh.

"We'll each take two extra tanks and two extra $CO_2$ [1] absorption canisters," Camellion said and reached for the lid of a compartment to the right. "I'll send the signal once we reach the surface."

"Man, we're going to be helpless upstairs if the ivans are around," Woo commented, unbuckling his seat belt. "We don't have any protection at all—and damn little after we reach shore. Dammit, I'm so hungry I wish someone would rape my taste buds."

"We'll have to chance it," Camellion said matter-of-factly. He took the special transmitter from the compartment and attached its ring to a snaplink on his swimsuit. The transmitter weighed only 10.6 ounces, measured 3.2 X 3.4 X 2.1 inches, and produced 30 watts of power.

Pushing themselves from the SDV, Camellion and Woo, twisting themselves around above the craft to have more room, went about unstrapping the extra air bottles in the sixth-seat space of the craft. When the tanks were free, Camellion and Woo slipped the straps through their arms to prevent the four tanks from floating to the surface, and went about releasing the watertight boxes containing the carbon dioxide absorption filters. After this task was completed,

---

[1] Carbon dioxide.

Camellion released the weapons' cylinder from the right side of the hull and started up after Woo, who was already on his way to the surface, 400 feet above.

Because of the air tanks forever trying to reach the surface, it was with effort that Woo and Camellion paused periodically for decompression; and when they finally did reach the surface of the sea, they were tired, cold, and apprehensive.

Darkness and the lapping of the icy water greeted them, although if one took time to look at the eastern sky, one could detect the first thin lines of light. To the west were numerous blue stars. The clouds were parting. Once the sun was fully risen, there would be mist and fog until the middle of the afternoon.

The Death Merchant slipped the small transmitter from his wrist, his movements awkward because of the two air tanks and the weapons' cylinder bobbing against him. He pulled up the 5-inch telescoping antenna, pried open the postage-stamp-sized plate, and, holding the tiny transmitter a foot out of the water, pressed the single button. That's all there was to it; the signal had been sent, a microsecond signal that was actually a short message. When the single frequency was picked up by the floating antenna of *Tirante* and decoded, the message would read, *"DISCOVERY. WE ARE LEAVING. MEET US."*

The Death Merchant let go of the small transmitter and watched it disappear beneath the water—*Another "Made in the U.S.A." object the ruskies will never find.*

Swimming to the shore, Camellion and Woo found that they could see well in the darkness. While Woo was surprised, the Death Merchant was not. For many, many hours they had been in the darkness. It takes the human eyes only an hour to adapt completely to seeing in the dark; once adapted, however, the eyes are about 100,000 times more sensitive to light than they are to bright sunlight. In fact, human eyes are so sensitive that on a clear night when there is no moon, a person sitting on a mountain peak can see a match struck fifty miles away.

Pulling along the air tanks and the weapons' container, the Death Merchant and Woo swam to shore and soon were moving over the wet sands and gravel. They had shut off the gas tanks and had lifted the faceplates of their helmets.

This part of the northwest coast of Wrangel Island was a jungle of boulders and wave-cut terraces, the savage water, over the centuries, having excavated caves at the bases of many of the larger pulpit-rocks. The entire region was as inhospitable as a cancer ward, not only because travel by foot was difficult but also because the rocks offered so many places for an ambush.

Camellion and Woo chose some rocks to their left, 100 feet beyond the waterline on the beach. Once in the rocks, they saw that behind the enormous boulders was a drift, that is, a mantle rock consisting chiefly of an irregular sheet of commingled clay, sand, gravel, and boulders of various sizes. This drift, showing its heterogeneity, was ideal for Woo and Camellion. Here Woo would wait with the extra tanks while Camellion moved inward to the cave where Ralph Hushan and Thomas Cholang were holed up. Woo wasn't at all happy; all he had for protection was a Colt .45 autoloader and six extra clips.

"You don't have to worry," Camellion said. He pulled the Auto Mag from the weapons' container. "If the ivans show up and you can't hold them off, all you need is one bullet to put through your head. Take it from me, it won't come to that."

Woo stared incredulously at Camellion. He knew that Camellion meant every word, that he was in deadly earnest—and it was frightening.

"Take it from you, huh?" Woo sounded and looked dubious. "How do you know?"

The Death Merchant, disconnecting the stock from the Auto Mag, gave Woo a quick glance. "Believe me. You're a long way from dying."

He handed the Auto Mag to Woo, who remained silent and watched as Camellion removed his helmet and began to get out of the swimsuit.

Camellion placed the swimsuit over the air tanks, tightened the straps of his gloves, and took the AMP from Woo.

"Keep down and don't answer anyone who doesn't first give you the code phrase. Repeat it to me."

" 'Hot swallows carried by angels,' " Woo said mechanically. "And you watch yourself." Woo suddenly felt ridiculous. Telling Richard Camellion to be careful was as silly as telling a crocodile to beware of minnows.

Camellion left the beach area and moved northeast, first

going over a large section of rounded bosses of rock known to geologists as roches moutonnees—gneissic rock that had been shaped by a glacier. The trek became easier as the light grew and the new day began to lengthen. Finally the clouds in the east, low on the horizon, were red-orange-yellow from the rounded top of the newly risen sun.

To the north, the east, and the south the various peaks of the Mammoth Mountains poked upward, their sides a mixture of rock, snow, ice, and unfriendliness.

With the Auto Mag in his right hand, Camellion moved as quickly as was possible and as cautiously as was necessary. He attempted to avoid those areas that offered the best positions for an ambush. At times he was able to take another route. Other times a detour would have taken him miles out of his way and he was forced to take the risk.

Where were the Russian forces?

The Death Merchant reasoned that it was halfway logical for the KGB to assume that they had killed him in the water. *If it weren't for the patrol I scratched out of existence up here! The KGB must consider the possibility that there's more than one of us and that it was we who neutralized their lost patrol. Surely they know that these foothills are honeycombed with caves. So where are they?*

Half an hour later Camellion reached the small, blocked-up entrance of the cave in which Ralph Hushan and Thomas Cholang were waiting. Kneeling to one side of the entrance, he pulled out enough snow and small rocks to make a small opening. For a moment, he listened. Nothing. All was quiet from within. He leaned closer to the small opening and called out, "Hot swallows carried by angels."

The reply came back in Hushan's voice, "The third temple will not fall."

Camellion put his mouth close to the hole. "Hurry it. The Russians know we're on the island." He began to pull snow and rocks away from the entrance.

Presently, Hushan and Cholang weighed down with their swimsuits, air tanks, and weapons, were standing beside Camellion. As he explained what had happened, Camellion slung the strap of the Auto Mag over his shoulder and took the spare magazine pouch which Hushan handed him and strapped it around his waist.

"But you did get the photographs?" queried Tom Cholang.

Camellion took the Red Chinese Type-64 submachine gun

from Hushan and checked to make sure the weapon had a full magazine and was ready to fire. "Affirmative. All we have to do now is get the film to the *Tirante*."

"And us with it," Cholang muttered disconsolately. A Czech Skorpion submachine gun in his hands, he had taken a fighting stance and was looking all around at the long slopes of the hills.

The Death Merchant took three hand grenades and three thermate canisters from Hushan and stuffed them into the front flap pockets of his snowsuit. Hushan then finished strapping the rolled-up swimsuit and the two air tanks to his back, and the three men began the journey to the beach, tension and excitement giving them a larger measure of extra energy.

The two Chinese-Americans and Camellion were engrossed in watching the slopes and the forward areas. They couldn't relax, all three knowing that the danger would not pass until they were safely in the SDV and headed toward *Tirante*.

The clouds had disappeared in the east and the full sun was visible. In some places, a blue fog hung heavily over the rocks, the mists barely moving. The higher slopes and cliffs, bathed in sunlight, were gorgeous with reflected color and light sparkling diamondlike off the snow.

The Death Merchant and his two men were halfway to the beach and moving along exfoliation on the slope of a granite hill when they heard the first helicopter coming in fast from the south.

"Dammit!" exclaimed Hushan. "Company's coming to call."

"Company's coming to die," intoned Camellion. "Let's hurry and get to the bottom of this rise before we're seen."

Almost falling down the incline, they reached the bottom of the slope and leaned around the closed anticlinal fold of another hill to watch the chopper that, by this time, was making a lot of racket.

The eggbeater was a Mi-12, the craft having been designed to meet a military requirement for a transport helicopter capable of transferring large cargos and troops to the frontline battlefield. The Soviet Union had felt this requirement could only be met by a twin-rotor helicopter if the size of the rotors could be kept within practical limit. A side-by-side rotor arrangement was adopted by the Mil design bureau, rather than the usual tandem layout. The Mi-12 had a large, completely enclosed fuselage, with a rear loading ramp giving access to the unobstructed cargo hold that could carry sixty men.

"Look at the size of that baby!" whispered Cholang. "He's too big to land in this local area."

"The one coming in behind him isn't," Hushan said grimly, sounding as if he were on the edge of an effectiveness he would never reach. "It can land on the tops of the larger hills or even on the beach."

Cholang gave his opinion. "All we can do now is run for it." He glanced expectantly at the Death Merchant, who was watching both choppers. The first big whirlybird had slowed and was settling to the ground a mile to the southeast. The second chopper, a mile or so behind the first craft, was a Kamov-25 (called "Hormone" by Nato forces), a twin-turboshaft specialized antisubmarine warfare helicopter for both shore-based and shipboard use. The twin side-by-side turboshafts were mounted above the cabin and powered three-bladed co-axial contra-rotating rotors. Other than the pilot and copilot, the K-25 could carry eleven other men.

"I say we make a dash to where Woo is waiting," Cholang said again, looking at Camellion.

"Always be at home where you are." Camellion was very calm. "The smaller chopper is a scout for the first. We have to see what it does and plan accordingly."

"See—hell!" grunted Hushan. "It's coming this way. We had better find some cover."

"Over there." The Death Merchant pointed to a mass of Precambrian fossiliferous slate, much of which hung out in laminated overhangs. Camellion and Cholang and Hushan ran across the area and were ducking down underneath the closest overhang as the Soviet K-25 chopper passed overhead at a height of several hundred feet, the racket of its rotors a roar that filled one's head.

The K-25 didn't continue northwest as the three men had hoped. Instead, it stopped three hundred feet to the north and hovered, its nose turning slowly to the west. Camellion and Cholang and Hushan could see that the large, square gunports on each side were wide open and that gunners were crouched behind 14.5mm KPV heavy machine guns mounted on horizontal rings in the center of the Dutch door openings.

"They couldn't have seen us!" Cholang said angrily.

Ralph Hushan, engrossed in watching the K-25 that was slowly moving south, didn't answer. A fierce expression on his face, Hushan watched the chopper come back . . . slowly seeking . . . searching.

The Death Merchant knew. There was no other answer.

"Heat sensors," he said. "The pig-farmers are using heat sensors. They're tracking us the same way they would go after a sub. They've picked up our body heat, but they're not quite sure where we are—not yet!"

Hushan made a sweeping motion with a gloved hand. "Well, dammit. We can't stay here. Those other Russian sonsabitches aren't going to hang around their big bird and play chess. That's for sure."

"And I was the idiot who had to up and volunteer for Special Services!" Cholang said in disgust. "At least I'll get rid of this nicotine fit before I'm dead."

He took a pack of cigarettes from his snowsuit and lighted one, inhaling deeply with great pleasure, noticing that the helicopter had turned completely around, had dropped lower, and was hovering at a scant 100 feet.

Hushan opened his mouth, inhaled, and started to speak. That's when the KPV heavy MG on the starboard side of the chopper roared and big 14.5mm projectiles began striking the slate, the line of slugs raking the outside wall several feet above the heads of the three men hiding inside the opening, which was 30 feet long, 6 feet deep, and 5 feet high. Chips and shards of slate rained down as Camellion and the two other men jerked back involuntarily.

"By God! Now they know!" snarled Cholang, speaking around the cigarette dangling from the left side of his mouth. He pulled back the cocking knob of the Vz61 Skorpion machine pistol as another blast of 14.5mm steel stabbed into the slate.

"They've got us bottled up—dammit!" Hushan yelled in frustration. "What the hell are we going to do?"

"You two go to the left and draw their fire," Camellion ordered. He had carefully estimated the distance of the helicopter and had taken the .357 Auto Mag from his shoulder. "I'll do the rest."

Ralph Hushan protested vehemently. "Man, you're out of your tree! You can't bring that chopper down with that!" He nodded toward the Auto Mag.

Not minding the criticism from such amateurs, Camellion

grinned like a mischievous gargoyle. "You had damn well better pray that I do! Now both of you crawl to the end of this damn slot, poke out your SMGs, and trigger off bursts. *Move!*"

The two men moved! They started crawling to the left, Hushan calling back over his shoulder, "We can't even see that chopper!"

"You don't have to, stupid!" snarled Camellion. "Just do as I tell you."

Hushan and Cholang did. They crawled to the left end of the slot, stuck their Skorpions through the opening, and triggered off short bursts. The starboard gunner in the Soviet K-25 chopper evidently didn't hear the firing because he again raked the entire length of the slit, the big 14.5mm projectiles chopping off more slate and rocks.

Ralph Cholang turned, looked at Camellion, and shrugged.

The Death Merchant made firing motions with his hands.

Once more Cholang and Hushan thrust their Czech machine pistols outward and upward—as much as they could —and triggered off long bursts. This time the Soviet machine gunner must have heard the firing, the evidence to the fact being that the next savage lines of 14.5mm projectiles were fired directly at the end of the slit. A hundred projectiles must have brought down a couple of hundred pounds of crushed shale; yet, because of the steep angle of the trajectory, the Soviet gunner could not fire directly into the slot. At best, he could only depress the weapon far enough to hit the wall several feet above the long horizontal trench.

At once the helicopter began its autorotational descent, the pilot expertly working the trim and cyclic controls. Simultaneously, the Death Merchant scooted out of the narrow opening, stood up, and, holding the Auto Mag in both hands, began firing police style, aiming by using the instinctive pointing technique.[2] He had two-to-four-seconds lag time and twenty .357 magnum rounds in which to do the job— *Or we're all dead!*

The Jurras noise suppressor began to cough as Camellion

---

[2] This means that the body is used to actually point the weapon, the barrel being placed and held so that the muzzle and the eyes are in the same perpendicular plane. This takes practice, success depending on one's natural ability for shooting. Or killing.

raked the starboard side of the helicopter. He knew that the powerful downdraft of the rotors would affect the trajectory and cause the projectiles to drift. For that reason, he had deliberately aimed a foot higher than the target mark. But the chopper was only 75 feet in the air and slightly over 100 feet in front of Camellion. Under ordinary circumstances a Jurras .357 AMP cartridge delivers a 137-grain bullet at 2150 fps. The special cartridges that Camellion was using sent out a 184-grain projectile at 2942 fps. Enough shock power to stop a rhino in its tracks!

Several .357 projectiles shattered windows to the rear on the starboard side; they screamed all the way across the cabin, zipped through the port side walls, and continued their journey into space. One bullet struck the steel ring mount of the KPV machine gun and ricocheted. Three struck the Russian gunner—one in the chest, one in the upper lip, and one in the right arm. Its face half torn away, the corpse bounded back, but jerked to a halt when the safety straps reached their maximum length. The two straps then jerked the dead body forward and it fell over the machine gun. The portside gunner was also down and dying. The bullet that had hit the starboard-side gunner in the chest had gone all the way through his body and had hit the other man in the middle of the back and had broken his spine.

Eight .357 projectiles struck the forward starboard side like lightning bolts. One went through a window and lodged in the mount of a window on the opposite side. Four tore holes in the aluminum fuselage. Three cut into the cockpit. Glass shattered into thousands of pieces. Karel Veronovitch, the pilot, jerked violently against the seat belt while parts of his head splattered against the control panel, the rear of the cockpit, and Basil Yutiz, the copilot and radio operator. Yutiz also jumped and yelled in pain and surprise.

Two .357 magnum slugs had struck Veronovitch in the right side of the head and had exploded his skull. The third bullet had entered the right side of his body just below the armpit. It had torn through the chest cavity, had bored out his left side, and, deflected by a rib, had gone downward and struck Yutiz just above the waist. With most of its power gone, the lead lodged in the right lobe of the liver.

A hideous sight, the torso of Veronovitch slumped forward, held in the bucket seat only by the seat belt while his stump of a neck pumped out huge gushes of blood.

Basil Yutiz, feeling only a great numbness in his body, had only a few seconds in which to experience horror . . . a couple of moments in which he saw the cockpit being repainted with blood and already decorated with gore and chunks of brain matter. The last thing in life he saw was a billion brain cells pasted like some gigantic gray-white amoeba to his right knee. Then Yutiz passed out from shock and internal hemorrhaging and rapidly began the final process of dying.

There were two other men in the doomed helicopter; one was an ammunition handler, the other, a KGB observer. By the grace of a sneering Fate neither man had been struck by the projectiles that had ripped through the windows toward the rear or the AMP slugs that had zapped out the two gunners. In an emotional daze, Dmitri Boiko and Vasili N. Krupskaya could only hang on to the handholds and gape at the two dead gunners and at the dead pilot and copilot.

*"Ne ayutsya, tu fronta'na ktivy!"* screamed Boiko.

He was so right. The helicopter was going to crash. Totally out of control, the Kamov-25 plunged to the ground.

The Death Merchant calmly watched the pilotless craft come down, the chopper wobbling from side to side, skidding in the thermals like a top winding down. With the dead pilot's hands off the controls, the K-25 came down at almost full throttle and slammed into the slope opposite the wall of fossiliferous slate. There was an enormous *wwwhhooommmmmm* and a big ball of expanding smoke and fire. A shower of burning wreckage rained to all the thirty-two points of the compass, some of the smaller debris striking the slate. A 3-foot-long piece of twisted framework shot 30 feet over the head of Camellion who, when he saw that the eggbeater was going to crash, had fallen flat and had buried his head in his arms. The piece of metal struck the slate, bounced off, and fell 10 feet behind, and 30 feet to the left of Camellion.

*Old friend, Death, you come at such odd times!* The Death Merchant got to his feet, turned to his left and saw Tom Cholang and Ralph Hushan coming toward him, utter amazement on their faces. He looked at the burning wreckage of the helicopter. Much of the framework had been blown all over the slopeside, yet some of the skeleton remained, crumpled underneath portions of the bent rotor blades. Camellion

63

could see three corpses roasting in the flames and, with the drift of the breeze, smell the smells of burning death—cloth, rubber, metal, plastic, and other material. All burning—and the odor of burnt gunpowder as 14.5mm shells exploded in series, like strings of big firecrackers. Now and then the distinct smell of burning flesh drifted to the south, the odor similar to burnt bacon.

"By God, you did it!" Ralph Hushan said hoarsely. "You brought him down!"

Camellion turned and looked toward the southeast, the familiar sound causing Hushan and Cholang to jerk around. The big Mi-12 helicopter was lifting off. . . .

# Chapter Seven

If the Death Merchant had not been the kind of pessimist who burned his bridges before he came to them, he would have been surprised when, through the increasing mist, he saw the Mi-12 rising into the air, its twin rotors revolving faster and faster.

"You'd better get that Auto Mag ready, Camellion," Tom Cholang said nervously, his eyes on the big chopper. "It looks like the entire force is coming after us."

Ralph Hushan turned and stared at the Death Merchant. "Can you do it? Can you bring it down with the Auto Mag?"

Camellion, shoving a full twenty-round magazine into the AMP, nodded.

"Yes, but I won't have the opportunity. The pig-farmers aren't going to make the same mistake twice."

"They're not going back to the base. That's for sure." Cholang sounded positive. "Call them 'pig-farmers' if you want. But they're fighters. On the ground, they never know when to quit."

"They're coming to have a look, to inspect the wreckage," Camellion explained pacifically. "The eggbeater will remain high. They don't know what kind of firepower we have, so they will keep out of range and use infrared with magnification. After that—"

"They'll drop men between us and the beach," interjected Cholang. "They know we have a midget sub or an SDV off shore."

Hushan sighed and wiped his freckled face with the back of his gloved hand. Looking at Camellion, he made sounds that could have been a blending of a snicker and a giggle. "Now tell us we're not going to have to make like road-runners!"

"With twice a roadrunner's speed," agreed Camellion, who had not taken his eyes from the Soviet helicopter. The pilot continued to pull up on the collective stick—"pulling in pitch"—the effect being to increase the angle of the blades and thus to increase the lift.

"But not until we see what that big bird is going to do," concluded Camellion. Let's get back inside the slot."

He turned and hurried over the short distance to the overhangs. First giving each other a worried look, Cholang and Hushan followed, Cholang saying desperately, "That chopper can drop low enough for troopers to jump out. The gunners could keep us down with cover fire."

This time it was Hushan who, crawling underneath the overhang, gave a rebuttal. "Yeah, but out there in the open we wouldn't have Chance One. I guess its a choice between damned now or doomed later."

The three men couldn't see the Mi-12 when it roared overhead, but they could tell from the sound of its rotors when it halted in its horizontal course and, at 300 feet, hovered over the burning wreckage of the K-25.

"They've probably got heat sensors, too," grumbled Cholang. His gloved hands tightened around the Skorpion SMG, and he lowered his body slightly when the muzzle of the Red Chinese T-64 sub-gun strapped to his back raked against a piece of low-hanging slate.

Not a single shot was fired from the Mi-12. It hovered over the slope a few more minutes, then the pilot changed the angle of the rotor pitch and the craft roared off to the southwest.

"Now we make like roadrunners," Camellion said agreeably and crawled from the slot. Once out in the open, he paused and turned to the two Chinese-Americans. "You're sure you're carrying the special Velet cartridges in those Red sub-guns?"

"Of course, just like you ordered," Hushan said in annoyance. Feeling insulted, he gave Camellion a dirty look. "We're not rookies in the middle of basic. We've got three box magazines of the Velets and four mags of the regular stuff."

With the Death Merchant out front, the group of three moved around the shale overhang and came to a wide but short cleft that wind, snow, and sleet had carved from the side of a huge hill. They were just in time to see the Mi-12 descending between two moundlike hills half a mile to the southwest. When the helicopter stopped its descent all Camellion and his two men could see were the top hubs and part of the blades of the twin rotors, as well as a cloud of snow being churned by the powerful downdraft.

Camellion and the Special Services team didn't stop to watch the big chopper, but forced themselves to move at a steady pace over ground that was rough and at times very slippery.

Several minutes later, the Mi-12 started to rise, the pilot quickly pulling in pitch and at the same time angling. Simultaneously, the helicopter rose and moved to the Southeast. Within the next five minutes it was descending 5 to 6 miles to the southeast.

"I'm beginning to hate that big bastard," panted Thomas Cholang. "The damn thing is like a vulture. It stays out of range and just waits."

Because they were moving single file and because the Death Merchant was in the lead, neither Cholang nor Hushan could see Camellion's face and learn from his expression what he might possibly be thinking. Both men were very worried about the Russians who had jumped from the helicopter and were now a barrier between them and the section of northwest beach where Dionysius Woo was waiting. To fuel their anxiety was Camellion's unnatural calm, his seeming lack of concern, as though the Soviet soldiers up ahead didn't even exist. To Hushan and Cholang, Camellion's attitude was actually frightening.

They continued to move forward, trekking along a route that went ever downward, an incline that could only be called a miniature valley. Several hundred feet on either side were ragged masses of rock cut and scarred by various limestone ledges filled with loose rock and snow. Assailed by frost and the bitter wind, their tops had worn away. But their inner spines and ramparts of concentric hogback ridges remained as monuments to the ceaseless conflict between the earth-shaping forces on Wrangel Island.

The tension screaming inside Cholang and Hushan was becoming unbearable when the Death Merchant changed course and motioned for the two men to follow him to a long, narrow opening between two large boulders that resembled monument rocks. Once the three had reached the icy sanctuary between the two ancient granites, Camellion got down to cases.

"You've both noticed how we've been going downward in a kind of valley," he said. His breath froze faster now. They were much lower in the foothills. The air was colder, but the mist was more dense.

"Sure, we've noticed," Cholang answered Camellion, his voice laced with tenseness, "and so have the Russians. It stands to reason that the first thing they did was to place scouts on the highest points to watch our progress. That's elementary. Once we're in range, they'll open up."

Hushan said slowly, "They know we have to move through the valley. They know we don't have time to take another route. It's reasonable for us to assume, too, that they have deduced we'll figure out their strategy and not be stupid enough to walk in like sheep. Those commie sons can't be more than a hundred yards ahead of us, probably spread out above on the ledges." His eyes jumped to Camellion. "If you're going to tell us that we're going to climb above them, I'd say that we don't have the time and that the ivans know it. They know damn good and well we're expecting their patrol boats."

The Death Merchant finally spoke, "First things first. Unless we get out of here, the patrol boats won't make a damned bit of difference. The pig-farmers know we've read them. They'll be on the lowest ledge as well as on the highest. The way these hills slope, they could snuff us no matter which route we took."

Hushan adjusted the hood of his snowsuit. "We sure as hell can't fly." He stared hard at Camellion. "I suppose you're going to tell us next we're going to have to climb to the very top of one side and get above the vodka-drinking sonsabitches?"

The Death Merchant ran the tip of his tongue across the edges of his upper teeth, then smiled and shifted the T-64 submachine gun in his hands. "The sooner we get started, the sooner we'll get to the top and then to the beach."

Cholang looked stunned. "A climb that will tack forty-five minutes to our schedule! You want the impossible, Camellion."

Hushan, too, was all instant concern. "By the time we get to the shore—if we get there—the water will be a convention of patrol boats!"

"There is no other way," Camellion said, his voice measured and authoritative. Without waiting for either man to reply, he stepped between Hushan and Cholang and headed west.

"He's really something," muttered Cholang. "But I don't know quite what."

"Yeah, but he knows what he's doing and that's what counts," Hushan said firmly. "Come on. Let's go."

In places the fog was so thick that vision was limited to a 20-foot radius. Just the same, the fog didn't interfere with the climb. The mist was neutral: it concealed Camellion and his two men from the Russians, and it made it impossible for Camellion and his men to see the Russians. At any given time, Camellion & Co. could see exactly where they were, and the climb itself was not all that difficult. Although the Death Merchant and his two companions had to be very sure of their footing because of loose rocks under the snow, the slope was not of such steepness that it had to be scaled in the usual way—by a climber's having to wedge his hands in cracks and pull himself up, while his feet desperately sought footholds. There were no straight-up walls or deep crevices to tear away life if one slipped and fell. The worst that could happen would be that the climber would slide down the rough slope until a boulder blocked his path and stopped his plunge. But in this particular situation, a broken arm or leg was the same as a death sentence.

The distance to the top was 350 feet. There were times when Camellion and his men could lean forward against the wind and practically walk up the jagged slope. Other times, as the grade steepened, they had to first make very, very sure of their footing and then, step by step, move up sideways, prepared to fall flat on their stomachs and dig in with their gloved hands and grab tight to rocks should they slip and start to tumble.

Their most dangerous enemy was the silent snow lying deceptively over the uneven surface. In some places where the snow appeared to be only a foot deep, it was four or five feet. Several times, Camellion or Hushan or Cholang sank in the whiteness up to their waists, Cholang once to a depth that reached the middle of his chest. In spite of these difficulties, the climb was nothing more than a hardy workout for the Death Merchant, who was a crack Alpinist.

The last hundred feet was the most difficult. Here the slope was very steep and scree-laden, so that the three men had to move very slowly and with great caution, a few times to the extent that they had to lie flat and squirm upward by reaching down into the snow and finding firm rocks protruding from the ground. In this manner they pulled themselves along until the slope became less steep and they could stand and plod onward.

The last 20 feet was fairly easy, the ground more level, the boulders larger. Then, the top of the ridge, another inhospitable wasteland filled with limestone and granite boulders . . . a bleak wasteland offering only enormous skies and limitless horizons, a total desolation of nothingness sparkling with snow jewels.

Toward the center of the ridge was another line of small, twisting hills, the sides packed with masses of snow that had been carved into weird shapes by the wind. In some places the snow and rocks climbed skyward for almost a hundred feet.

At this height, the fog had been dispersed by the direct rays of the sun, this marriage of sun, snow, and ice so intense that the glare could not be tolerated for very long.

The Death Merchant and the two Chinese-Americans went behind a boulder and put on snow goggles.

"At least most of the Russians are below us," Cholang said, adjusting the elastic band behind his head. "Except for maybe two or three up here on the top, just in case." He adjusted the goggles over his eyes and pulled up the hood.

"Well, getting to the other side and down won't be a cakewalk," Hushan said. He adjusted his own goggles and glanced at the Death Merchant who, having finished securing his own goggles, had taken out the Webber-4B dart gun. "What about the Russians on ridges on the other side across from us?" he asked Camellion. "They'll be able to see us. It's only four or five hundred feet from here to there. We'll be too small a target for them to open up on us, but they'll contact the Russians on this side, just below us and the few who are probably on top with us."

"We'll have to go from rock to rock and hope for the best," Camellion said. He unscrewed the Jurras noise suppressor from the barrel of the Auto Mag and placed the silencer in one of the flap pockets of his snowsuit. "I'll take the point. You two take the rear and the flanks. Any questions?"

"I don't suppose we'll stop for a midmorning breakfast?" Cholang said with mock seriousness.

"We'll have brunch as soon as we get to the beach," Camellion said gravely. Then, "Let's get on with it."

They began the dangerous task of crossing the ridge, going south in a loose formation that resembled a horizontal pyramid, the Death Merchant at the apex. They moved swiftly in those places where the wild, undisciplined wind had swept the rocks clean of snow, but were forced to a slower pace in other areas covered with huge drifts and partially covered rocks. All the while they moved closer and closer to the north end of the hills in the center of the plateau-like ridge, their approach accompanied by occasional faint cracking and popping sounds. This was the reaction of the rocks to the summer sun. For months the conglomerates had known temperatures as low as 50° below zero. With the summer season had come some warmth and the rocks had slowly begun to expand. Before the summer was over, there would be very large snow slides, not only here but all through the Mamontovvye Gory. Winter would come, and with it more bitter cold and snow and ice. The process of rebuilding would begin all over again.

The Death Merchant and his crew did have some luck on their side, in that they could thrust forward on a crooked route that kept large boulders between them and the enemy troops on the opposite ledges of the small valley; and a route that helped blend their navy blue snowsuits against a multicolored background of sandstone and granite boulders, small stones, large stretches of gravel, tumbled masses of broken shale, and shattered roches moutonnées. The snowsuits should have been gray-white, but some inefficient boob had made a mistake—and a nuclear submarine does not turn around and return home to exchange snowsuits.

When he was not far from the north side of the center hills, Camellion motioned for Cholang and Hushan to follow him to slabs of slate sticking up at various angles. On their hands and knees, the three men crawled the short distance, stopping only after they had burrowed in like termites.

"The edge is not a hundred feet to the east," Camellion

71

said. "Now those hills are a couple of hundred feet in length. We'll—"

"Why not go past them on the west side?" interrupted Cholang. "Hell, if there's ruskies up on top and some of them are just below the rim, we could be caught in a crossfire and pinned down."

"Good point, good point," agreed Hushan.

"Dumb thinking, dumb thinking," Camellion growled, annoyed and impatient. "Don't you two turtle butts realize I've thought of the west side? I've studied satellite-made infared maps of this area for days, and I can tell you that the west side is impassable. The slopes of the hills go right down to the edge of the rim, so steep they might as well be perpendicular."

Cholang's imperious expression faded.

Hushan scratched the right side of his face. "All right. So why did we stop here?"

"I'm going out to make a sort of recon of the hills." The Death Merchant shoved the Auto Mag into a long holster on his hip; the big weapon was not flexible enough for his immediate needs. He made a motion with the dart pistol in his left hand. "The pig-farmers should have a man or two at the north end and a couple at least on top. If I can terminate the ones on this end, we might be able to crawl past the ones on top without being seen."

"What we need is a miracle," Hushan said in a harsh, bitter whisper. He watched the Death Merchant take one of the captured Stechkin machine pistols from his carryall bag, snap a cartridge into the firing chamber, then thumb on the safety and push the firing selector to semiautomatic. *A helluva lot of good a Stechkin will be against AK-47s!* he thought.

"What do you want us to do, stay here?" Cholang asked Camellion.

"Negative. You two follow me in at ten yards. Be sure to keep low, on lower ground than I. Those packed swimsuits and bottles on your back make quite a hump. We don't want some eager ivan putting a slug through them. Ready?"

Cholang and Hushan nodded slowly.

"I wish to God I could smoke," muttered Cholang.

The Death Merchant had bellycrawled for ten minutes. Cold, tired, hungry, and hating the Russians—*If it weren't for those communist pigs I wouldn't be here!*—he stopped by the side of a large drift that reminded him of a large scoop of whipped cream and looked around the left side. Seventy-five feet in front of him the first rocks of the center hills waited malevolently—more boulders and chunks of ragged slate—*The perfect place to station a guard. Or guards.*

Camellion stared at the rocks. He could risk crawling up to them. He could but he wasn't going to. He became angry at himself. All he had been doing was screwing off the noise suppressor, then screwing it back on. He searched for a bare spot, found one, lay down the Stechkin and the Webber dart gun. and pulled the Auto Mag from its holster and the silencer from the carryall bag. Again he screwed the noise suppressor onto the specially threaded muzzle of the AMP. The plan might work. Again, it might not. But there wasn't going to be a turkey shoot, not up here on this stretch of barrenness, Too many X-factors were in the stew. Suppose there were more than one pig-farmer but only one reared up? The Death Merchant didn't think there would be more than one, if there were any scouts at all in that area. The big Mi-12 had a capacity of sixty men. By the time these men were dispersed on several ledges on both sides of the valley and on top, the total force would be spread out very thinly.

To make the mission more difficult was the lack of instant communication between Camellion and his men. But walkie-talkies would have only helped the Russians, who would have deduced from the conversations what Camellion's plans were. Even sealed frequencies could not be used since the Russians had very sophisticated electronic equipment on Wrangel Island—so Camellion had been told by the CIA. How could the Company be so sure? It was none of Camellion's damned business. OK, so maybe the Company had a mole in the KGB or perhaps even on Wrangel itself.

Camellion looked around the drift and once more studied the various kinds of conglomerates sticking out at all angles. He found what he wanted: a big chunk of long shale sticking out over the boulders and shale below. The only problem was the possibility of the screaming noise of a ricochet. But perhaps not. Shale was soft and a .357 AMP packed a TNT punch.

Camellion turned and looked behind him. He could see part of Hushan lying prone in the snow. He couldn't find

Cholang. He looked again at the projection of shale, raised the AMP, aimed at a spot a foot from the slopeside, and pulled the trigger. The noise suppressor coughed slightly and the powerful .357 magnum projectile hit right on the mark. There was no ricochet. And if the projectile had made a noise in entering the shale, any Russian below would have attributed the sound to the rocks which groaned and popped a few times every three or four minutes. The long slab of shale sagged slightly. The Death Merchant got off two more rounds. The third shot did the trick. With a loud cracking sound the 10-foot length of shale dropped 40 feet to the ground and, with a loud noise, shattered into a couple of hundred pieces.

Camellion first gave the very top of the slope a brief look, then dropped his eyes to the boulders and slabs of slate 15 to 20 feet in front of where the shale had fallen.

Having anticipated finding an ivan eliminated all surprise when Camellion did see not one but two parka-clad figures jump up from behind a boulder on the east edge of the rock mass and stare at the shattered shale.

*Bye-bye, cockroaches.* Camellion, both hands around the AMP, pulled the trigger. As one Russian jumped, threw up his arms, and was slammed forward, Camellion pulled the trigger a second time before the second ivan could drop down. The second man, a hole in his body the diameter of a rolling pin, fell beside the first corpse.

Camellion pulled the magazine from the AMP, extracted the big cartridge from the firing chamber, and inserted it into the top of the long clip. He put the magazine into the carryall bag, pulled the bag around to where he could look into it, and took out a magazine whose end was painted red. From now on, he would use the Velet cartridges. With a quick motion he shoved the clip into the AMP, pulled back the slide, felt the explosive cartridge slip into the chamber, and put the weapon on Safe. He unscrewed the silencer from the AMP, dropped it into the bag, picked up the Webber dart gun, placed it in the bag, then zipped the cover. The last thing he did was pick up the Stechkin machine pistol.

With the Stechkin in his left hand and the Auto Mag in his right, Camellion left the whipped-cream snow drift and began to snake toward the pile of rocks hiding the two dead Russians, pulling himself along by digging in his elbows and shoving with his feet and legs. The only sounds were the cracking of the snow-ice, the wail of the wind, and an occasional snap, crackle, and pop of the temperature-tortured rocks.

Reaching the edge of the rocks, he snuggled down and waited for Cholang and Hushan to catch up with him. After they did, the three of them crawled into the boulders and slate and soon found the two dead Soviet soldiers lying on a frozen, red carpet of their own blood. Camellion rolled over one of the corpses, jerked open his parka, and looked at the blood-stained uniform. It was light blue.

"They're KGB," said Camellion, "members of the Chief Border Guards Directorate."

Hushan and Cholang couldn't have cared less; to them, a Russian was a Russian. They tossed aside their Type-64 Chinese Red SMGs and ammo pouches and exchanged them for AK-47 assault rifles that had belonged to the Russians. Just as quickly they removed the AK-47 ammunition containers from the corpses and strapped the belts around their own waists. The rate of fire of the AKs more than offset the explosive value of the Velet cartridges.

"We'll go single file, eight feet apart, and keep as close to the hills as we can," Camellion said quietly. "By snuggling up to the hills, we'll make it almost impossible for anyone on top to see us without their leaning over the edge."

Smiling, Hushan and Cholang nodded enthusiastically. For the first time they seemed to have confidence in the plan and to exhibit hope that the escape plan might succeed.

The route in front of the hills was far easier than the climb up the north side. The ground at the bottom of the steep slopes was not too uneven, though pebbles and chunks of granite of all sizes made walking difficult. The most annoying obstacles were the immense snowdrifts which, underneath a foot of actual snow, were still frozen as hard as concrete from the long winter's freeze. Many of the drifts had been frozen for scores of years. At this height, the strong wind had been blowing for centuries against vertical rock faces. Wind scour had undercut cliffs, this sandblast action eventually forming sculpture-balanced rocks, pedestal rocks, mushroom rocks and other weird residual forms. The wind had cleared some of these forms of snow, but others had snow packed around them. The total effect was that the slopes had the appearance of a gargantuan cake whose frosting had been played with by a madman.

By no means did the bottom of the slopes end at the same place, this meaning that the distance between the end of the slope and the edge of the top varied. Sometimes the distance was as much as 150 feet. Then it would narrow to 50 feet or less.

The Death Merchant and his two men moved ahead, always watching the mottled face of the steep slopes. They were three-fourths of the way across the top when Thomas Cholang, last in line, looked up and saw the Russian on the slope. The KGB border guard had just spotted Cholang and, 40 feet above him, was standing to fire down on the Special Services commando.

"They've seen us!" yelled Cholang. He ducked instinctively to one side, swung up his AK-47, and fired a split second before Stephen Delyusin pulled the trigger of his own AK, the twin blasts, ringing across the face of the slopes, sounding extra loud. Delyusin's slugs *zip, zip, zipped* into the snow close to Cholang, but none struck his body. Some of Cholang's 7.62mm hit only rock, snow, and ice. Three caught Delyusin in the front of his body, in the right shoulder, in the forehead, and in the hollow of his throat. The KGB hog was ninety percent dead a second after the three antimonial lead alloy slugs struck him.

At the head of the line, the Death Merchant swung around, darted to the side of a limestone boulder, ond raised both the Auto Mag and the Stechkin machine pistol. Ralph Hushan jumped, then half fell behind a slab of rock as he prepared to get into action with his AKM.

Only by sheer accident had Delyusin seen Cholang. Now the other Soviet border guards—startled by the sudden firing —reared up, some equipped with AKMs, other's using PPS submachine guns.

Hushan and Cholang proved immediately that their training was superior to that of the Russians by killing two KGB who had reared up from a small ledge 25 feet above. Cholang and Hushan, spotting other Russians, dropped down and snuggled behind the rocks. They knew that before they could snuff out the Russians, the border guards would smoke them. A couple of hundred 7.62mm AK-47 projectiles zapped into the snow and ice, thudded into softer rock, and *zinged* with whines from the hard granite, such a deadly rain of lead that the two commandos had no choice but to paste themselves to the ground and hope that Camellion could somehow divert the stream of projectiles hitting the rocks.

The Death Merchant did. He opened fire with the Stechkin and the Auto Mag, the big AMP booming, the Stechkin only half as loud. A .357 AMP bullet hit a KGB man in the right side and kicked him against a giant icicle hanging from a tiny ledge. The icicle broke and went down with the man. Two 9mm Stechkin projectiles hit another KGB guard in the right collar bone and the right jaw and slammed him back as other border guards, aware of the new danger, swung their weapons toward the Death Merchant who dropped down a split second ahead of a tornado of AKM and PPS slugs which tore through the air, through the space where his head and arms and shoulders had been.

Camellion's worry now was that the Russians on the ledges below would climb over the rim and come in behind him and his two men.

*Hushan was right. We do need a miracle!*

He got it! Already weakened by the expansion of the rocks, the snow and ice began to break loose with a low, long rumble, a sound that the Death Merchant had heard before. *It's an avalanche. The sound waves from the gunfire caused it!*

The Russians trapped above knew what the sound indicated, and so did Cholang and Hushan. Along with the Death Merchant, they knew that all they could do was snuggle up to the side of the boulders and hope that the coming tons of snow and ice and loose rock didn't take them over the rim which, at this point, was only 30 feet away.

Now much louder, the rumble was accompanied by loud snapping and cracking sounds. The rumble became a roar and the avalanche began. The snow and ice started thundering down the slope.

The KGB men were doomed, a thought that was not at all consoling to Camellion, who was worried about his own two men and himself. He gripped the Stechkin and the AMP, kept his face down, and made himself small against the boulder. There was one major rule that had to be obeyed: lie still and breathe lightly. If a man doesn't panic, he can breathe for as long as two hours underneath the snow.

To the horrified Russians on ledges across the valley, it appeared as if the entire slopeside had plunged downward and pushed itself over the east edge into the valley below. For a few moments, the entire west side of the valley was blanked out by dirty whiteness.

The boulder protecting the Death Merchant was very large; nonetheless, he felt it shudder and act as if it might break free as snow, loose rocks, and other debris smashed against it. The boulder shuddered again, and Camellion had visions of the enormous mass of rock rolling over on him. The result would be like a hammer falling on a bedbug. *I'd be squashed flatter than tissue paper.*

Within a few seconds the roar was behind him, to the east, and he felt a weight pressing down the length of his body, starting just below the shoulders, not a crushing weight but one that was evenly distributed. *How much snow is on me?*

Camellion was very careful of the Auto Mag and the Stechkin as he pushed himself up slightly with his elbows, making sure that the muzzles pointed downward, to prevent snow from clogging the barrels. With an effort, he hunched his shoulders and continued to rise, the weight of the snow on his back telling him that it was only loose snow and not too deep at that.

He stood up. He was in snow up to his lower chest. All around him the landscape had changed—and so had the slope to the west. What now existed was a long expanse of snow glistening in the sun, sparkling with diamond-fire, depending on how Camellion turned his head. Rocks decorated the snow—boulders of various sizes, slabs and other kinds of debris. Everywhere was a fine mist, like pale gauze. Not far from the Death Merchant the trunk of a dwarf mountain birch protruded from the snow, its end twisted and splintered. Only 8 feet from where he stood, a large, long piece of slate stuck up like a long, gray finger. If it had fallen to the right, it would have stabbed him like a tremendous spear.

As he stared at the projection of slate, he saw Ralph Hushan pop up through the snow fifteen feet away. Hushan brushed snow from his goggles with his left hand and, with his right, pulled the AK-47 from the snow, stock first.

With a very quick motion, Hushan brought up the AKM. Then he spotted the Death Merchant, who was standing with his arms above the snow, a weapon in each hand.

"Have you seen Tom?" Hushan called.

Camellion was about to reply that he had not when he saw a white-hooded head push itself up through the snow 30 feet to the left of Hushan and 40 feet behind him. Below the head came the shoulders and arms of the KGB border guard, one hand holding an AKM. The Russian was brushing snow from his goggles as Camellion exploded his head with a .357 AMP bullet. The Russian dropped down into the snow, the only evidence that he had been there the splattered red marks on the snow and bits of cloth and flesh and bone and gray-white brain matter.

In snow up to his waist, Hushan looked frantically around him. So did Camellion. But the surface of the snow was quiet. Cholang and some of the Russians might still be alive; if they were, they were buried too deeply to crawl out or had been killed by rocks, or carried over the edge.

With an effort, their breath fogging constantly, Camellion and Hushan waded through the dry snow until they stood together, in a position that was a short distance to the west from where Camellion had risen from the snow.

"Tom must be dead," Hushan said. "He almost has to be."

"Do you remember where he was before the snowfall."

Hushan pointed with his finger. "Back there. Maybe fifteen feet to the north from where I was. I think he got down behind a lot of slate that stuck up."

They stared at the spot. There wasn't any slate, only an incline of snow.

"He was either crushed or was carried over the rim," Hushan said. "But we don't have time to look for him." He looked hopefully at Camellion. "Do we?"

"You know we don't. The living can't help the dead by dying themselves."

Alert for stray KGB border guards, Camellion and Hushan pushed their way through the thick snow until they were several yards beyond the edge of the avalanche.

The Death Merchant stopped and began looking around. "Keep a sharp eye," he said. "Where are your grenades and thermate canisters?"

Hushan's eyes raked the slopes above and to the left and the right.

"The bag. Left hip. What are you going to do?"

"Bring down more snow. If any pig-farmers are alive on

the ledges below us, they won't be for long." Camellion shoved the AMP into its holster and dropped the Stechkin into the carryall.

Hushan stiffened with alarm, glanced at the Death Merchant, then looked at the long slope above them. "What about us? We're right in the path. You sure you know what you're doing?"

"Yeah, I'm sure." Camellion pulled two grenades and three canisters from his own bag and placed them on the ground. "We're safe here. It's a simple matter of engineering. All the snow that could come down above us has already fallen. There'll have to be another buildup before it becomes dangerous. I'm referring to the snow piled on the edge of the rim. If just a little of it goes over, it might start another big slide on the slopes that go down into the valley."

He dug into Hushan's hip bag, took out two demolition grenades, and put them on the ground. First he threw the three canisters of thermate, spacing them so that after they exploded, there were three brightly burning areas, each 20 feet apart.

Camellion threw the four grenades, each explosion rolling out across the valley and making the entire slope, above Camellion and Hushan, groan and creak. The fourth grenade did the job. A hundred-and-fifty-foot section of snow, lengthwise across the rim, started to slide, that snow that had not been melted by the intense heat of the thermate. For several hundred feet back, the snow started to move, its path made easier in that there was no barrier where the thermate had melted huge sections of snow to bare rock. The snow sliding down from the west moved faster, pushing at the snow on the east rim. With another roar, a solid snowfall cascaded over the rim and crashed down on the ledges that had not been torn away by the previous larger avalanche.

"Now we'll get to the shore and suit up," Camellion said. He paused and for a moment looked up at the ocean of deep blue sky. "Not today, old friend . . . not today. . . ."

"What?" Hushan looked perplexed.

Faint surprise flowed over Camellion's face. "Nothing. Nothing at all."

They moved west. They stumbled through snow and over bare gravel, at times half slipping and half sliding on half-frozen scree. Gradually the way led downward. The west slope of the ridge was much longer, hence less steep. Movement became easier after they were off the slope and in the region that would take them to the beach.

The deep, muffled explosion was not totally unexpected. Just the same it did come as a slight surprise to Camellion and Hushan. They knew that the sound was that of an underwater explosion, but still not the kind made by depth charges.

"Could it have been a ruskie mag-torpedo?" said Hushan. He then answered his own question. "But if a mag-torpedo hit the Trass, the sound wouldn't be that loud."

The Death Merchant, 6 feet ahead of Hushan, called back, "Magnetic mines and torpedoes won't work against the SDV. The shield prevents heat and sound from getting out; it also neutralizes any magnet effect. I think we heard an M-mine taking out an L7."

"You mean that Woo—"

"Did what he had to do! He heard the firing and explosions back here. He knew he could only wait. Then he saw the L7, swam out to Trass, and let go with an M-mine. If a depth charge doesn't get him from another L7, he'll be OK."

"Yeah? Well suppose a depth charge gets him and Trass? What then?"

"We die . . ."

Camellion and Hushan soon found themselves in an area that once had been touched by the ever-patient, ever-working sea. In a very long process the innumerable chisels of the sea may carve bedrock into a variety of strange, grotesque, or beautiful forms—sea caves, sea arches, hanging valleys, and the lonely columnar monoliths called stacks. None of that had taken place in this particular region, not yet. Here and there the rocks were channeled and there were patches of sand and cobbles that had been wave-tossed by storm-whipped water. The beach lay ahead. Even now Camellion and Hushan could hear the music of the surf.

A few minutes before they reached the beach, they heard the loud *blam, blam, blam* of depth charges. Neither man slacked pace. Why bother? It was all too clear what was happening. An L7 patrol boat was lobbing out D-charges in an effort that one of them might find and destroy the SDV.

Then they were running across the crescent-shaped beach and saw the L7 3 miles to the southwest. Only a single nautical mile south of the SDV!

Camellion and Hushan's worst fear was realized: the prow of the L7 turned to the south. *Blam! Blam! Blam! Blam!* And with each D-charge explosion, a mound of water rose on the surface of the sea.

*Whooommmmmmmm!* An M-mine!

The bow of the L7 rose suddenly out of the water, rose so fast that within a few seconds the bow was almost vertical! Quickly, then, the vessel plunged beneath the water.

"You're right," panted Hushan, running behind the Death Merchant who was headed for the place where he and Woo had stashed the swimsuits and the air tanks. "It's Woo. He just blasted the patrol boat with a mine."

It did not take long for them to find the section in the boulders and the heterogeneous drift where the equipment was neatly stacked. Suits, tanks, and weapons' cylinder were there. Dionysius Woo was not.

"We'll suit up and meet Woo at the SDV," Camellion said harshly. He bent down and picked up one of the deep-dive suits. "Be sure to use the gas bottles that are full. The *Tirante* will come in closer to the north side of the island. We'll have only thirty-two miles to go, but you never can tell."

They had suited up, closed and secured their faces plates, turned on the air tanks, and were running across the beach, almost to the water, when they heard the helicopter coming in from the east. Judging from the *chub-chub-chub-chub* of the twin rotors, the Mi-12 was coming straight at them.

*Oh, gee whiz and all that sort of worried stuff!* The Death Merchant kept right on going, the weapons' container over his right shoulder. Soon he was in water up to his knees, then to his hips. He dropped the hard plastic cylinder and threw himself forward in the water, pulling the line of the plastic cylinder with him.

By then, the Mi-12—200 feet up and several hundred feet to the east of Camellion and Hushan—was close enough to open fire. The gunner from the starboard side did so, getting off a long burst from a 14.5mm KPV machine gun.

Ralph Hushan might have lived if he had been as fleet of foot as the Death Merchant, if he had not been 15 feet behind Camellion and if he had not stopped to turn around and look to see where the big chopper was.

*Zip, zip, zip, zip, zip!* Hundreds of slugs started hitting the sand, then throwing up tiny spurts in the water. Hushan turned and attempted to throw himself to one side. A useless effort. One 300-grain bullet hit him in the shoulder and half amputated his left arm. Another projectile exploded the left side gas bottle on his back. A third and a fourth projectile stabbed in between the two tanks, bored through his back, came out his chest, and zapped into the water. The 1-2-3-4 impact slammed Hushan face down in the water, and there he lay, bobbing with the waves, streaks of red flowing out into the water and quickly disappearing with the roll of the waves.

For three or four seconds the Death Merchant heard the *zulpp, zulpp, zulpp* of projectiles stabbing into the water around him and saw the bubble traces of their passage. Then the *zulpp, zulpp, zulpp* was above him as he clawed deeply into the protective water and started swimming toward the Trass, using his wrist compass to guide him southwest. He could locate the SDV without the homing signal, but he knew it might take hours. Although the sun was shining brightly, the water was very dark past 60 feet. But if Woo were dead, he wouldn't have any choice in the matter.

*Let's see if he's alive.* Camellion pressed the button underneath the rubber and activated the Harmonica Box. He waited for the return signal. There wasn't any. Twice more he pressed the button and sent out the special C-note impulse.

*Beep, beep, beep, beep.* Woo's return signal started coming through the headphones. *Just like Christmas, even if it is summer!*

To the one-note accompaniment of Woo's H-Box beeps, Camellion at length located the Trask-III, the front seat of which was occupied by Dionysius Woo. Camellion, still pulling the weapons' container, swam to the front of the undersea vehicle and looked at Woo, who was slumped over in the seat. He reached out and shook Woo by the shoulder, and the commando raised his head and grinned with effort at Camellion who was reaching for the communication's wire floating from behind Woo's helmet. Before Camellion connected the line to his own helmet, he looked at Woo and in the dimness saw that blood had flowed from his nose and ears and was caked around his mouth and on his cheeks.

Concussion!

The Death Merchant plugged the line into his own helmet. "How bad is it, Woo?"

"Nothing that a few weeks in the hospital won't cure." Woo said thickly. "But I never want to hear anyone beating a drum. You'll have to pilot us out of here. I'm too disoriented."

"I'll help you get into another seat." Camellion said. He disconnected the communications line and attached the line of the weapons' cylinder to a clip on a ring fastened to the top rim of the SDV. Woo unstrapped his seat belt, pushed upward, and Camellion helped him move above the vehicle, then pulled him to the second seat and assisted as Woo worked himself downward into the space.

Once Woo was strapped in, the Death Merchant eased himself into the front seat, pulled in the floating plastic cylinder, and secured it to the hull. He strapped himself in and plugged in the line that Woo handed him, wondering when the man would ask him about Hushan and Cholang.

He didn't until Camellion started the electric engine. "How did they get it?"

"A snowslide got Cholang," Camellion said. "The pig-farmers cut Hushan down on the beach. They had a helicopter. By the way, that was smart work the way you handled the patrol boats."

As Camellion blew water from the tanks, then turned the SDV and headed it north, Woo explained that he had only done what he had felt was necessary: seeing the Russian patrol boats, he had swam out to Trass-III, and had released the mines. "I knew that if their depth charges got lucky, we'd be stranded on this damned island. It's too bad that Ralph and Tom will never see home again. Well, that's how things are."

"At least you will," Camellion said.

"I was born in a little town in northern California," Woo said. "I haven't been there in years. It doesn't make me any difference if I never see the place."

Camellion increased speed. There was always some nostalgia. And faces. And ghosts. Sometimes even sentiment and a few memories to smile at. Or weep for. Always a little to remember.

# Chapter Eight

Oray Rigdon, the CIA psychologist aboard the *Tirante*, recalled the time he had been teaching personality theory to a group of fresh clandestine operators and of the "grapefruit exercise" that was supposed to measure and improve their sensitivity. The trainees had been required to turn in written contact reports. Some had developed meaningful relationships with their grapefruits. One nonconformist, however, had merely drawn a large grapefruit and in the center of it had placed a large question mark.

A tall, thin, 47-year-old Pennsylvanian, Rigdon was fairly certain that Richard Camellion and John Connery would probably have written "bullshit" across the first page. Rigdon was not at all surprised that the two men were responsible for the tension in the wardroom, and for making the other men uncomfortable. All except Rigdon who found the two men fascinating and welcomed the chance to study Camellion and Connery, both of whom he considered enigmas.

Rigdon had welcomed the chance to go on the mission as psychological evaluation officer. His job as psychology specialist at the Company's headquarters in Virginia was interesting, but it could be boring, although what he did was vital and very necessary.

A CIA case officer's prime duty was to recruit agents among foreign citizens around the world, and the Company had a vital interest in any method that promised to reveal weaknesses, vulnerabilities, and psychic pressure points in possible recruits. Few people realized that the CIA had become one of the world's foremost laboratories for unusual psychological techniques. Rigdon's office in the Company's Technical Service Division had a mandate to test anything —from hallucinogenic drugs to computerized handwriting analysis—that would help case officers manipulate their agents or other unsuspecting potential agents. It was Rigdon's job to show them how to accomplish these psychological operations.

A trained scientist, Rigdon did not attempt to make any judgments in regard to either Colonel Connery, the CO of the Special Service unit, or Richard Camellion, who was a totally unknown quality. The odd part was that no one on board *Tirante* knew who Camellion was. All they had been told was that Camellion had the final word.

Occupying a position on the left center of the metal table, Rigdon compared Connery and Camellion to the paradox of the irresistible force meeting an immovable object.

Colonel John Connery, the irresistible force sitting at one end of the table, wanted to cancel *Operation Stringbean*.

Richard Camellion, the immovable object sitting at the opposite end of the table, insisted that Stringbean proceed as planned.

Rigdon was not a gambling man; if he had been he would have bet everything he owned or would ever own that the "immovable object" was not going to be moved. He was equally as positive of some other facts. Totally unburdened by the ordinary fears of ordinary people, Connery and Camellion knew who they were and were complete pragmatists. This meant that they could not be intimidated by the unknown and the mysterious and weren't afraid of death. Unlike 99 percent of people, they were not threatened by themselves.

*Yes,* Rigdon told himself. *I'm certain.* Camellion and Connery were men who had developed their vocational potential in accordance with their personality needs; men who, while respecting people and society, still relied fully on themselves and on their own capabilities and capacities. Intuitively, Rigdon sensed that this was particularly true of Richard Camellion. He was a man who was governed by his own inner directions, his own nature and his own needs, rather than by the dictates of society and environment. He would always make his own decisions, even in the face of controversies and popular opinions. He would always maintain his own point of view and would not be swayed—a man who was his own master. But there was an X-factor, a quality about Camellion that made Rigdon vaguely uneasy, a mode that defied analysis.

"Mass suicide!" Colonel Connery's voice was as firm as

iron. He stared the length of the table at the Death Merchant, his dark eyes like two black marbles underneath the V of his thick, shaggy eyebrows. "You're proposing mass suicide, Camellion. The Russians know that Wrangel was reconnoitered a few days ago. They don't know who it was or why you were there, but you can damn well be sure that they'll be watching their shores the way a mother bear watches her cubs. You can't tell me differently. This mission must be aborted."

"They'll bring in reinforcements from the mainland," Colonel Gordon said warningly, looking at Camellion. "There's a Red Army barracks at Pevek and an air base at Ambarchik."

The Death Merchant, dressed in white submariner's coveralls, surveyed the grim faces around the rectangular table. To his right was Captain Donald Coffey, the pleasant-faced skipper of *Tirante*. Next to Coffey sat Lieutenant Ed Forrestil, the second-in-command of the sleek nuclear sub. Beside Forrestil was Colonel George W. Gordon. Well-muscled with suntanned, aquiline features, he spoke little and was not given to superfluous motion.

Across the table from Gordon and the two naval officers, and starting from Camellion's left, were Sergeants James Strope and Paul Virone, the two mean-looking Special Services noncoms. Both men wore expressions as if they were looking for a fight and scared stiff they wouldn't find one.

Oray Rigdon, the CIA observation officer, sat between Sgt. Virone and Special Services Captain Allen Dunmerser. Rigdon had thick white hair and was a nervous chain-smoker. Captain Dunmerser was a well-made collegiate type in his early thirties, but with horn-rimmed glasses he looked out of place.

Captain Coffey and Lieutenant Forrestil avoided looking at either Camellion or the Special Services men. Why get involved? It didn't matter to them whether or not Operation Stringbean was aborted. Either way, it was not they who would have to go ashore and face the Soviets. Coffey and Forrestil only furnished the transportation.

It was the direct opposite with Colonel Connery and his men, all of whom stared at Camellion with angry, resentful eyes, waiting for the Death Merchant to answer.

Camellion said in a pleasant voice, "Colonel, I agree wholeheartedly with your conclusions." Amused at the surprise in the five pairs of eyes, he went on, "By now the KGB think-tanks in Moscow are working overtime. But I don't think the KGB or any part of the Soviet General Staff will send reinforcements to Wrangel Island. The last thing the Soviets expect is an actual invasion."

The two Sergeants glared at the Death Merchant; anger burned more fiercely in the eyes of Colonel Gordon and Captain Dunmerser. Rage and frustration battled all over the broad face of Colonel Connery, who now tried a new angle of attack against the Death Merchant's proposal.

"Tell us, Camellion. How much military experience do you have under your belt?" Connery sounded almost solicitous. "It's facts that count here, not half-baked theories of civilians."

Camellion didn't mind Connery's intended insult. It was the old story of the professionals resenting what they believed to be armchair amateurs. He was almost sorry about how he was going to verbally slaughter Connery and his group.

"Far more than any of you in this kind of attack, far, far more experience, even if I'm not wearing a uniform. And I know the Russians, especially the KGB. I know I have more experience because I've read your P-files. You were a hotshot in the Korean War, Connery, and in Nam. The rest of you were damn good in Nam. Because you're experts in sneak-in operations, you're going to attack Wrangel Island."

Colonel Connery was too self-controlled to let rage dominate him, and in this case, too stunned. "Very well. You're more experienced," he said, acting as if it pained him to admit it. "Since that's the case, your experience should tell you I'm right, that our casualties will be at least sixty percent."

"Casualties could go even higher," said Captain Dunmerser. He looked directly at the Death Merchant and adjusted his horn-rimmed glasses. "We don't know how many patrol boats are scattered around the southern tip of the island, not only in Rodgers Harbor but in the other harbor on the southeast side. We can't ignore that fact."

"Nonsense," Camellion said lightly.

"Gentlemen, Mr. Camellion is right," spoke up Oray Rigdon. He had spoken without thinking, and now he felt slightly embarrassed as all eyes pounced on him. "Any statement can be called either an opinion or a fact. If you label it an opinion, you are admitting the possibility of error. If you call it a fact, you are then stating that the premise is never to be questioned."

Colonel Connery gave Rigdon a condescending look, the kind of glance one gives a small child who has just said something impossibly ridiculous.

"You might be right, Mr. Rigdon. But when a bullet hits a man in a vital spot and he dies, that's not an opinion. It's a fact. That's about as subjective as anyone can get. Only the man doesn't think he's dead. He is dead."

Rigdon remained silent after giving Connery a disdainful look.

"Camellion could be right about the Russians not sending reinforcements to Wrangel," announced Colonel Gordon. "I'm inclined to think that to them, an attack on the island is not possible. After all, the only nation that could mount such an attack would be the U.S., and the KGB knows damn good and well we wouldn't attack anyone, certainly not any part of the Soviet Union."

"But they know a recon was carried out on the island," pointed out Sergeant Virone, exhaling cigarette smoke through his nose. "Who else but Big Uncle would do that?"

"The theory is supposed to be the Chinese." Connery's tone was scornful.

"A recon doesn't have to be the prelude to an all-out attack," the Death Merchant said levelly. "For a moment, try to think from the Russians' point of view. They know that *Foxfire* is eighty miles to the east of Wrangel and have to presume she's on an intelligence mission. There's two laboratories on the island where the Soviets are conducting experiments in mind-murder, torture, radiation and only God knows what else. I ask you: if you were the KGB, would you not assume that the enemy was after information about the installations and that they came from *Foxfire*?"

"Hold on. The Russians are monitoring *Foxfire*." Captain Coffey turned and looked at Camellion. "Their technology and hardware will tell them that whoever was on the island didn't come from *Foxfire*."

Camellion shrugged. "It adds up to making the Russians all the more confused. Since they can't detect *Tirante*, they won't know what to think, which is fine with us."

"I doubt if the men who get killed on the beach will call

it 'fine,' " Captain Dunmerser said, scowling at the Death Merchant. "Machine guns will blow us up the second we step out of the water."

"There aren't going to be any machine guns around," Camellion thrust back. "In a moment I'll show you why."

He got up from the table, walked across the ward room and pulled down a 50" X 50" motion picture screen from its round metal housing on the wall. He locked the screen in place, walked six feet to the rear of where he had been sitting at the table, and picked up a slide-cube projector from a chair.

"The first stills were made from the motion pictures I took on the recon," he said, carrying the projector to the table and setting it down at his place.

"Why the stills? We've already seen the motion pictures of the Soviet base," Colonel Connery said briskly.

"The stills will give us more time for evaluation." Camellion pushed the prongs of the plug into the electric outlet built into one of the legs of the table. "Captain Coffey, you're closest to the light switch. Dim them please."

Captain Coffey got up, went to the wall behind him, and turned off the main lights in the ceiling. He flipped another switch and turned on the green night-lights on the walls. He returned to his chair as Camellion turned on the machine and projected the first slide onto the silver lenticular surface of the screen.

"Gentlemen, you are looking at the north side of the main prison," Camellion said. "Before I continue, let me state that the pictures I took were compared with the photographs taken by the satellite. There's only a one percent margin of doubt that the buildings are not what they are supposed to be."

"The one on the screen is a prison," Captain Dunmerser said. "Chain-link fences, concertina wire, the works. What's the smaller building to the right of the prison, then the larger building to the right of it?"

"Notice the large conduits?" the Death Merchant said. "The smaller building is the generating plant. The much larger one is one of the laboratories in which underwater experiments are carried out—on live subjects, I might add."

Colonel George Gordon suddenly expressed interest. "But you only took pictures from the north, looking toward the south?"

90

"Affirmative. Yet we can still learn a lot from the photographs. You will notice that some of the buildings are taller than others. By comparing the horizontal shots I took with the vertical photographs of the satellite, we can deduce the layout rather well."

He switched to the next slide, to one that had been made by the satellite, an enlargement of the entire base. The enlargement was not the usual kind of color photograph but consisted of various-sized dark patches streaked with lines of light. Still, if one looked closely with a magnifying glass, there were distinct details. The photograph was infrared and had been made from a height of 273 miles.

The Death Merchant got up from the table. In the dim light he went to the screen, picked up the pointer from the groove, stood to one side, and placed the tip of the pointer on a dark rectangular blob.

"I believe that this building, which is as long as the first lab and the generating station combined, is the second laboratory. I believe it is in this building that experiments in behavior modification—brainwashing—mind-murder—are being conducted."

Camellion tapped the tip of the metal pointer on another dark area. "I think this is the torture center, the 'Palace of Laughter.' " He could see that most of the men were interested, with the exception of Colonel John Connery, who sat staring at the screen with his arms folded.

The pointer moved to the left. "Here are the barracks and the other buildings necessary to maintain the Soviet base. And here in this area"—the pointer moved back to the right —"is the administration building, perhaps the officers' quarters, and the radio station. The sea-sensors watch may or may not be in the radio station. As you men can see the entire complex covers an area the size of a city block. Two city blocks if we include the prison."

"Why shouldn't we include the pen?" asked Sergeant James Strope. "What the hell, it's there!"

"It might as well not be," Camellion said. "We're not going to free the prisoners. We don't have the time and we don't have the transportation."

"Camellion, I think it's time I told you we're wise to your tactics," Colonel Connery said bluntly. "Instead of showing us photographs of the objectives, why not tell us how we're supposed to reach the beach without being cut to ribbons by enemy fire."

The others quickly agreed, nodding their heads.

"You were going to tell us why there wouldn't be any machine-gun fire near the beach," Captain Dunmerser reminded Camellion, his voice reproachful. "But all we've gotten from you so far is a photographic tour of the Russian base."

Without a word, the Death Merchant strode back to the projector and started pressing the change button. Slide after slide flashed on the screen. In a very short while he came to the slide he wanted, a scaled drawing of Wrangel Island. Camellion had drawn a series of squares to the south of the island. South of the line of squares were three rectangles, side by side, their lengths vertical on the screen.

"If this picture show is going to continue, I'm going to have to have some popcorn," Colonel Gordon said with a little sneering laugh, relishing the chance to get in a dig at Camellion who was walking back to the screen.

"I'd like to know when the cartoon starts," growled Sergeant Virone.

Most of the men laughed, including the two officers of *Tirante*. Oray Rigdon only smiled.

Camellion didn't mind. Just as one does not refer to a man as stupid because he is not a master of calculus, neither does one become angry with those who have the mentalities of highly intelligent children.

The Death Merchant picked up the pointer and turned to the men at the table. Good men. Their only fault was that they were suffering from trained incapacity: their learned attitudes dominated and even eclipsed natural talents for original thinking.

*Especially Colonel Connery. But he's still in better shape than Rigdon. His work with the Company has turned him into a terminal case of paranoia. Poor joker.*

"Gentlemen, I suggest you close the amusement hour and pay close attention," Camellion advised. "Within the next few days, some of us might be dead. But let's get one thing clear, once and for all. We are going to attack Wrangel Island. Period! *Finis!*"

"Listen, Camellion, we—"

"Zip your mouth shut, Connery! Playtime is over!"

Before Colonel Connery could make a reply, Camellion

turned to the screen and moved the pointer over the squares. "As you may have guessed, these small squares are the Swimmer Delivery Vehicles. These thirty SDVs will carry one hundred and eighty men. Forty will stay close to the shore and guard the diving suits. The other hundred and forty men will move inland to the Soviet base."

"That's sure some explanation about enemy beach fire!" thundered Colonel Connery. "You're doing what you did before, putting the cart way out in front of the horse."

"I'm coming to the machine guns right now!" snapped the Death Merchant. He turned to the screen and moved the pointer in a semicircle across the small squares.

"These ten SDVs will surface half a mile from the beach and bombard the beach and the area just beyond with forty millimeter XM175 grenade launchers. This action should effectively take out any heavy machine gun emplacements the Soviets may have close to the beach."

"But can grenade launchers work effectively from those SDVs?" Captain Dunmerser sounded interested; his voice was amiable.

The Death Merchant turned and faced the group. "The range of such launchers is 2,500 yards. That's 7,500 feet, more than enough distance, since the launchers will be only 2,640 feet off shore. The Soviet base is about 5,000 yards from where the launchers and the SDVs will be—or 2,360 yards from the shore."

Chimed in Sergeant Strope, "Well, an XM175 can fire something like four hundred and twenty grenades a minute. Hell, such firepower could be as effective as an air bombardment."

"Mounting the launchers on the SDVs isn't a problem," Camellion said. "The Navy experts tell me that the launchers will be sealed with waterproof plastic."

"What about the total weight," inquired Colonel Connery, all belligerence gone from his voice.

"Each launcher weighs forty-four pounds," Camellion said. "The real weight will be in grenades, around a thousand pounds of grenades for each SDV. I'm told that much weight does not present a problem. The Navy is going to use fifteen-passenger 'Arrowhead' vehicles for the job."

Colonel Connery said quickly, "It could work. We pepper the beach area with thousands of grenades as we move in. The men in the SDVs can extend the range as we move inland. No problem there. We'll be in communication constantly with the men in the Arrowheads."

"I still think we're pursuing the negative," Colonel Gordon said accusingly. "Your scenario seems to have left out the Soviet air base at Ambarchik. Fighter-bombers could blow us right out of the water."

"Let's not forget the Soviet patrol boats on Wrangel," tacked on Sergeant Virone.

"I suggest you let me finish," Camellion said in tones of reprimand. "Ten other SDVs will patrol south of Wrangel. They'll be moving fifty feet under the surface and will take care of any L7s with M-mines. The three subs"—he turned to the bright screen and pointed at the three rectangles he had drawn—"will use surface-to-air missiles against any aircraft that flies over from Ambarchik."

"I was wondering about those three subs," remarked Captain Dunmerser. "I guess one is *Tirante*. What about the other two?"

As the Death Merchant turned from the screen, Colonel Connery spoke, "Didn't *Foxfire* leave her position just after you came aboard, Camellion?"

In the semidarkness, Captain Donald Coffey cast a brief indignant glance at Connery. "Affirmative, Colonel. *Foxfire* left her position after Mr. Camellion and your commando came aboard *Tirante*. *Foxfire* is now a hundred and forty-six miles east of Wrangel. She has the Unit on full power. She'll rendezvous with *Sea Tiger* at twenty hundred hours. The two submarines will then proceed to this position, which is forty-six point four NMs north by west of the island."

"We then proceed to the south of the island?" asked Colonel Connery. He turned from Coffey to Camellion. "How far will the subs be from the south shore?"

"What about the fifty SDVs?" Colonel George Gordon asked in measured tones.

"*Sea Tiger* is bringing them," Lieutenant Ed Forrestil said. "I should think the SDVs are strung out behind her like a metal tail."

The Death Merchant cleared his throat, partly because he had to, partly to gain attention. "Seven miles due south, Colonel Connery. However—"

"Seven miles is damned close!" intruded Colonel Gordon gravely. "I don't put that much faith in the cloaking device.

Just because the Russians can't hear us with sonar doesn't mean they can't see us!"

"Lights, please," Camellion said, thinking of how pleasurable it would be to let Gordon have it in the mouth with a knife-hand *shuto* chop. Watching Lieutenant Forrestil get up from the table and go to the light switch, he stared down at Gordon who was looking up at him.

"Negative, Colonel," he said. "The device does make us invisible. Don't ask me how. It has something to do with the bending of sound and light waves."

"Fantastic!" muttered Sergeant Strope, as if talking to himself.

"Only *Tirante* and *Foxfire* will lie seven miles off the coast," the Death Merchant said, walking back to his place at the table. "The *Sea Tiger* will take a position a hundred twenty-five miles south of Wrangel, after she discharges her troops. *Sea Tiger* will be the first line of defense against aircraft."

"What's the max on the TF?" asked Sergeant Virone.

The Death Merchant pulled out his chair and sat down, his eyes moving to Virone, who had taken out a Sportman's Pencil from his shirt pocket and had popped out its six-inch steel needle by pressing the eraser on top.[1]

"The maximum time factor is two hours," Camellion said. "From the time we leave the SDVs and begin the swim to shore, we have a hundred and twenty minutes to do the job and get back to the underseas boats."

"What time do we go in at night?" Colonel Connery's crimson tongue drifted behind wolfish brown teeth. His chin jutted, and he had little grog blossoms on his cheeks and wrinkles scattered like jackstraws at the corners of his eyes.

"Day after tomorrow, at twelve hundred hours." Camellion expected resistance and he got it.

Connery and the Special Services men stared at him in astonishment.

"Why dammit, man! That's high noon!" Connery put his big hands on the arms of his chair and acted as if he might get up. His body looked as tough as a wharf rat's.

Camellion hooked his hands behind his head and smiled.

[1] A genuine article. While the Sportsman's Pencil looks like a genuine pencil, it contains a six-inch-long steel needle than can be brought into instant action.

"That's right. High noon! When the Russians will least be expecting company to drop in."

Captain Dunmerser addressed himself to Captain Coffey, "What's the weather report for Thursday?"

"Like a virgin's heart," smiled Coffey. "All fair."

"Hell, what's the difference whether we die in the rain or the sunshine," murmured Virone, who was cleaning his fingernails with the point of the Sportsman's needle. "Dead is dead. . . ."

# Chapter Nine

In any military operation, the element of risk is always present. The size of the operation and whether or not it is clandestine is never the issue. There does come a time when the planners realize that they have done all they can do, that from then on, fate, luck, or whatever one wishes to call Chance, takes over. A religious person could say the "will of God." Sometimes a wrong movement or as little as a wrong word can bring total defeat. Or a single wrong guess.

It was not any different with Operation Stringbean. On Thursday morning at 05.00 the final major briefing was held in the main wardroom of *Tirante*. Watches were synchronized. The various lieutenants and platoon sergeants were briefed in the greatest detail as to the terrain of the south portion of Wrangel Island; they were told over and over what was expected of them; they were told also that speed was essential.

The three submarines—the Special Services men were distributed among *Tirante* and *Foxfire*—proceeded to Point-Y. Behind each submarine, trailing along like calves following mother whales, was a string of Swimmer Delivery Vehicles, each SDV attached to a steel cable. All three subs and the SDVs had their Gf-Mechanism on full power. For all practical purposes, the strange underseas armada was not in existence. It could neither be seen nor heard.

At 10.00 hours the three subs arrived at Point-Y, the area that was 7.1 miles south of Wrangel Island. The subs stopped all movement at a depth of 50 fathoms. Lieutenants and platoon sergeants reread their orders, then burned the sheets of yellow paper. Weapons and various kinds of grenades and ammunition were distributed. A final, short briefing, after which the chaplain on each vessel said a short prayer and invoked the blessing of God on Operation Stringbean.

Finally the order came to suit up and disembark. Commandos stepped into diving chambers, each man holding his weapons' cylinder. Valves opened. The chambers, were flooded with water, hatches opened, and men swam out into the cold, dark waters of Proliv Longa—the Long Strait. Hatches closed; water was pumped from the diving chambers. More commandos stepped in and the process was repeated.

Operation Stringbean had begun. Spread out in a line, the fifty Swimmer Delivery Vehicles had their blunt noses pointed toward the southern shore of Wrangel Island, their electric motors purring. Every man knew that he might be going to his death, and every man wondered why such a tiny piece of real estate was so incredibly valuable. What secret was on the island, of such importance that the U.S. was mounting an attack against Wrangel, a strike that, conceivably, could lead to World War III?

The two regular commandos in the Death Merchant's SDV had been told the full facts. They had been told because they were part of the ten-man camera force that would go with Camellion into the Palace of Laughter and later into the two large laboratories. The ten would photograph everything in sight, including files, with special high-speed cameras.

The SDV in which Camellion was seated was toward the center of the line, its control in the able hands of Commander Newel Ledbetter, a United States Navy UDT[1] and amphibious craft expert. It was Ledbetter who would direct the commandos who would surface and bombard the shore area with 40mm demolition grenades. Every tenth grenade would be thermate.

Behind Ledbetter sat Colonel John Connery. The Death Merchant occupied the third seat. Behind him was Captain Allen Dunmerser. Two regular commandos were behind Dunmerser. The six could communicate by means of the talk-wire stretching from helmet to helmet, beginning with Ledbetter and ending with Chuck L.J. Lilmuten, the commando in the last seat.

The five men with Camellion had a lot of normal doubts, but one thing was clear in their mind: they were in for a short but brutal battle. The KGB troops on the island were well

[1] Underwater Demolition Tactics—or Teams.

armed and well trained. And nobody fights as well as a Russian when he knows his motherland has been invaded. The Commandos were aware of still another fact: their best friend was speed.

Snug and warm in his electrically heated snowsuit, the Death Merchant mentally sorted the various components of Operation Stringbean, arranging them in orderly A, B, C fashion

A. *Alfa-Blue Group,* under the command of Colonel Connery, would destroy the radio station and fan out to the barracks.

B. *Bravo-Red Group,* led by Colonel Gordon, would strike out straight for the power house and blow up the generators. BRG would then turn and go back to help Richard Camellion and his group.

C. *Delta-Green Group,* which would attack the Palace of Laughter and the two laboratories.

Kill every Russian who showed himself!

Photograph every available file!

Blow up the Palace of Laughter and the two labs!

Race back to the beach, get into deep-dive suits, swim back to the SDVs; get back to the subs, set the time charges on the SDVs and get the hell out of the area.

There was only one big problem: *Suppose the Russians had SDVs?*

"Commander Ledbetter, this is Camellion. How far are we from the half-kilometer mark?"

"Another three minutes," replied Ledbetter calmly. "In another minute the 'Nellies'[2] with the launchers will spread out and surface and begin giving the ivans our first 'Hello!' "

"And the other ten SDVs with M-mines," added Colonel Connery solemnly, as if reminding Ledbetter.

"Affirmative," said the bearded Ledbetter. "Those Nellies with the M-mines will move out at the same time the others spread out and surface. Don't worry, Colonel. It's when we get to the island that the real fun will start."

The Death Merchant reached down and picked up the underwater infrared Night Sight Viewer, his thoughts on the message he had received from the Company center. The

[2] A UDT colloquialism for SDV.

*Tirante* has sent up its antenna every eleven hours, the ball floating on the choppy waters for twenty-two seconds, more than enough time to receive "squirted" messages from the U.S.

Adjusting the focus of the Night Sight Viewer, Camellion reflected on the short message. *And the only Italian food I like is spaghetti. I'm not too crazy about it. But first things first.*

With the other men in the SDV—except Commander Ledbetter—he raised the Night Sight Viewer to his faceplate. He was just in time to see the ten large Arrowhead SDVs spreading out and rising to the surface. Along with the Arrowheads, ten other SDVs were spreading out, five going to the west, five to the east, each vehicle loaded with M-mines.

The majority of the underseas craft were headed downward to the bottom of the strait which, at its deepest a half-mile from the shore, varied in depth from 300 to 400 feet.

"Get your cylinders ready," Ledbetter said. He began to guide the underwater craft to the surface, the rise accompanied by a hissing sound as high-pressure air forced water from the trim tanks. Since Ledbetter was the coordinator of the grenade attack, his SDV would not rest on the bottom of the strait. It would surface, and he would keep in contact with the commandos at the launchers by means of radio.

The last thing that Camellion and the others saw before they put down their Night Sight Viewers was scores of commandos leaving the SDVs, each man pulling his weapons' cylinder on a short line, so that it would not bob to the surface before he did. Those commandos would pause halfway for decompression as would the larger Arrowheads and the craft in which Camellion rode.

The Death Merchant and the others hooked their viewers onto rings in the cockpits and proceeded to unstrap the plastic containers from the rim of the craft. Once the cylinders were free, Camellion and the four men connected them by a snaplink to a ring on the top of the vessel's rim.

Like the rest of the commandos, Camellion and the men with him were walking arsenals. They carried four kinds of grenades: the Mark-2 fragmentation grenade, whose fragments could cause casualties within a radius of 30 feet; the Mark-3A2 offensive grenade, which was very effective against personnel in closed-in places because of its shock effect; the M18 smoke grenade; and finally the AN-M14 incendiary grenade whose filler was pure thermite that would burn at a temperature of 4330 degrees F. for thirty-five seconds.

Each commando carried an Ingram submachine gun, twenty magazines for the deadly little SMG, a gas mask, a 9mm Browning, and ten clips for the autoloader. They also carried a variety of knives of their own choosing—everything from stilettos to big, broad-bladed bowie knives.

The Death Merchant had two .357 International Auto Mags in special holsters around the waist of his snowsuit and a nineteen-shot L.E.S. 9mm P-18 autoloader in a right shoulder holster. In a sheath on his belt was a deadly Dwarf. The knife was a bastard from the mating of wormeaten wood with twisted steel, an evil companion you wouldn't take home to mother but would gladly introduce to your favorite enemy. Slightly under seven inches overall, it was a deadly little devil, especially when used by a kill-expert like Richard Camellion.

Commander Ledbetter brought the craft to a standstill at 22 fathoms from the surface of the water. Time for decompression, time to make sure that there would be no air bubbles in the tissues when the men surfaced.

The Death Merchant and his people waited, knowing that on each side of them, stretched out for a sixth of a mile on either side, other commandos were halted in the water . . . waiting . . . and telling themselves that no matter what happened, they would live, that death was far far away.

The sole exception was Richard Camellion, who knew that life was far more mysterious than death . . . who knew that while the Cosmic Lord of Death rules the Universe—*He does not rule alone!*

Charles "Chuck" Lilmuten, the commando in the last seat of the SDV, spoke. "When the first Arrowheads reach the surface will they start lobbing grenades or wait for us?"

Camellion said, "Tell him, Commander Ledbetter. The Arrowheads and the launchers are your department."

"The Arrowheads will begin the bombardment the moment they get to the surface," Ledbetter said. "Two will zero-in on the Russian base."

"If we're lucky, grenades will disable the radio station and prevent the Russians from transmitting an alert to the mainland," Camellion said. "It will take Delta-Green Group, which is us, an hour to get there, and I presume that Alpha-Blue won't be able to move inland any faster."

"I estimate forty-five minutes for my group to reach the

base," Connery said coldly. "Even so, I don't think we're going to prevent the Russians—what do you call them? 'Pig-farmers?'—from contacting the mainland."

"I agree with you, Colonel," conceded Camellion. "Almost certainly there's another transmitter at the airfield in the center of the island."

"And attack helicopters," said Captain Dunmerser in a gloomy voice. "They'll be all over us, like a swarm of bees. Even you have admitted that intelligence hasn't the slightest idea what's on that air base."

"We've been all through that," Camellion snapped. "The LAAWs[3] will take care of any choppers that show up. Twenty of the men have LAAWs and five 'Homer' rockets for each one."

"There's no guarantee the LAAWs can do the job," Captain Dunmerser said. "You got to admit, Camellion, this is a weird, offbeat kind of attack. You might have followed a lot of luck on the recon and fooled the Soviets into thinking you were Chinese, but everything is 'Made in U.S.A.' on this trip. Dammit, we could be triggering a war that could escalate into the end of civilization as we know it."

"We could, but we won't," Camellion said. "Once we have proof about what the Soviets are doing on Wrangel, the old fossils in the Kremlin will be just as anxious to keep quiet about this as we are."

"The photographs. You mean the photographs," Colonel Connery said.

"I mean the photographs."

They floated in silence, seemingly suspended in a universe of velvet, a soft blackness of gentle pressure pushing equally on all sides. But only a fool would think that the seas are a friend of man. They are not.

Commander Ledbetter's voice was a welcome relief. "Time to see the sunshine, chaps. Up we go."

He turned on the motor and pulled one of the air levers. There were more sounds of air hissing and valves opening as air forced water from the trim tanks. He pulled back on the stick, the diving planes on the port and starboard sides tilted, and the vehicle started upward at a short slant.

3  Light Antiaircraft Weapon.

Minutes later the SDV popped up out of the water into the bright sunshine. The craft shook slightly from the effect of lowered resistance, then settled into the rhythmical movement of the waves as Ledbetter shut off the engine.

The water was still flowing down the face-plate of Camellion and his five companions when they heard the first 40 millimeter grenade explode. The first Arrowhead SDV had gotten into action with its launcher. A second and a third and a fourth Arrowhead opened fire with their launchers, one after another. By the time the Death Merchant and the four men had unstrapped their seat belts, released the weapons containers, and were in the water, all ten Arrowheads were throwing hundreds of grenades at Wrangel Island—eight at the rocks and low hills directly behind the beach; two firing grenades at the Soviet base itself.

The series of explosions were as rapid as strings of firecrackers going off, only hundreds of times louder. Often entire sections of the beach, lengths as long as 100 feet, exploded, geysers of sand and rock and earth spewing upward, the constant explosions a barrage of shattering noise.

Little wonder! The XM175 40mm grenade launcher[4] is motor-driven and belt fed. In this sense the XM175 is a grenade launcher machine gun, although the twelve-ounce projectiles are not fired as rapidly as ordinary machine-gun bullets.

To the left and to the right of the Death Merchant the other commandos were in the water, all one hundred eighty of them, each fighter pulling his weapons' cylinder as he swam toward the shore, some men, with the help of their fellows, pulling as many as three containers, one of regular size and two that were twice as large. These much larger cylinders contained the LAAW rocket launchers and the Homer rockets. Each LAAW launcher was only 34" long and could be fired easily by one man.

The half-mile to the shore seemed more like 50 miles. Swimming between Captain Dunmerser and Chuck Lilmuten, Camellion knew from experience that if Soviet machine guns were firing from concealed positions, it was impossible to

---

[4] The XM175 was developed for use in the Viet Nam war and was mounted on the AH56A Cheyenne high-performance helicopter.

hear them because of the thunderous racket of exploding 40mm grenades.

Tension and fear always produces extra adrenalin, so necessary for additional strength, and surprisingly soon Camellion and scores of other Special Services commandos were wading through the surf, moving clumsily in their bulky deep-dive swimsuits.

They unscrewed their faceplates and, with the water lapping around their knees, then their ankles, moved up onto the beach which was thick with gravel and cobbles scattered in piles amid the sand. Looking like men who had just stepped out of a spacecraft, they headed for a long row of sandstone stacks, dozens of 30-foot-tall monoliths set in no certain pattern, the towers of rock fronting a jumble of rain-and-wind-cut low hills.

All this time, Commander Ledbetter had been watching with binoculars from the SDV. Now, seeing the commandos crossing the beach, he ordered the commandos firing the 40mm launchers to extend the range by forty yards. "But not all at once," he said, speaking into the mouthpiece of the hand-held AN/PRC-6 radio receiver and transmitter. "Keep fifteen yards ahead of them as they advance. Then pepper the hills—out!"

Sweating profusely from the heat of the sun on their rubberized swimsuits, Camellion and the commandos reached the staggered monoliths and began to rid themselves of the cumbersome swimsuits. Men worked rapidly to remove air tanks from their backs, to unscrew bulky helmets, and to unzip the rubberized skin enclosing them—an undressing that required less than five minutes. Even so, during that very short time, Camellion and the entire force were almost helpless. Cognizant of this weakness, the Death Merchant and the commandos hastily opened the plastic cylinders. Their tension wasn't lessened by the Ka-25 ASW helicopter that passed a mile to the east at a height just under 1,000 feet and moved out to sea. Once the chopper was a mile to the south, it made a wide half-circle and started back toward the north, on a course that would take it directly above the monoliths.

Putting the strap of a grenade sack over his left shoulder, Camellion looked up and down the line, at the commandos in "Snow-Bush" camouflaged snowsuits who were pulling

SMGs, sacks of grenades, and bags of spare SMG magazines from cylinders. At least six commandos had pulled LAAW rocket launchers and rockets from the containers.

But Colonel Connery beat Camellion to the yell.

*"You men there!"* yelled Connery in his bull voice. "Three of you use a vertical spread on that damned chopper."

Well trained, the three commandos were very fast in turning the fin fuses on the rockets and dropping them into the mouths of the launchers, then putting the tubes to their shoulders and sighting in on the Russian helicopter.

The Ka-25 was headed straight for the monoliths, *chub-chub-chubbing* in at an altitude of less than 800 feet. Whether the craft was only scouting or getting ready to attack was anyone's guess. Camellion figured it was half of the first and both of the second.

The three commandos fired together, the Homer rockets streaking upward from the force of their monopropellant fuel. The Soviet pilot, seeing the three streaks coming at him, tried to pull up and swing to port. But the helicopter was doomed. The electrically guided Homer rockets hit the chopper at the same time. There was one tremendous explosion, a bright, brief burst of ball fire, then nothing but parts of twisted wreckage raining down into the water.

There were three more explosions, these muffled—two in quick succession, the third ten seconds later, the last to the east, the former toward the west. M-mines! Three Soviet patrol boats no longer existed.


Dressed now only in their warm snowsuits and combat Pak-boots, the commandos began forming into their different units, a task facilitated by the colored 4-inch square each man wore on his chest below his right shoulder—blue for Alfa Group, red for Bravo, green for Delta.

Colonel Connery and Colonel Gordon hurried toward the Death Merchant, who had taken the PRC-6 from his belt and was talking to Commander Ledbetter.

"When we move north, concentrate your grenades on the base. K."[5]

"Wilco," Ledbetter's voice came back. "I estimate we have only five thousand grenades left. It's best to use them against the base. K."

---

[5] Means: "You must transmit now."

"Roger and out." Camellion switched off the radio and placed it in the leather case on his belt, securing the flap and turning his attention to Connery and Ledbetter. Behind the two Special Services officers came seven commandos with green patches on their snowsuits; these were the other seven of Camellion's force. To the other side of Camellion, Captain Dunmerser and Chuck Lilmuten and Bruce Tuby were readying their gear.

"Our groups are set for the push." Connery didn't sound unfriendly, but he acted as if he expected some kind of argument. Colonel Gordon—in his snowsuit he looked all tough and twice the size of Camellion—seemed to be on the defensive.

"I think you need more than one LAAW man," Gordon said gruffly. "You'd better take one from each of our groups."

"Negative," replied Camellion. "One is all I need, and he'll slow us down." He looked up and down the rocks. Commandos crouched and waited. "Get back to your groups and move out. Standing here is like wishing upon a star. It won't get the job done."

"Luck, Camellion." For a moment Connery looked knowingly, almost compassionately, at the Death Merchant who nodded and twisted his mouth into a half-smile.

"Come back alive, both of you," he said, "and we'll have an all-day argument once we're on the way home. You two put up a pretty good one."

Touching the fingers of his left hand to his hood in a gesture of farewell, Colonel Gordon turned and followed Connery. Unlike most of the men who carried Hi-Power Brownings, he had two O.F. Mossberg stainless steel .45 autoloaders in flap holsters on his belt.

Camellion turned and walked over the gravel the short distance to Captain Dunmerser, who was checking to make absolutely certain the other nine men of Delta-Green Group had everything in order.

"All you have to do is give the order," Dunmerser said, his breath turning to fog in front of him.

Camellion inspected visually the two commandos in charge of the LAAW rocket launcher. One man carried the tube slung over his shoulder, the way one would carry a rocket. The second man carried the rockets in a special bag on his back.

The man with the rockets let the cigarette in his mouth

fall to the ground. "If you're worried, sir, that a stray slug might touch them off, forget it. They're TOT.[6] Detonation can take place only after the fuses have been set."

"I didn't know, but I do now, thanks." Camellion frowned. "What's your name?"

"Willard Scaggs, sir."

"Well, Will, don't call me 'sir.' I can bleed and die the same as you."

Scaggs looked surprised, and Camellion gave Bruce Tuby a thoughtful look. "Don't use those rockets unless you have to. We don't have that many. We can expect hell in double doses from the ivans the closer we get to the base. Any questions?"

The ten men only looked at him.

"Then let's do it. Diamond formation whenever possible. Rocket launcher men to the rear. And don't be afraid to be gun-shy and show it. You'll live longer. The marble orchards are full of halfwitted heroes."

With his Ingram SMG in his hands, the Death Merchant took the point and led his Delta-Green Group around the side of the low hill. To his right, Alfa-Blue and Bravo-Red Groups were already moving north between the low mounds and over the low hills, dodging from rock to rock, both groups 25 to 30 meters ahead of Camellion's tiny force.

Ahead of Camellion, several meters past the field of gravel, was an almost flat section of ground covered with patches of snow, scree, and clumps of indigo-colored monkshood. Very high overhead a group of arctic terns flew straight south to escape the sound of the bombardment going on several miles to the north.

Camellion led his group to some large masses of rock to the west of the open area, each rock so gigantic it was almost a drumlin, a tiny hill. He suddenly thought of the words in a certain passage of the *Bhagavad Gita*.[7]

*Now I have become death, the destroyer of worlds.*

The thought was leaving his mind when the first Russian AK-47s opened fire and the three helicopters appeared.

---

[6] Touch-on-target.

[7] Means "Song of the Lord" in Sanskrit. As the exalted and often translated statement of Hindu beliefs, it is part of the *Mahabharata*, which is the Hindu "Bible."

# Chapter Ten

*"Hit the dirt!"* yelled the Death Merchant. He and the other commandos flung themselves behind the closest rocks, the harsh staccato firing of AKM assault rifles, PPS submachine guns, and the deeper roar of Soviet heavy machine guns pounding against the ears of the attacking force. Unable to take cover quickly enough, four men of Alfa-Blue Force and two fighters of Bravo-Red were killed instantly. Two of the men had been almost cut in two by the rain of projectiles.

The second half of the double trouble was the three helicopters, two YAK-24Us and one Ka-25. To the Death Merchant and his people, the plan of the Soviets was obvious. The Ka-25 was an attack chopper, loaded with machine guns and rockets. The YAK-24Us were troop carriers. The idea was for the twin-rotored YAKs to hang back while the Ka-25 blasted the Americans with machine-gun and rocket fire. Then the two YAKs would come in, drop to within a few feet of the ground, and discharge the eighty KGB troopers.

On the ground the commandos hugged the rocks, except for eight of the men who quickly loaded Homer rockets into steel tubes. But they never got the chance to fire at the Ka-25. The Russians, in their haste, had not taken into consideration the trajectory of the 40mm grenades streaking in from the Arrowheads. The commandos on the SDVs had the launchers pointed upward, in a mortar position, so that each grenade followed a course that was an enormous loop.

The Ka-25 roared in, getting lower with each second. At 300 feet the chopper intersected the last of the stream of 40mm grenades pouring in from the Arrowheads. Several dozen grenades struck the port side of the helicopter and exploded. A microsecond later the chopper exploded, the thirteen explosions so close together they sounded like one gigantic blast. The Russian whirlybird vanished in one giant flash of red-orange flame, concussion scattering wreckage and chunks of pilot, copilot, and three gunners all over the sky. The explosion had been of such magnitude that burning and smoking debris rained down not only on the Special Services commandos but also on the Russian machine gunners who had dug in on the tops of the low hills several hundred feet to the south.

The KGB troopers with AKMs had stopped firing when the commandos had ducked down in the rocks. Now, as burning material and twisted metal dropped from the sky, the DshK heavy machine gun stopped throwing its 12.7mm projectiles at the rocks. As fate would have it, none of the wreckage injured any of the Americans or the Russians.

The two YAK-24Us started to swing south, the pilots calculating that they could set down close to the beach. The KGB troopers could jump the 6 feet to the sand and then come in behind the invaders.

The Russian plan dissolved in violent chaos when a Homer rocket struck one YAK in the rear rotor housing that protruded from the craft's stabilizer. There was a fleeting flash of fire. The rotor blades, now twisted, shot to the right. The large helicopter jerked, rocked from bow to stern, wobbled again, then started going down at a very steep angle toward the south. It reminded the men on the ground—both Russians and Americans—of a giant bird that was mortally wounded as its forward rotor, just to the rear of the control compartment, fought to keep it in the air. Wobbling from port to starboard, the half-destroyed chopper headed over the first line of hills, all the while dropping sharply.

The second YAK disappeared from the sky in two bright flashes. One Homer had hit center starboard. A second missile had slammed into the control compartment, blowing it and the pilot and copilot into hundreds of fragments. The remainder of the helicopter fell in two pieces, KGB troopers tumbling out of both ends of the middle section. Their arms and legs moving frantically, the men resembled little dolls as they fell screaming to their deaths.

The sky rained junk and bodies. Some of the chopper bounced when it hit the rocks. The KGB troopers did not. There were only loud thuds and the breaking of bones and pieces of equipment. Each corpse then was mashed in a sort of flat shape, looking like things in white-gray parkas that

109

had been stepped on, useless lumps of flesh from which bones protruded.

None of the Russians to the north were hurt by the wreckage or the bodies of their comrades. But a part of a turboshaft engine struck a commando in the back of the head, ripped through the thick material of his snowsuit hood, and split open his skull. The man's body went limp. Dead, he sagged against the boulder he had been using to protect himself from Soviet machine-gun slugs.

The Ka-25 attack chopper, now as low as 50 feet, passed over the commandos guarding the deep-dive suits. Completely out of control, the helicopter headed sharply downward, the front tricycle landing gear barely missing the top of a sandstone stack.

"Some of you men get down there to the beach," ordered Lieutenant Ed Percy. "It will either crash on the beach or just beyond."

Lieutenant Ebenezer "Ed" Percy was the officer in charge of the forty commandos. Several seconds later, he and the other men heard the loud explosion when the chopper hit the beach just ahead of the surf.

Five of the commandos stopped, turned around, and looked questioningly at Percy. "Check it out anyhow," he said. "If any of them are still alive, kill them."

The silence was unusual. Unable to see the commandos, the Russians were not firing. Not knowing the exact size of the invading force and unnerved by the quick destruction of the three helicopters, the Russians waited for the enemy to come to them.

Crouched to the right of the Death Merchant, Captain Dunmerser no longer wore his hornrimmed glasses; instead he wore contact lens.

"They're spread out on the tops of the hills," he said. "They don't have mortars or they would have used them by now. I guess that proves they haven't brought in reinforcements from Siberia." He glanced hopefully at Camellion who remained silent. "We could use a Homer to blast the ivans on this end, then lay a cover of smoke and charge."

"Negative," Camellion said. "If we missed the first time with a Homer, the Ruskies might fall back. Maybe next time they'd catch us out in the open."

On Camellion's left, Nel Spaulding whispered, stuttering

110

as usual, "E-E-Either we-we advance, or stay-y h-here or re-retreat. But h-how are we going t-to charge f-forward without e-ending up as c-c-cold c-cuts?"

"It's a good hundred and fifty feet from here to there," said Dunmerser, who wanted to use the Homer rockets.

The Death Merchant's PRC-6 buzzed in its case. Camellion reached for the radio, a scowl on his face. All the PRCs had been locked to the very low frequency of 299 KHz. At such a low frequency very little radio energy is radiated into space. By the lock and the VLF of 299 KHz, Camellion and Connery hoped the Russians would not have time to cut into the single channel and pick up any of their transmissions. Nonetheless, there was some element of risk to each transmission. the danger was always there.

Camellion switched on the PRC, held the instrument close to his mouth, and flicked the push-to-talk switch. "This is C. Execute."

"A-Blue," Connery said. "The only way is to use rockets followed by smoke. Do you concur? Over."

"Negative. I repeat: negative," Camellion replied. "Such a plan would require too many Homers. Hold your positions. We're closer to the enemy at this end. I'm going to try to get to the top of the hill ahead. When I do, I'll open fire on Russian positions on the hills east of me. That's when you and Bravo-Red use smoke and advance; not before. Now open fire, so I can keep track of the Russian positions. Over."

"All you're going to accomplish is get yourself splattered," Connery said in alarm. "Over."

"That's the plan. Out."

Camellion switched off the PRC, shoved it back in its case, and turned to Captain Dunmerser, who was staring at him through his goggles in a kind of dumb wonderment. "It's one hell of a risk you're taking. You're just begging for a bellyful of Russian slugs."

Ingram machine guns began firing sporadic bursts to the east. Soviet machine guns fired in response, including the heavy DshK. The scream of ricochets soon became a constant annoyance. Full-metal-jacketed 7.62 semispitzer projectiles zinged off rocks protecting Camellion and his tiny Delta-Green force, testimonials that the KGB troopers on the hill ahead knew they were there.

"You can't lose when you never take a chance," Camellion said to Dunmerser. "But you never win either."

He looked around the side of the rock and saw that the hill in front was hardly more than a large, rounded mound, with the longest slope on the west side. This west slope merged into a small, lopsided, rock-strewn plain. The east slope curved into the west incline of the next hill to the east. Camellion estimated that the gap between the two hills, from summit to summit, was around three hundred feet. All the slopes were rock covered, patches of snow and vegetation spread out like a crazy-quilt.

Camellion turned and spoke in a louder voice to the other commandos, "Fire short bursts at the hilltop. But once I start up the side make sure you fire ten feet above the peak of the hill."

Six of the men belly-crawled to better positions, shoved their Ingrams between rocks, and triggered off short bursts at the hilltop. Quickly then they pulled back, in time to escape the rain of Russian projectiles that struck the rocks and made chips of stone fly.

The Death Merchant took two Mark-18 smoke grenades from his bag, pulled the pin from the first grenade, and threw it as hard as he could over the rock. It landed halfway up the slope, went off, and began spewing out violet smoke. He tossed the second grenade. It fell 20 feet behind the first one and began hissing out a violet cloud.

The Death Merchant didn't rush out from behind the rock and try to dart up the grade. He wasn't ready to commit suicide. Instead, he crawled to his left, to the west, down on his hands and knees behind the commandos. Captain Dunmerser stared after him, wondering what he was going to do. Dunmerser soon found out.

Camellion crawled 150 feet to the west, stopped, then looked out at the west slope of the enemy hill. If any KGB pig-farmers were on the west slope, they weren't firing and were keeping well hidden. All the firing was coming from the boulders and slabs on the summit, most of it from a Degtyarev light machine gun. Here, to the west, the odds were better. *I'll still be running on a muddy track, but I'll have more of a chance to win by a nose.* Maybe! From this point, where he was crouched, it was a good 250 feet to the top of the mound.

He slipped his right arm through the leather sling-strap

of the Ingram SMG, placed the strap over his left shoulder, and moved the slip-type buckle resting against his chest, tightening the SMG to his back. As small as the weapon was, it was still not right for his purpose, even when on semiautomatic fire. For one thing, the SMG was not a balanced weapon; for another, the weapon had a tendency to jerk upward when fired by one hand only.

The Death Merchant unsnapped the straps holding the Auto Mags snug in their holsters, pushed up his goggles, pulled the AMPs from the oiled leather, and switched off the safety catches. Keeping as low a profile that would still permit him to run with maximum speed and movement, he darted out between two large rocks and, running straight north as hard as he could, raced to gain a position on the west slope, his eyes darting every now and then to the jumble of rocks on the summit.

The KGB at the top spotted him when he had gained a fraction more than a hundred feet. He had time for only a glimpse of four Russians—or was it five?—swinging to their right and poking the barrels of AKMs through rocks. He ducked to the left with such speed that he almost crashed into a monument-sized boulder in his haste to escape the flood of high-powered slugs. Coming seconds later, the projectiles struck the ground where he had been only moments before, the impacts all doing a John Wayne number, the snow and pebbles kicking up in a regularly spaced series of spurts. Some *whanged* off tough granite. Others buried themselves in loose graywacke. One 7.62mm projectile hit a chunk of granite to the Death Merchant's left, ricocheted ten feet, smacked the side of a boulder only a foot from his face, then screamed off into space, missing his left cheek by only six inches.

Camellion dropped the AMPs into the hip holsters and took three smoke grenades and one M2 fragmentation grenade from his explosives bag. It was a shame that he couldn't present the ivans with one of the half-pound blocks of RDX he carried, but the high-powered stuff was needed to destroy the base. Each commando carried ten half-pound blocks of RDX.

He tossed the first smoke grenade in front of the boulder, throwing it with all his strength. The second and third went to his left. Then he threw the hand grenade. No matter what the Russians were, they were human. When the grenade exploded, they would react by instinct and duck down. Camellion would use this lag-time to his advantage.

He did so the instant the grenade exploded with a big bang that seemed to shake the hillside. He left the protection of the boulder and plunged to the left in a northwest direction. He couldn't see the top of the hill. He couldn't even see the upper ramparts of the grade. Blocking his view—and the Russians'—was a weaving wall of violet smoke, some parts of the dense fog so intensely colored they appeared to be solid.

Angered at Camellion's slick strategy, the KGB fired frantically, AKMs and PPS sub-guns chattering. But the Degtyarev light machine gun continued to rake the area straight downward, the Russians determined to make it impossible for the other Delta-Green men to advance.

The Death Merchant ducked and weaved, his goal a snow-coated mound of gravel chunks and soil that rose from decayed limestone resting on the uneven surface of the rock beneath. A bullet struck one corner of his bag of explosives, ripped through the tough plasto-canvas material, and jerked the bag violently. Another piece of hardcore lead streaked through the tough nylon fabric of the top of his snowsuit hood. That bullet made him angry; he could feel it going through his hair on the crown of his head. A third semi-spitzer slug cut across his right knee while his leg was raised in a long step. Again Camellion heard a quick tearing sound, and he knew that the $450 snowsuit had received another rip. How close had the slug come to his knee? It didn't make any difference: the ones that missed didn't count.

His breath coming in slight pants, he reached the mound of gravel and soil and got down, the thudding of slugs striking the front of the mound and the ground on either side stirring his feelings toward the Russians to a greater pitch. But his anger did not interfere with his logic or his talent for estimating distance and remembering the enemy's position. According to his calculations, he was within 24.4 meters —80 feet—of the KGB gun-nest. Eighty feet to the west and slightly to the north.

*Piggy boys, I have a surprise for you!*

In turn, the KGB had a surprise for him!

*Blammmmmm!* The first frag grenade exploded 20 feet ahead of the small mound. The blast pounded at his ears as shrapnel peppered the other side of the mound. Camellion fell flat, reached inside the hood, and shoved the tips of his fingers into his ears.

The second grenade exploded 30 feet to his left and 5 feet to the front of the mound. The third and the fourth explosions were to his right, the third 70 feet away and 10 feet to the north. The fourth was much closer, 50 feet and parallel to the Death Merchant. Lying there, his face down, Camellion felt a dozen tiny stabs as shrapnel bored into the right side of his snowsuit and was stopped by the thin but tough insulation.

The explosions were replaced by a hail of machine-gun fire, scores of slugs screaming off in ricochets. Camellion pulled his fingers from his ears and listened to the firing. Now the KGB was using the Degtyarev light machine gun. *Oh boy! The big show is getting hotter than the balls of a Gila monster in a New Mexico desert in August!*

Listening to the tremendous firing to the east, between the KGB machine gun nests on the other hills and the Alfa-Blue and Bravo-Red forces, Camellion thought of all the questions for which, as yet, there was not a single answer. For instance, the road in the middle of Wrangel Island that ended on a plain of tundra—a road that led nowhere. The answer to that riddle, as well as to the secret of the radar station that appeared to be a sophisticated weather base of an experimental nature, would have to be found at the Soviet complex only a very short distance away. The radar-weather station was to the east of the airfield in the center of the island and, therefore, inaccessible to the Death Merchant and his attacking forces.

None of the Special Services people knew it, but all of Wrangel was targeted to go *boom*. But again, first things first.

Camellion took the last four Mark-18 smoke grenades from his bag and went to work, the acid of the drifting smoke beginning to burn his eyes. Before he pulled the pin of the first smoke grenade, he took out his gas mask, pulled back the hood, slipped the mask over his face, then readjusted the hood.

The smoke ahead was thinning and he hurried, not wanting the Russians to see the smoke canisters sailing through the air, or they'd be able to pinpoint his position. He threw the first smoke grenade far to his right, to the east. The second went in the same direction. He threw the third grenade 40 feet in front of him. The fourth went 50 feet to the west. Within several minutes the entire perimeter was thick with intensely violet smoke.

Camellion didn't have any doubts that he could have wiped out the KGB machine gun nest with several incendiary grenades. But he wanted to do more than neutralize the enemy. He had to use the rocks for protection when he fired at the rest of the enemy on the other hills to the east; and he wanted possession of the Degtyarev light machine gun. There was only one way to get the job done: the hard way, the dangerous way. The KGB might again try a grenade barrage in an effort to turn him into blown-apart dead meat. *They probably will if I toss a grenade close to them now.*

To the din of projectiles ricocheting from hundreds of rocks and thudding into the front of the small mound, Camellion took a frag grenade, pulled the pin, and tossed it far to the east, aiming it so that it would explode 75 feet in front of the estimated position. The grenade went off with a flash and a bang, and for a few moments the enemy machine gun stopped firing.

This time Camellion left the rear of the mound and, an Auto Mag in each hand, darted straight up toward the enemy position, so intent in counting off the seconds, so intent on getting close to the Russian position that he hardly noticed the thick smoke swirling around him. He swerved to the left and got down behind a rocky frost heave mantled with lichens, some snow, and patches of grassy vegetation, his quick movement to safety almost concurrent with the roaring of five or six AKMs and PPSs and the light machine gun.

Camellion had harbored the fear that the KGB might have heard his feet on some of the loose rock. They hadn't, or they wouldn't now be firing in great sweeping arcs. They knew he was somewhere, but they didn't know where.

In spite of his delicately balanced position between life and Death, Camellion felt elation surge through his body. To judge from the sounds of the firing, the Russians were only 40, maybe 50 feet in front of him and perhaps 20 feet to his right. He grinned in anticipation. Two more steps to execute. The grenade. Then surprise the pig-farmers. After that it would be root-hog or die—as the natives of the Big Thicket region of Texas are prone to say.

Camellion pulled a frag grenade from the bag, measured the distance to the Russian position, then remeasured the imaginary line from point A to goal B. He had to be right.

He had to drop the grenade from 5 to 15 feet in front of the rocks. Concussion would do the rest. If he got lucky, shrapnel might take out one or two of the ivans. On the other hand, if he dropped the grenade in the laps of the KGB troopers, he could wreck the light machine gun and end up wading in blood and torn-apart bodies. It would be a gory mess, and Camellion didn't like disorder.

He pulled the pin of the grenade, mentally calculated the distance once more, and threw the grenade just so, just with the right amount of pitch and power. He pulled the Auto Mags, tensed his legs, and heard the grenade go off with a deafening roar. With the explosion came a high shriek of pain. *Ah! Sweet success!* His legs might have been springs as he reared up from behind the frost heave and charged straight up the incline at the KGB position. He didn't dodge or zigzag. He couldn't afford the time. Either the grenade had done its work or it hadn't. If it had not and the Russians began a sweeping fire—*I'm a dead man!*

Fifteen more big steps and he found himself beyond most of the smoke and catching the first glimpse of the KGB "rock nest." During that thin slice of a second, he saw that the fragmentation grenade had done its work well. Smoke was still curling from the small crater whose north rim was only seven or eight feet from the rocks. The outside surface of the granite rocks was newly pitted, the white chop-marks left by shrapnel showing vividly. And from the way the KGB troopers in the rocks were acting—as if dazed and out of contact with reality—the concussion had dislocated their awareness, an alertness they were only now recovering.

Two Russians, fear and astonishment on their faces, died a few seconds after they spotted Camellion and tried to drop the muzzles of their PPS submachine guns toward him. Now ducking and weaving from side to side, the Death Merchant fired both Auto Mags on the run. One big projectile stabbed into the upper chest of one man, exploded, and slammed the man all the way back to the boulders on the east side. The projectile from the left AMP hit the other KGB trooper in the right shoulder, exploded, and tore off his arm. He screamed in horror, fainted from shock, and crumpled at the base of the rock. A third Russian was reaching for a hand grenade when Camellion fired again and blew away his entire face with an explosive slug.

Another KGB guard bravely jumped behind the deadly

Degtyarev light machine gun whose muzzle was pointed in Camellion's direction. Camellion ducked far to the left and fired both AMPs at the same time that the Russian grasped the handle, swung the weapon on its bipod, and pulled the trigger. The LMG roared, but the stream of 7.62mm slugs passed a foot or more to Camellion's right. The Russian couldn't fire again. One of the .357 magnum bullets exploded in his neck, blew apart his throat, and sent his Adam's apple flying like a bloody golf ball. The second bullet struck the right side of his chest and pitched him back against the other rocks. Since his finger was on the trigger and the upper part of his hand around the trigger guard of the light machine gun, the weapon went with him. The Degtyarev chattered out a final burst of slugs that arced up to the sky, then clattered to the ground. It fell beside another KGB trooper who was down on both knees, sobbing, his hands over his eyes. Shrapnel from Camellion's grenade had sliced his face to ribbons. Blind, in pain, and feeling the sticky blood oozing from between his fingers, Boris Gorvendivitch was as helpless as a day-old baby.

The two remaining Russians weren't cowards; they weren't fools either. Their decision that discretion was more logical than suicidal heroism was immediate and automatic. Unnerved by the swift, violent annihilation of their comrades, Illarion Dashkov and Leon Ungern Vilenski had only a quick look at the gas-masked Death Merchant, who wore snow goggles on his forehead and, only 7 or 8 feet away, had two long-barrelled pistols in his hands, shiny weapons whose stainless steel reflected colored sunlight.

Dashkov and Vilenski dropped frantically behind the boulders and reached for their AKMs which they had dropped when the grenade had exploded. They assumed that the Death Merchant, to save time, would charge in straight from the west. Accordingly, they thrust the barrels of their AK-47 A-Rs around one boulder and fired upward to the west, expecting that one of their bursts would blast the lone enemy into the next world.

From the way the two men had dropped, it was obvious to the Death Merchant what they had expected him to do. So instead of doing the expected, he did the unexpected. He ran around the rocks to the north, decidedly uncomfortable over the prospects of the Russians on the hill to the east catching sight of him, if only for a few moments. By now the KGB troopers on the next hill had to have noticed the firing going on to the west and have realized that something was very, very wrong. But if the Russians on the other hill fired at him, the Death Merchant didn't know it. Or maybe they didn't have time. Within six seconds he had stormed between two rock columns, leaning so that they resembled a large V, and was inside the Soviet machine gun nest.

Leon Vilenski and Illarion Dashkov, trapped by their fatal miscalculation, did their best to jerk their AKMs from beside the boulder and swing the muzzles to Camellion, fear giving them supernormal speed. Both KGB men had half executed the swing around when the Death Merchant fired both Auto Mags. One .357 magnum bullet, going in at a steep angle, hit Vilenski in the right chest, exploded, and set up a tiny cloud of cloth, foam padding, bits of flesh, and pieces of rib bone. The expanded projectile came out the left side of his chest, then smacked Dashkov in the right forearm at the same time that the Death Merchant's second big bullet bored into Dashkov, just above the humerus of his right arm. The bullet exploded, tore the humerus from the scapula, or shoulder blade, then, travelling downward, shattered the end of the right clavicle, broke six ribs on both sides and finally left the Russian's body via his left side.

With their mouths half open and the peculiar glaze of approaching infinity clouding their eyes, Dashkov and Vilenski collapsed, Vilenski falling forward, his skull cracking against the boulder in front of him. Dashkov tumbled sideways, his body twisting so that he fell on his back.

*Damn!* The tiny, natural citadel was thick with bodies. *Messy! Very messy!* Camellion stepped over the corpses of the first two pig-farmers he had whacked out and moved toward the Degtyarev light machine gun. He reached the LMG, holstered one Auto Mag, removed the PRC-6 from its leather case, and was about to switch on the set when there was a giant blast 300 feet or so to the east, the concussion a wave of force that reached around the rocks and pushed against him.

"*Vsio svet tu'stvuite,* Connery!" ("Damn your blood, Connery") Camellion muttered aloud in Russian. He hunched down and looked around the side of a large granite boulder at the next hill to the east. The rocks were smoking—small rocks on the ground. But the boulders were gone. So were the KGB border guards who had been using the monument rocks for cover. The Homer rocket had blown rocks and men into nothingness, unless one wished to count the thousands and thousands of pieces of cloth and flesh and other debris lying scattered all over the hilltop and slopes.

The Death Merchant switched on the radio and punched the attention button. This time he used the emergency code he and Connery had worked out while still aboard *Tirante*, the call-letter and number based on the international morse code. He first pressed -.-., the letter C, then .----, one short and four long for the numeral 1.

Colonel Connery responded immediately. "I ordered a Homer used because time is running out," he said menacingly. "We're pinned down. Over."

If malevolent thoughts could kill, Connery would have dropped dead. "It's damned thoughtful of you not to have chosen this hill I'm on for your target," Camellion said, his voice as sweet as his face was bitter. "Now that you've begun to use the big stuff, you might as well—" He broke off at the sound of another big blast to the east, of another Homer rocket exploding. "You might as well blow the tops of the other hills. I'll cut down those you don't get. Over."

"You've secured the position on the last hill? Over."

"Affirmative—including a light machine gun and plenty of ammo. Over."

"They've stopped firing. Maybe they're in retreat. If they are you'll be able to see them. Alfa and Bravo will move forward when we hear your LMG. Verify. Over."

"Wilco and out."

Camellion again worked the attention button, this time signalling, .-/-../.....—A.D.5. Almost at once Captain Dunmerser's voice came over the set. "A.D. here. Execute. Over."

"Bring Delta-Green up the slope. I have the hilltop and the ivans are cleaned out. Verify. Over."

"Wilco. Over."

"Out." Camellion turned off the set, put it back into its case, then picked up the Degtyarev by its top carry-handle. More mess. There was half-frozen blood on the top of the barrel and on one leg of the bipod. By the side of one dead Russian was a crate of round-drum magazines. Like all modern Soviet weapons of automatic purpose, the DLMG had a chromed barrel and was characterized by ruggedness and simplicity of maintenance.

The Death Merchant turned, stepped over corpses, carried the LMG to the north, placed the bipod on one of the shorter rocks facing the east, and looked down the long slope. Scores of KGB were in full retreat down the north-side slopes of the hills. The Homer rockets had done the trick. Camellion saw also that KGB reinforcements were coming in from the north, moving out from a chain of even lower hills. These men were moving south toward their comrades who were in retreat. Seeing that help was on the way, the KGB in retreat stopped, sought cover behind boulders and slabs of slate, and waited for the invaders to reach the crest of the hills.

To Camellion, the situation had developed into something as fine as frog hair. He hurried back to the ammo crate and, with some effort, picked it up by the rope handles and carried it to the light machine gun. He pulled back the cocking lever of the LMG and waited for the Russians, coming in from the north across a rock-strewn plain, to get closer. There must have been a hundred of the enemy; at least fifty to seventy more hiding behind rocks on the north slopes. When the reinforcements were within a 150 feet of the lower edges of the northside slopes, he opened fire. The Degtyarev screamed out its 7.62mm projectiles at the rate of 630 rounds a minute when on cyclic burst fire, 1500 rounds a minute on full automatic. Since there were only 480 rounds in the round magazine, Camellion fired cyclic, the LMG chattering furiously.

The Russians from the north, now out in the open, went down by the dozens, the semispitzer slugs knocking them to the ground, kicking and screaming. After the first thirty of them were sprawled out dead—or dying—some of their comrades dropped and attempted to conceal themselves behind rocks far too small for the purpose, while others pinned their hope for life on reaching the larger rocks on the slope sides. Only a dozen reached the hillsides, then only because the Death Merchant had to stop to place a fresh drum in the LMG.

Most of the Russians trying to make themselves small by the rocks did not fare any better. Camellion raked them mercilessly with hundreds of slugs, moving the light machine gun back and forth on the swivel of its bipod. Sometimes a 7.62mm bullet found only a hand or foot, but such stabs were as effective as a bullet in the head or the chest, for they effectively made the victims useless. Some Russians jumped when hit in the foot or hand, exposing vital areas of their bodies. They died moments later when projectiles struck these vital areas.

By now the Russians on the hillsides, using large boulders for concealment, had determined Camellion's position. They too were at a fatal disadvantage. If they moved from the north side of the rocks to the east side, they would expose themselves to fire by the Alfa and Bravo groups. If they remained where they were, north of the boulders, Camellion would cut them to pieces. In desperation, the KGB turned three Degtyarev LMGs to the west and opened fire. Hearing the first slugs zinging off the granite around him, Camellion said, "Dammit to hell," dropped down, and pulled the LMG after him.

While Camellion searched for another rock to place the SMG on, Alfa and Bravo groups reached the tops of the hills and started tossing fragmentation grenades down the slopes. Rocks shattered and Russians screamed and died. Bones broken, bodies somersaulted upward, came down, crashed on the hard surfaces, and lay still. Many of the doomed were dismembered by the explosions, so that the slope was littered with arms and legs, heads, and other parts of the human body.

The Death Merchant was placing the bipod of the light machine gun on a rock and at the same time watching some of the commandos start down the north-side slopes. He turned and looked upward when he heard the familiar sound.

The Tupolev-28P fighter appeared in the northwest, moving with such speed that within seconds the sound of its two axial afterburning turbofans were a howling scream. In most respects the world's largest fighter, the TU-28P came down out of the sky like a silver arrow marked with red stars, its speed so great that none of the commandos had a chance to use Homers. At an altitude of a thousand feet, the TU-28P let loose three of its "Alkali" air-to-ground missiles. The pilot was either the worst marksman in the Soviet Air Force or else he had orders to get the invaders at all costs because the first Alkali exploded three-fourths of the way up on the north slope of the second hill to the east. There was a big bang, then a rolling ball of red and white fire. That was all. But it was enough. The second and third missiles zipped over hills and exploded at the bottom of the wall in back of the commandos on the beach. As fast as it had appeared, the TU-28P was gone, was only a dwindling killer in the southeastern sky. At its great speed, it took 10 miles of sky for the fighter to turn around. Back it came, becoming larger and larger, its engines louder and louder.

Suddenly behind the fighter there was a long dartlike object. Either *Tirante* or *Foxfire* had released a HAWK-1 (Homing All-the-Way Killer) missile. Warned by his instruments, the pilot tried to gain altitude in an effort to outclimb the missile. He might as well have tried to reach the moon. The HAWK had greater speed. The Russian fighter jet was climbing steeply at mach-1 and almost to 30,000 feet when the HAWK caught it.

Camellion and the men on the ground—friend and foe alike—didn't hear much sound from the explosion. HAWK and Russian plane were too high. There was only a muffled boom and a brief, bright flash, then specks of wreckage tumbling down, over and over, in the sky.

The signal came on Camellion's PRC-6 in International Morse code. The Death Merchant took out the set, switched it on and pushed the push-to-talk button. "C-1. Execute."

"We've cleaned out the Russians," Connery said, his low voice all business. "The missile killed twenty of our boys. But from here it appears that the way is open to the base. How is the situation with your group? Over."

From where he stood, Camellion could see the first of his Delta-Green Group coming up the last lap of the hillside.

"We're in good shape and will proceed to the base at once. Any problems with Alfa-Blue or Bravo-Red? Over."

"Negative. Colonel G. is upset. Sergeant T. was one of the men killed by the missile. Over."

"Death and taxes are a fact of life. Out."

Camellion switched off the radio, shoved it back into its case, and, taking off the gas mask which he had pulled down around his neck, watched Captain Dunmerser and Nel Spaulding edge themselves sideways between two boulders facing the south. The two men first stopped and looked at the dead KGB border guards before fastening their eyes on the Death Merchant, staring at him as if he had just risen out of hell with his hair on fire.

"It would seem you've been rather busy up here," Dunmerser said callously, spitting on one of the corpses.

"Where are the others?" Camellion asked.

"Going around to the west. We can catch up with them at the bottom of the slope. Any special orders at this point?"

"Search the dead pig-farmers and take any grenades you might find. We'll need them."

"W-What about t-the AKMs-s-s?" asked Spaulding.

"Take what you want," Camellion said.

Two other commandos came through the rocks and began to help Dunmerser and Spaulding search the bodies of the dead Russians.

Camellion looked toward the north, at the unfriendly land. In the lower parts and hollows the mists hung like white breath. Nothing moved. There was no sound, the birds and other animals having been frightened off by the firing and various explosions.

A thin smile slipped across the Death Merchant's face. It was also natural. Death worked in silence. . . .

# Chapter Eleven

General Walter Vatutin and Colonel Josef Milovanov, standing in front of the main entrance of the stress evaluation center, surveyed the destruction with professional interest and that peculiar kind of never-forget Russian hate; and watched the activity going on around them: men and some women climbing up to, and down from roofs, or setting up machine guns at strategic points or putting various kinds of coverings over empty windows.

Not a single building of the complex had escaped damage by the thousands of 40mm grenades that had rained down and blown holes in the slanted roofs. The barracks buildings had burned to the ground. But the fires on the roofs of the stress evaluation center and the two laboratories had been put out, at the cost of a dozen men who had been killed by explosions while extinguishing the flames. The administration building was half-destroyed, the officers' quarters a burned-out shell. The tower of the radio station lay crumpled, a twisted mass of steel girders.

"My evaluation of the situation is that the *Amerikanskis* will reach us before help arrives from the mainland," Colonel Milovanov said in measured tones. "But we should be able to contain them in the southern half of this station. Before they'll be able to reach the prison the paratroopers will have arrived."

Milovanov remained silent about the greater part of his gloomy thoughts: that if General Vatutin had asked for reinforcements and the proper kind of weapons and other materiel, all this destruction could have been avoided. Vatutin had given an in-depth radio report to Moscova, but when he had been asked if he required more men, he had replied that the KGB forces on the island could handle any future reconnaissance an enemy might undertake. Fortunately for General Vatutin, the big brass in Moscova[1] had agreed with him. Like Vatutin, the big shots had not even anticipated an actual invasion. The tragedy was that the forces on Wrangel Island lacked mortars and other kinds of materiel necessary to repel an invasion by even a small force. The largest weapons available were heavy-caliber machine guns. There were fourteen helicopters, several large Tu-70 cargo planes, and three fighters. And two of the fighters were having their engines overhauled. There had never been a valid reason to have a lot of weapons on the island. It was not of strategic importance. For that very reason the KGB Directorate of Science and Technology had chosen it as a site for an experimental station. Somehow the *Amerikanskis* had found out about the experiments. But which ones? How much did the CIA know?

It pained Josef Milovanov to think of the deadly effectiveness of the enemy forces. The *Amerikanskis* were weak and dominated by a lust for luxury, but they were terrible fighters, brave and vicious fighters, in spite of their leaders who simply couldn't grasp the power of Soviet propaganda.

So far some 150 KGB guards had been killed. Rockets had blown up three helicopters, and some kind of missile had destroyed Lieutenant Oskanin and his fighter plane. Submersibles of some kind had destroyed five patrol boats. Now the invaders were coming straight at the base.

"We are faced with a paradox," Vatutin declared, buttoning his greatcoat. "The helicopters were low enough to be brought down by one-man rockets fired from bazooka launchers. It was very different with Lieutenant Oskanin. Radar proves he was 28,740 feet when the missile blew him out of the sky. A missile of that capability—it had to be a heat-seeking one—had to have been fired from a submarine."

"Our sonar shows that there aren't any submarines in the area," Milovanov said, emerging from his black room of thoughts. "For that matter none of our coastal sensors have indicated the presence of any craft. I don't understand it. The enemy had to come past the sensors in order to get ashore."

Milovanov stepped back with Vatutin to make room for

[1] Russian spelling of Moscow.

fourteen troopers who were about to carry four PKS[2] machine guns and seven cases of ammunition belts into the Stress Evaluation Center.

Milovanov stared after the troopers going into the massive building of the Stress Evaluation Center. "The *Amerikanski* submarine that was there for so long left day before yesterday," he added. "Even so, we were monitoring the sub and can be positive that it left the area."

General Vatutin glanced annoyingly at Milovanov. "I know the submarine departed from the area, dammit. Therein lies the incongruity—missiles fired from a nonexistent submarine. A further contradiction is that if our airplanes and surface craft can't find a target, they can't bomb it. And to bomb blindly would be foolish. The Proliv Longa is far too vast for such random tactics."

Lighting a cigarette, Colonel Milovanov exhaled smoke through his mouth and nose and looked up at the cloudless azure sky. The fighter planes from the air base at Ambarchik had perfect flying weather. He gave Vatutin a brief, speculative glance. "Comrade General, I would say that another problem is how the Central Intelligence Agency learned of our experiment with the Cosmic Generator."

"Da, but not our problem." Vatutin made a deprecating gesture, then pulled a handkerchief from one of the pockets of his greatcoat. "Let counterintelligence solve that mystery. To me there isn't anything puzzling about it. It shouldn't be to you either." He blew his nose loudly several times and stuffed the handkerchief into his pocket.

"Photographs from one of the *Amerikanski* spy satellites," Milovanov said promptly, feeling that Vatutin had expected a definite answer. "They are curious about what they believe to be some advanced type of experimental weather station. It is also possible that the CIA might have picked up some information regarding our behavior modification program and our other experiments. It might be a combination of

[2] A general purpose machine gun. The PK stands for "Pulomet Kalashnikov"—machine gun Kalashnikov. The S, as in other Soviet machine guns, stands for "Stankovy"—mounted. When used on a bipod the weapon is designated a PK; when on a tripod, a PKS.

reasons." A serious expression crossed his face. "But to invade! Those *Amerikanskis* are unpredictable!"

General Vatutin turned and studied the south end of the base, a quarter of a block away, where Major Konstantin Rinchino was shouting orders at squads of KGB guards and some regulars of the Red Army, directing them to place machine guns behind the barrier of heavy Rostov trucks that were parked horizontally, end to end, on the perimeter. The gas tanks had been drained and the south side of their deep beds had been armored with loose steel plating taken from the prison.

"It was that dummy weather station with all those stupid towers that caused the Americans to move." Vatutin's low voice was bitter and angered. *"Blyatskaye Dyeluh!*[3] I warned General Lorgendonev and Major General Ankuochien! I told them that station would be like waving a red flag under the noses of the Americans. Their opinion was that we needed some disguise to justify the existence of such a large landing strip."

Colonel Josef Milovanov thought of his wife and four children who lived in Moscova. That would be the first Soviet city to vanish in a mushroom cloud of deadly radiation. He looked up at the sky again and thought of how easily it could be darkened with ICBMs.

"Comrade General, I wonder if we will strike first? I suppose it doesn't really make that much difference."

Vatutin turned to Milovanov, a frown on his bulldog face. "Strike first? What do you mean?"

"A full scale war. World War Three."

His brow clearing, General Vatutin smiled. "There will not be a major war over what is happening here on Wrangel Island. There will only be secret meetings and arguments between our high officials and theirs."

Milovanov nodded thoughtfully and slowly rubbed his mustache with the tips of his fingers. "What about Europe, Comrade General?"

"The key to Europe is the oil of the Saudis and they will soon be ours. Once we have the Arabian oil, we'll be able to dictate terms to the Europeans. Enough of that. Our concern is the here and now. We must hold the American commandos until troops arrive from the mainland."

---

[3] "Goddammit!"

Milovanov cleared his throat and sniffed at the air which smelled strongly of burnt materiel.

"We still have time to bring in the men from the airfield," he offered. "By so doing, we'd have several more men in our force here."

"*Nyet*. We can't leave the strip undefended. The attack from the south might be a diversionary tactic. Another force could still come in from the east or the west. We can't take the chance. The Cosmic Generator takes precedence over anything we have here." General Vatutin looked at the prison building in the southeast corner of the installation. "The explosives have been placed?"

"All around the foundation. I can detonate them by remote control." Milovanov patted his left breast pocket. "I have the device with me. All—"

The shriek of a siren cut him off. The lookouts, posted a quarter of a mile to the south, had reported to the command center that had been established in the behavior modification laboratory.

The American force had been sighted.

# Chapter Twelve

From where the Death Merchant lay belly-flat on a slab of granite, he could see very clearly the south side of the Soviet installation. He and the other men of Delta-Green Group were only a quarter of a mile from the base—and about 125 feet above it on a flat-topped hill. His gloved finger barely turned the focus wheel of the Bushnell compact binoculars. Good. The image was clear. Camellion wasn't disappointed. The Soviet compound was every bit as big as he had expected it to be. The destruction by the 40mm grenades was better than he had hoped for. Every room had large gaping holes, with jagged ends of ripped lumber sticking out around the edges. The roof of the Palace of Laughter and the roofs of the two laboratories appeared to be smoking. The smoke was actually vapor from the action of the sun on the still-wet roof. Where the barracks had stood were several acres of ashes and blackened frames, most of them sagging. All the other buildings had taken a severe pounding. Only the prison and its fence seemed untouched.

Lying to the right of Camellion, Chuck Lilmuten sniffed and rubbed the back of his hand under his nose. "Man, I tell you, Ledbetter and his guys sure blew hell out of them," he commented to no one in particular.

"You'd better believe it," said Will Scaggs, who was next to Lilmuten. "The radio tower might as well be tangled up spaghetti. And that other building next to the radio station. Hell, it's burned out and nothing more than a shell.

"I-I-It has a-a f-flagpo-ole in f-front," stuttered Nel Spaulding. "It's t-the-the administration build-i-ing." He carried a broad-bladed Gladiator in a leather sheath worn transversely on his back. Now he unbuckled the holster and snapped the huge knife in back of the right hip holster filled with a 9mm Browning autoloader.

"It looks rather peaceful down there, like the morning

130

after the night the tornado struck," Captain Dunmerser said, staring through his Bausch & Lomb binoculars. "By God! I can't see a single pig-farmer."

"It wasn't raining when Noah started to build the Ark," Camellion said quietly. "They haven't retreated to the airbase. They're down there and waiting for us."

"I guess you're right," conceded Dunmerser. He moved his binoculars slightly. "Their first line of defense is the trucks. The Russians know we have to move down from the hills and cross that empty plain. That's where they hope to cut us down."

"We can't be positive that they haven't retreated," offered Will Scaggs, a note of hopefulness creeping into his voice. "The few scouts we saw in the distance didn't offer to fight. Hell no, we can't be positive."

"Oh yes we can," the Death Merchant said stubbornly. "Communists are like all fanatics: they take willing leave of their wits for the sake of their faith. Faith over fact and common sense and science is one of the fatal flaws of human nature." Camellion sighed and put the binoculars into their case.

Captain Dunmerser looked at his watch. "Another twenty seconds." He looked up and down the line. "Everybody get ready to move to the west."

The Death Merchant put on a pair of Ray-Ban green sunglasses, then stared down at the open space to the south of the Soviet base. East of the plain were small hogbacks of broken rock, strangely beautiful with the half-melted snow and the vivid red of bearberry leaves. KGB troopers had not been waiting there for an ambush or heat sensors would have revealed their presence.

West of the plain and west of the entire base the undulating tundra moved straight to Rodgers Harbor, the whole area alive with flowers, all growing profusely among ancient granites and sandstones large enough to conceal a man, large enough to conceal the men of Delta-Green.

Colonel Connery and Colonel Gordon began the attack on the mark. As Camellion and his group watched, a storm of Mark-2 fragmentation grenades appeared out of nowhere and exploded almost in unison against the steel sides of the heavy-duty trucks, and in front of the trucks. Some of the grenades fell short and only succeeded in blowing big holes in the ground. But some of the trucks were half-demolished, whiles others suffered less damage, losing only wheels or the side doors of cabs. One truck, hit by four grenades, had been blown apart, its smoking wreckage scattered—along with six dead KGB guards—over a wide area.

Immediately, the Russians opened fire with machine guns, some from underneath the trucks and others from the reinforced beds, the mystified gunners firing at the masses of lopsided monument granites 50 to 500 feet to the south. Hundreds of 7.62mm slugs from Degtyarevs and AKMs screamed out a raucous aria of ricochets. There were louder solos from deeply cannelured 14.5mm projectiles as they attempted to penetrate rock, couldn't, and glanced off into space. The KGB were also using several KPV heavy machine guns.

Captain Dunmerser laughed with unrestrained glee and clapped the Death Merchant on the back. "Camellion, I've got to hand it to you. In an area like this, crossbows can't be beat!"

The Death Merchant didn't reply. Calmly, his tanned face expressionless, he watched the destruction taking place below and thought of the type of crossbow that thirty of the commandos were using. Called the Cobra, the crossbow was of rugged alloy construction, with an effortless, self-cocking mechanism. The draw weight was 150 lbs; muzzle velocity 295 fps; range in excess of 300 yards. One could even mount a scope on a Cobra. For the job to be done, Camellion had decided on aluminum bolts or shafts, with a three-bladed broadhead—just right for wiring either a grenade or an incendiary. To end-balance the extra weight, tiny lead bars had previously been attached to the rear of the shafts.

Colonel Connery had been against the idea from the beginning. Back on the *Tirante*, he had argued: "It can't be done! How in hell do you expect a man to put a shaft on the bed, pull the fuse, and aim and fire in six seconds? Crap! They'd blow themselves up!"

But, Camellion had persisted, and the colonel had finally given in to the Death Merchant's taunting. "Maybe your men can't handle it? . . ."

"Don't worry about that!" Connery had exploded. "I've got men who could hit an ant's butt with a crossbow at a thousand feet. They'll beat the hell out of ivans with hand axes if they have to."

Colonel Connery had not exaggerated. The men selected by Connery, who was in charge of Special Services, and by Colonel Gordon, who was boss of the Navy SEALS (for Sea, Air, Land), were now proving that they were indeed experts with a crossbow.

The Russians continued the savage firing, confident that it was impossible for anything or anyone to cross the open space and live. And they were right. Scores of submachine guns and heavy MGs were hosing the area with thousands of slugs, so many that already small clouds of dust had risen from the rocks protecting the thirty commandos who didn't dare leave their positions.

The KGB guards braced themselves for another barrage of grenades. Instead they received something even worse— thirty M14 thermite grenades. This time the commandos aimed to a slightly higher trajectory. This time none of the incendiaries fell short. Most struck the trucks, many exploding within the beds of the vehicles. Seven fell just beyond the trucks and burst into hideously beautiful flowers of bright-burning death whose many petals fell on doomed Russians.

One was compelled to feel sympathy for the shrieking men, many of whom began to dance as though they were being stung by invisible hornets. Reflex demanded that those who hadn't been splashed with molten thermite and were already dead try to extinguish the white fire eating through their clothing. But every effort was a waste of time. Within seconds the thermite had burned through their parkas and uniforms and was eating through flesh to the bone, then through the bone. A single drop of molten fire was enough to put a man out of action and even kill him, depending on where it had fallen. The KGB border guards screamed and shrieked, danced and died.

"Shake, rattle, and roll, you rotten pig-farmers!" muttered Bruce Tuby, who had gotten into the habit of using Camellion's colloquialism.

The Russians weren't shaking, nor were any of them rattling. But more than a dozen were rolling on the ground in an effort to extinguish the flames consuming their clothing. One by one, they stopped their movements and lay still.

133

In a short while they too would be blackened corpses.

The thirty commandos with the crossbows were not finished with the Soviet force. They fired another thirty frag grenades and while these exploded and tore trucks apart and sent charred corpses tumbling into the air, the commandos loaded the beds of their Cobras with shafts to whose ends smoke grenades were attached, each man lowering the trajectory before he fired. A short time later when these grenades exploded each one was a different distance from the blasted and burning trucks. Soon the clearing was filled with thick, drifting clouds of violet smoke, plus black, oily smoke drifting from the trucks.

Seeing the smoke, Alfa-Blue and Bravo-Red Forces made their move. All this time the forces of Colonel Connery and Colonel Gordon had been concealed in the boulders and broken rocks of the hogbacks to the east. Now, as quietly as possible, the commandos raced to the west side of the Russian base while the thirty commandos to the west secured their crossbows, left the rocks, and zigzagged like crazy men to the east, anxious to link up with the two other groups.

The Russians were firing only two light machine guns, the gunners raking the clouds of violet smoke at ground level. They were positive that the enemy was about to attack straight on. Another waste of ammunition. All thirty commandos escaped without a scratch, although one man had tripped and fallen and had a sprained arm.

The Death Merchant and his men slid back from the rock when they heard Ingram submachine guns firing and grenades exploding toward the east. Bravo-Red and Alfa-Blue had succeeded. The commandos were storming into the base.

"Well, the first big casualties are the Russians," Chuck Lilmuten said.

"Negative," said Camellion, who was checking his Auto Mags. "The first casualty was truth. Truth is always the first to die in any war." He shoved the AMPs into holsters, secured the straps over the trigger guards, then looked at the men who were giving their equipment a final once-over. "Make sure those special cameras are locked tightly in their bulletproof cases. The ivans didn't deploy all their men behind those trucks. There'll be plenty more of the pig-farmers in the Palace of Laughter and in the two labs."

"I'd just as soon eat a pork chop as go down there," muttered Nick Sternberg who was Jewish and built like a baby bull.

"We all would," agreed Captain Dunmerser. He took out the second hard-chrome .45 Enforcer he carried, an autoloader that, smaller than the standard .45, had been designed for the professional, for combat shooting. Lightweight, powerful, and deadly accurate, the Enforcer[1] was a savior to anyone who might happen to find his life on the line.

Dunmerser pulled back the slide and felt the cartridge jump into the barrel and lock in place. He thumbed on the safety and shoved the weapon into its holster, thinking that within half an hour he might be dead and in eternity.

"Let's do it," Camellion said. "Let's go down and terminate all the pig-farmers we can find."

They moved from the top of the hill, each man knowing that while it was more than likely that any KGBs posted to the west would now be moving east to reinforce their comrades, there would still be stiff resistance on the west side of the Soviet base.

They left the hill and moved in single file to the northwest, creeping around boulders and slab and monument rocks. Finally they reached a point that placed the burned-out administration building around several hundred feet to the north, 70 yards or so filled with foot-high sax grass, bright red saxifrage, pink-purple lousewort, and long, but not very tall, ridges of gravel and sand known as eskers.

"Well, it's not a lot of cover but enough," Dunmerser whispered to Camellion. "We can leave these larger rocks and crawl to within fifty feet of the buildings."

The Death Merchant didn't answer; he continued to study the depressing looking apron.

"None of this would be so bad if we had some beer to drink on the way in," Clark Ochsner said to Amos Huckaba who was lying next to him. "Beer makes you smarter."

"You're out of your tree," growled Huckaba, shifting the plug of tobacco in his mouth. "The only thing beer will do is make you fat and turn your liver to rock If you drink enough of it."

"I don't know about that," said Ochsner cheerfully. "It made Bud Wiser."

---

[1] The Enforcer's internal parts are even coated with Teflon to eliminate lubricant problems in cold or dusty areas.

"Oh, hell!" Huckaba half laughed and jabbed Ochsner in the ribs with his elbow.

Camellion and Dunmerser smiled. Dunmerser turned and was about to tell Ochsner and Huckaba to knock it off, then changed his mind. It was only their way of letting off tension, their way of pretending that none of the slugs had their names on them.

The crawl through the grass and between the ridges of the esker went without incident. There was only the slight breeze and the sounds of gunfire and exploding grenades, plus the sickening stink of burning metal and rubber, cloth and leather, burnt TNT and gunpowder—and roasted flesh.

Close to the edge of the grass, the Death Merchant belly-crawled to a chunk of igneous rock sticking up from the ground, looked underneath the bottom edge, and sized up the buildings at close range, none of which had been built with beauty of architecture in mind. Most of the buildings were constructed of concrete blocks, double-walled with 6 inches of insulation between the two walls. But the huge Palace of Laughter and the two even larger laboratory buildings were tremendous slabs of reinforced concrete. Like the other buildings, all three were painted dark gray.

Not a single Russian was in sight!

The Death Merchant drew both Auto Mags. "Pass the word and make it a respond-back," he ordered Captain Dunmerser. "We're going straight to the southwest corner of the administration building. Tell them to watch all the windows."

Dunmerser crawled back half a body length, turned, and whispered to Nel Spaulding, who turned and stuttered out the message to the next man. A few minutes later the verification had returned to Camellion, who looked behind, turned to the front, inhaled deeply, got to his feet, and suddenly was off like a bolt of lightning. Captain Dunmerser and the nine commandos, amazed at the incredible speed of the Death Merchant, raced behind him, determined not to let this old man, ten years their senior, show them up.

Camellion and the rest of the Delta-Greens were only a short distance from the administration building when two machine guns started roaring—a KPV heavy from the roof of the Palace of Laughter and a SG 43M light from the second floor of the partially burned out officers' quarters building.

Slugs *zip, zip, zipped* all around Camellion and the other men, many of the big 14.5mm and smaller 7.62mm projectiles hissing so close to the zigzagging men that half an inch more would have meant annihilation. But Camellion and his force of ten reached the side of the administration building without as much as a graze, all of them, including Camellion, breathing heavily. Dunmerser didn't waste time. He sent three men to the southeast corner and ordered Lyle Skimbus and Roy Jack Hood to watch the rear. He then went over to Camellion who was standing right at the edge of the southwest corner.

"We could go to the right." Dunmerser rubbed his jaw, thick with two days growth of beard. "We could keep several men here to draw their fire while we slip around to the first objective, the torture building. Sure, it's risky."

"Too risky," Camellion said. "What's to stop them from outguessing us and moving over to the east side? You don't shuck corn with a dull knife. We're going to take them out before we advance. Our force is too small to split up."

Dunmerser looked disappointed. "OK. How do you want to do it?" he said soberly, his eyes as intense as his low voice. "We'll have to use a Homer against the machine gun on the roof. Hell, that building's forty feet away if it's an inch."

Camellion leaned around the corner of the building and fired a single round from one of the Auto Mags. He quickly drew back as the two machine guns began to roar. Some of the slugs thudded into the west side at the corner, sending up a cloud of dust and chips. Other slugs hit, then screamed off into space.

He swung around again to Dunmerser, who had pulled back his hood and was putting on a U.S. Navy watch cap. Perspiration ran down his face. "Captain, you stay here and keep the pig-farmers busy. Make them think all of us are still here. And watch the windows on this side. They could try to sneak in from the north side and blast us from either floor. I doubt it. This building is so burned out, they'd make too much noise trying to cross over."

"What are you going to do?" Dunmerser straightened the watch cap, adjusting the thick, woolen bottom over his forehead.

"I'm going to the other side." Camellion looked at the

137

anxious faces of the commandos and jabbed the stainless steel barrel of his right AMP at Spaulding, Sternberg, and Lilmuten. "The three of you come with me."

Camellion turned and the three followed him to the southeast corner where Huckaba, Ochsner, and Tuby were crouched. Camellion next turned and looked back at Dunmerser who, with Will Scaggs, was at the other corner. Camellion then motioned that he wanted them to draw fire from the two Russian machine guns.

Dunmerser and Scaggs nodded, turned, stuck their Ingrams around the corner, and fired short bursts, Scaggs on one knee, Dunmerser shooting over him. They jerked back in time to avoid a hail of slugs from the two machine guns.

Camellion said to the three commandos who had followed him, "I'm going to stop at the northeast corner of this building and try to take out the machine gunner. When I fire, you three run across to the south side of the building the machine gun's in and use several frag grenades and an incendiary."

Sternberg, a well-muscled young man, didn't think much of the idea. Neither did Lilmuten and Spaulding, their deep frowns evidence to that fact.

"The length of the building is at least sixty feet," Sternberg said. "Throwing grenades from one end to the other and getting them into the opposite corner is impossible."

"Yeah, you need a guy who can throw a curve ball!" protested Lilmuten.

The Death Merchant made an impatient gesture. "I'm not asking you to lob the grenades into the exact position of the machine gun, just the general west end of the first floor. That building is so firegutted that a few grenades will bring the whole damn end of the second floor down. Those Russians are perched up there on a partially burned section. They've got nerve, but that's all they've got."

"Now you're talking sense," Lilmuten said. "Those ivans won't even see us!"

Sternberg heaved a big sigh. "Well, as my grandmother would say, *'Zehu hakoach hapoel lemaan hatsedek hanitschee[2]'*. I hope she was right."

"Look, pal," Lilmuten said drily, "your grandmother can't help us here. In case you don't know it, we're on our own."

2  Hebrew: "There is a power that works for ultimate Justice."

138

With a slight smile, the Death Merchant turned and looked at Sternberg. "If your grandmother were here, I think she would say, 'Shmor alecha vhaya muchan lebeeltee tsaffvy.' "

Sternberg raised his eyebrows. "Hmmmm. 'Take care and be prepared for the unexpected.' Yeah, I guess she would." He blinked at Camellion. "I didn't know you were Jewish."

"Judaism is far more than being able to speak Hebrew," Camellion said. He listened for a moment to the chattering of Ingrams and the roaring of the two Russian machine guns. Far to the west, there was more gunfire. "Let's go," he said lazily.

He and the three commandos moved along the east side of the burned-out administration building, the commandos watching the west in case any of the enemy spotted them. Evidently, Colonel Connery and Colonel Gordon's forces had either killed all the Russians to the southwest, or else had pushed them back to the other buildings. The firing on that side had slowed, had lessened, and all the commandos with Camellion could see were their own forces running toward the north, dropping down at times behind rubble to fire at targets far ahead.

The Death Merchant saw that the door to the main entrance of the building was open. He jumped onto the small porch, crept to the doorway, looked around the opening and down a hallway filled with charred beams and studding that had fallen from the ceiling. He crossed the porch, jumped down, turned, and waved the three forward. He then ran to the northeast corner and darted a look around the edge of the north-side wall. The long building, 20 feet away and several stories tall, was half-gutted. Part of the slanted south roof was burnt through, and there were burn streaks around almost every south-side window on both floors. The barrel of the machine gun was sticking out of the last window on the second floor, in the southwest corner. And he could see portions of the man doing the firing—and was there another KGB guard on the other side of the machine gun? Camellion couldn't be sure.

"How does it look?" asked Lilmuten.

"It's o-o-only twenty feet to the other s-side," Spaulding offered. "T-That's just a g-good j-jump."

"When I open up, you three run for it," Camellion said. "One of you use the grenades. The other two watch the windows. Got it?"

139

"Got it," Sternberg said. "Anytime you're ready."

Camellion thought of the Russians in the corner of the opposite building. "They're as good as dead!" An odd glow shone in his eyes. *Ani mevee klaya!*[3]

The firing had stopped. Camellion waited until Dunmerser and some of the other commandos fired and the Russians fired back. Smoke was still curling from the muzzle of the SG-43M, at the southwest corner, when Camellion leaned around the edge, raised both Auto Mags, and began pulling the triggers.

At the sound of the first round from the Auto Mag, Sternberg, Lilmuten, and Spaulding raced across the 20-foot space. Reaching the south wall of the officers' quarters building, they began to creep west. Sternberg and Spaulding watched the windows, not only the windows on the south side, but those on the north wall of the administration building as well. Chuck Lilmuten, the first man, reached into his kit bag for grenades.

The Death Merchant emptied both AMP magazines. One powerful .357 Magnum slug struck the barrel of the machine gun and exploded with a loud pop. The stab of the slug pushed the barrel west while the rear part of the weapon moved east, a foot of it slamming against the Russian who was handling the drum magazines. Without thinking, Erofei P.S. Khorchiv reacted in reflex. He jumped to his feet, reached for an AKM leaning against the wall—and died! One of the .357s had zipped through the window and exploded in his left side. Five more projectiles screamed in at a very sharp angle. Three exploded against the side of the machine gun and knocked it over. Another hit the wall. The fifth projectile exploded against the inside of B. K. Cukovin's forearm. Bits and pieces and patches of parka, uniform, and shirt flew into the air. So did Cukovin's right hand and wrist. Cukovin yelled in surprise and fear of death when he saw the blood spurting from the stump. He stepped back, tripped over his own two feet, and fell through the hole in back of him. With a loud crash his body landed on the first floor, the smash sending up a shower of ashes mixed with blood.

There had been four KGB border guards in the tiny area,

3 Hebrew: "I bring only death."

perched on a floor that, while substantially solid, was braced only by half-burned 2″ X 6″s. The back stairway was intact, but much of the floor to the east had been burned through. The sections still intact were now as fragile as an eggshell. What remained of the floor just hung there, waiting for a strong wind to whip through the shattered windows and pull it down.

Dmitri Bogomolov and Georgi Korii, the last two Russians, grabbed PPS submachine guns, Korii snarling, *"Vennym ornik dnei, Dmitri. Sti ronu tu roniali!"* ("Take the window, Dmitri. I'll watch the rear.")

At the same time that Korii was speaking, Lilmuten lobbed a fragmentation grenade through the window directly below. Bogomolov was swinging toward the window and Korii was leaning down toward the edge of the giant rip in the floor when the grenade exploded and shattered the 2″ X 6″s below as though they were toothpicks.

Bogomolov and Korii, machine gun, floor, and the corpse of the man hit in the hip crashed downward, and with all of the mess came a section of the wall from the area in which the Russians had set up their machine gun.

Dazed to the point of conscious immobility, Korii and Bogomolov found themselves buried under burnt boards and heavier studding. Korii tried to wriggle free and found that he was pinned by boards, but not impossibly so. Korii almost screamed when he attempted to move, the agony in his left thigh shooting all the way up to his ribs.

*"Dmitri, venibor kumen!"* Korii said weakly.

But Dmitri Bogomolov couldn't help even himself. Chuck Lilmuten tossed in the second grenade. The explosion that followed turned the two Russians into two unrecognizable lumps of bloody flesh, and the thermite grenade, tossed in by Lilmuten moments later, would further reduce the four corpses under the rubble into a hideousness seen only in life's most malignant tragedies.

Pleased with the speed and the professionalism exhibited by the three commandos, the Death Merchant reloaded the AMPs and, as flames began crackling louder in the west end of the building, watched Sternberg, Lilmuten, and Spaulding creep back east, then run back to the corner where he was standing.

"How did we do, Boss Man?" joked Lilmuten with undiminished enthusiasm. Only the bright gleam in his eye betrayed his keen sense of anticipation.

"I don't have any complaints," Camellion reassured him and meant it. "One of you get Tuby and Scaggs, and tell Captain Dunmerser and Hood and Skimbus to keep up the firing at the machine gun on the roof."

"I'll go." Sternberg hurried to the south along the front of the building. Camellion, Spaulding, and Lilmuten dropped flat to the ground to wait and to watch the areas to the east and the north. From where they lay, they couldn't see all of the base. Six hundred feet to the east, commandos were attacking the kitchen and the auditorium buildings, as well as lobbing grenades through the windows of the mess hall which was one big square of a building. The two warehouses were burning fiercely, flames and gray smoke boiling up to the sky.

To the north, 30 feet from the north wall of the officers' quarters, was The Laughing Palace, its east side on a line parallel with the east side of officers' building and the administration building. But it was twice the size of both buildings, a huge rectangle, 100 feet long and 60 feet wide, its front facing the east.

North of the Palace of Laughter was the first experimental station, the insidious behavior modification laboratory, its front facing the south, its 200-foot length stretching from east to west. Due to the mind-murder lab's length and height, the Death Merchant and the men with him couldn't see the second laboratory building or the generating station east of the second lab. They could see half the south side of the prison and its high fence. And any time they glanced upward there were the layers of oily, black smoke hanging over the collection of burned, burning, and battered buildings.

Some of the tall steel poles that carried power and telephone lines leaned sideways, having been damaged by the earlier rain of 40mm grenades. Lines lay scattered on the ground in spiderweb patterns, many of the broken ends spitting blue-white fire.

There was no warning. Suddenly there were several colossal explosions to the north, then several smaller explosions from the same region. More smoke began to rise from the area to the northeast of the second laboratory.

The broken power lines quit spitting fire!

"By golly, they've done it!" Lilmuten sounded as if he might jump up and start dancing. "They've blown up the powerhouse."

The Death Merchant, forever on guard, turned and saw Sternberg, Tuby, and Scaggs hurrying along the front end of the building. As soon as the three had joined him and the two other commandos, Cammellion said, "We're going to first scratch the machine gun on the roof. Then I think we'll put a few rockets into the south wall of the Laughing Palace."

"T-That sure ma-makes m-more sense than k-knitting w-woolen warmers f-for bowling b-b-balls," Nel Spaulding managed to get out. "I m-mean that attack-i-ing the f-front door would be s-suicide."

No one answered Spaulding. The men were too engrossed in watching the Death Merchant. Camellion ran across the 20-foot space to the southeast corner of the officers' building. He stopped, looked up at the windows on the east end, then motioned for the rest of the men to come ahead.

The five commandos raced across the short area, Bruce Tuby carrying the rocket launcher in one hand and holding a Browning autoloader in the other. Next to him, Will Scaggs carried the bag of Homer rockets.

Camellion moved to the northeast corner of the officers' building and looked around the corner, his ears filled with the roaring of the KPV heavy machine gun as its gunner responded to the pesky and useless firing of Captain Dunmerser and the other men.

There it was, the barrel of the big piece, sticking out between spaces in a short, low wall made of sandbags. Camellion's lips moved back over his teeth—*A turkey shoot!*

He turned and motioned with an AMP to Bruce Tuby.

"Take a look. Tell me what you think."

Tuby came forward, stuck his head around the corner, briefly studied the position of the KPV, then pulled back.

"A turkey shoot!" He grinned. "I can blow that gun all the way to the moon."

Camellion nodded. "If I didn't know better I'd say it was mental telepathy."

Tuby frowned. "Mental telepathy! What the hell do you mean?"

"It's nothing. Go ahead and blow those pig-farmers off that roof."

Tuby turned to Scaggs, held up the firing end of the launcher, and Scaggs dropped a Homer through the funnel-shaped deflector. Tuby pushed the lock button, lifted the tube to his shoulder, took a practice aim through the Y sight, stepped out around the corner, and zeroed in on the KPV.

Spaulding and Lilmuten stepped out with Tuby, Lilmuten looking up at the roof where the KPV was firing, Spaulding checking the center and the east ends of the roof. They didn't have to worry about anyone firing from the south-side windows of the Palace of Laughter—there weren't any windows!

A second before Tuby pulled the trigger, several KGB guards on the roof by the machine gun spotted the three commandos, shouted a warning, and attempted to swing their PPS sub-guns over the edge of the sandbags and fire. Too late! The Homer rocket was on its way.

A big boom! An instant's flash of ball-fire! Sandbags, machine guns, and men went tumbling up, back, and sideways.

"Hot diddle damn! How about that?" shouted Kilmuten. He moved back to the east side of the officers' building, got down with the other men, and saw that Camellion was already on the PRC-6 and in contact with Colonel Connery whose metallic voice was saying, "We're holed up in what used to be the garage. We're only a few hundred feet from the south side of the prison. It's odd, but no one's firing at us from the prison. You'd think the place would be filled with guards. Over."

A grim warning stabbed in the center of Camellion's precognitive system. He punched the push-to-talk button. "Stay away from that prison. I repeat: do not—DO NOT—go near the prison. Where's Bravo-Red?"

"Sergeant Virone and some men blew up the power station and are in what's left of it," Connery said. "They're under fire from the enemy on the roof of the second lab. We'll—"

"I'm here in the kitchen," Colonel Gordon horned in, peeved that Connery had not given him a chance to reply. "We can see the east and north sides of the torture chamber dump and the east end and the south side of the first lab. You and your guys OK? Over."

Chimed in Connery, "We can attack from three sides.

144

You know—all of us do—that they're waiting for us in those three big buildings."

The Death Merchant had already made the decision. "Bravo-Red, put two Homers into the northeast end of the Palace of Laughter. Then use RDX packs to gain entry into the first lab. Alfa-Blue, rescue Virone. Then go to work on the second lab, west of the power house. Verify."

"I verify," Connery and Gordon said together. Connery then said, "Out."

Camellion switched off the transceiver, laced it in the belt-case, and snapped the flap. He felt as if he had just stepped into a hot shower, his body soaked with perspiration—not so much from tension but from heat. The snowsuit was almost air tight and the sun was hot. He shoved the other Auto Mag into its holster.

"Where do you want the Homers placed?" Tuby asked. He had lighted a cigarette which was dangling from the left side of his mouth.

"We're not." Camellion pulled back the hood of the snowsuit. "We're going to use RDX. I'll place the charges while you men cover me. After they go off, we'll—"

"Here come Captain Dunmerser and the rest of the guys," Scaggs said in a businesslike tone.

"After the charges go off, we'll all go in." Camellion adjusted the Ingram machine gun on his back, pulled out the two Auto Mags, and jerked back slightly at the crashing thunder of the extraordinary explosion to the northeast. Definitely not the explosion of Homer rockets! The single detonation had really been a series of smaller explosions, of charges connected and set to be detonated from a single origin.

Camellion and his men stared at the prison. For several moments the big building seemed to shake and quiver, as though it were a photograph being projected from a motion picture film that had jumped the sprocket wheels and was out of time sequence. A few more flickerings and the entire building started to sag and crumble downward. With a growing roar and growing clouds of dust the prison collapsed into a gigantic pile of rubble. Whole sections crashed against the fence, smashing it as though it were made of tissue paper. More rumbles and sounds from final falling rock. And a cloud of gray dust so thick that the wreckage could not be seen.

The Death Merchant's warning system had been right on target.

"Suppose the goddam Russians blow up the Palace and the labs?" Lyle Skimbus asked in an odd voice.

# Chapter Thirteen

*Skimbus has a valid point. Suppose the pig-farmers do blow up all the buildings?* The possibility was like a baby. Once you have it, it won't go away. The trouble was that the Uncertainty Principle was at work. It always was.

All one could do was hope for the best. And that is what the Death Merchant did as he raced to the south side of the Palace of Laughter, flattened himself against the wall, looked up first at the end of the roof, then scanned the ten commandos who, prone on the ground in front of the officers' building, were covering him. As he watched, he saw Roy Hood and Lyle Skimbus raise their Ingrams and rake the roof—toward the center—with slugs. Captain Dunmerser looked at Camellion, pointed up at the roof, and held up three fingers.

Camellion nodded. He wasn't too concerned about three ivans on the roof. In order to see him and get off clear shots, any enemy would have to lean over the edge and look down—an impossibility with the commandos watching.

Keeping to the side of the building, he darted almost to the center, pulled the paper from the stick-tape, pressed the tiny circuit button of the RC box stuck into the end of each block, then slapped the two half-pound blocks of RDX against the concrete, at a height of about six feet. *Now for the four toward the end.*

He was moving toward the southeast corner when Bravo-Reds's first Homer rocket exploded in the northeast corner of the building where the giving of maximum pain had been refined to an exact science. The second Homer went off with the roar of an eighteen-inch coastal gun when he was 15 feet from the corner. Again Camellion shoved the Auto Mags into holsters and his hands reached into the bag of explosives.

One hundred and forty-two seconds later the four half-pound blocks of RDX[1] were in place. The ten commandos had crossed the short space—killing two KGB guards on the roof in the process—and, with the Death Merchant, were running along the south side of the Palace. They turned at the southwest corner, stopped on the west side, and looked up toward the roof. All this time they could hear grenades exploding around the front of the building. It was a happy feeling to know that Colonel "Iron Jaw" Gordon and his Bravo-Reds were getting ready to charge the inside of the vast structure.

Camellion pulled the remote-control detonating device from the left breast pocket of his snowsuit, flipped back the spring-action cover, and pressed the red button. The six blocks of RDX[1] roared off with a crash that should have put cracks in the sky. The big blast didn't break any of the blue, but it did demolish into broken blocks and dust the southeast corner and a large section of the center. Five feet of the east side and fifteen feet of the south side were gone. Where the corner had been was now a huge smoking opening. In the center was another smoking gap, a jagged hole twenty feet in diameter, the edge a crooked mess of broken concrete blocks, bent ends of steel reinforcing screen, and, toward the center of the rim, fiberglass and foam insulation.

With the rumbling echo of the explosions crashing back and forth from horizon to horizon, the Death Merchant and his Delta-Green boys raced from the west side of the Palace, charged around to the south side, and, each man holding an Ingram, ran toward the hole in the wall.

"We do it after the fifth grenade," Camellion said when they reached the west side of the hole. "Allen, you and I will go in first with a grenade and cover for the others. OK?"

"Why not?" Dunmerser shrugged. "I'd rather be first than last."

Camellion, Dunmerser, and six of the commandos stood cover while Tuby, Scaggs, and Roy Jack Hood lobbed fragmentation grenades around the edge into the hole, throwing as fast as they could. Tuby and Scaggs had left the rockets and the launcher by the west wall. But if any stray Russians found the rockets and tried to use them, they'd find them useless. Scaggs had the tip fuses in his pocket.

---

[1]  This is actually Cyclonite, one of the most powerful of all military explosives. Used only by experts.

The shattering explosions were almost a solid wall of force that smashed at the men, who knew they were only getting the edges of the waves of concussion! Think of the poor ivans—the communist bastards!

The last pieces of shrapnel were falling from the fifth grenade as Camellion shouted, "Let's go spit on the fires of hell!" He and Dunmerser stormed through the hole, Ingrams in one hand, grenades with pulled pins in the other, their hands down firmly on the safety levers.

During those few brief moments they spotted cover, then threw the grenades, Camellion tossing his to the left, Dunmerser throwing far to the right. Both men were diving down behind sections of concrete wall by the time the two grenades exploded. Immediately, to give the other nine cover, Camellion and Dunmerser opened fire with their Ingrams at the forward area; at the same time, they analyzed, as best as they could, the interior of the first floor.

Toward the southeast there were fourteen dead bodies on the floor, their green uniforms covered with gray dust and chunks of concrete. A moron could see what had killed them: driven inward by the RDX, the exploded walls had smashed them into the next world.

Sixty feet to the north, the Russians had used 2″ X 6″ boards to construct triple-thick partitions, eight feet long and six feet high, held up at each end by filing cases and other pieces of office equipment. The Death Merchant was startled to see that by one end of a partition was what appeared to be a modern version of a medieval rack, only instead of the victim having his bones dislocated by ropes being circled around hand-turned drums, the pulling power was furnished by an electric motor at each end of the metal bed.

Through a foot-wide opening between the ends of two wooden partitions, the Death Merchant could see another barrier that the Russians had thrown together, stretching from north to south—more filing cabinets, desks, chairs, and other odds and ends, behind which scores of KGB border guards were firing at Colonel Gordon and the Bravo-Reds who had managed to get inside through the hole in the northeast corner of the building and were down behind chunks of wall that the RDX had tossed inward.

The other KGB troops behind the wooden partitions opened fire on Camellion and his group. Some of the ivans—determined to kill the invaders or die in the attempt—leaned around the sides and triggered AKMs, PPs, and even Stechkin and Kalashnikov machine pistols, while others, standing on boxes or chairs, fired over the top of the partitions.

The Death Merchant didn't like the deal. *We are in one jolly mess!* Russian slugs screamed and ricocheted by the dozens from chunks of large pieces of concrete, the firing of such magnitude that the commandos had little opportunity to rear up and fire back, much less expose enough of themselves to throw grenades.

*This is one helluva way to fight a war!* A .726mm AKM projectile hit the edge of a concrete block 6 inches above and to the left of Camellion's head and showered his face with dust. He flattened himself more, wished he were a clerk in Vallie West's tire shop in Du Quoin, Illinois, and looked to his right at Amos Huckaba and Clark Ochsner.

"Listen, I'm going to put some Auto Mag slugs through those boards," he said. "The odds are that I'll scratch two or three of the pig-farmers. The moment the firing quits, you guys toss frag grenades. Let me know as soon as you have the pins out, and make damn sure you keep a tight grip on the saftey levers. You got it?"

Huckaba, who was the closest, nodded and shifted the quid of tobacco in his mouth. Seldom without a plug, he often boasted that he could hit a dime at 8 feet with a stream of tobacco juice. He would then prove it after the bets were high enough.

Camellion turned his head to the left and looked at Lyle Skimbus, 6 feet away. "Skim, when I start firing, you try to rake the top of the partitions with the Ingram. Think you can?"

Skimbus, who had an Oriental cast to his eyes but was a Czech-American, looked insulted. "What the hell do you think I am, an amateur? Of course I can!" Like the rest of the men, Skimbus resembled a ghost, gray dust sweat-plastered to his face.

His cramped position forced Camellion to pull the AMP from the right holster awkwardly. But he managed to bend his elbow and bring up the Auto Mag to where he could use it.

"We're set. Anytime you're ready," Huckaba called out.

Camellion switched off the safety and waited until there

was a time lag in the firing from the Russians behind the partitions.

Now! *And let's hope I don't get my hand blown off by a slug!*

He leaned out to the right, aimed by intuition and got off six rounds as fast as he could pull the wide trigger, spacing the projectiles three feet apart.

*"Ohhhhhhhauhhhhhhhh!"* A Russian screamed as one of the .357 Magnum bullets exploded, zipped through the 6 inches of the three boards, struck him in the shoulder, and left his arm hanging by only thick tendons. A second bullet missed the Russians behind the partitions; it streaked across the wide area and struck a Russian in the side—sixty feet to the north. The men grunted, staggered to the side, and went down.

The other four slugs found Russian flesh. One bored through the boards, banged into a man's chest, and knocked him to the floor. Another KGB goon caught a .357 in the stomach. Doubled over, he did a two-step jig of death and fell to the floor. The fifth slug hit a guard who was half turned. It went through his left side, cut through the lower lobe of his left lung and took its exit via his back. The sixth .357 hit a man who was standing on a chair and leaning over to put a fresh banana-shaped magazine into his AKM automatic rifle, the flattened-out slug stabbing him in the left side of the face, several inches below the ear. After his lower jaw and upper teeth exploded out into the smoky air, along with blood and chips of bone and flesh, the man passed out from shock and crumpled faster than soggy tissue paper.

No sooner had Camellion fired the sixth shot than Skimbu reared up and calmly started lacing the top of the partitions with 9mm Ingram slugs. Luck was with him, for the other Russians behind the partition, seeing five of their number get stabbed by AMP projectiles, paused in alarm, not knowing exactly what was happening. Three even forgot to duck down. Skimbus's projectiles caught two of them in the side of the face. The third was knocked back after a slug had gone through his neck. Falling in a spray of blood the three KGB men went down simultaneously with the two grenades, thrown by Huckaba and Ochsner, that landed behind the partitions and exploded with thunderous roars, showering the corpses and the men still alive with shrapnel.

The explosions of the two grenades increased the fears of Major Konstantin Rinchino and Captain Valdimir Kakich, both of whom shared a horror of having their men trapped in a pincer; splitting up their force was the last thing the two officers wanted. Now they had no choice. Captain Kakich hurriedly gathered men and started toward the south where the Death Merchant and his force were charging through the opening blasted out by the two grenades, both Americans and Russians dodging and darting from side to side and firing short bursts from automatic weapons, pistols, and revolvers. The Russians were good, but the Death Merchant and the commandos were better. Nor was the morale of Captain Kakich and his men helped as they heard grenades explode behind them and realized that the other American force was charging Major Rinchino.

Four Russians went down, riddled with Ingram slugs. And so did Clark Ochsner who caught two 7.62mm bullets in the chest from a Tokarev pistol. Very quickly the two forces came together, a choice desired by both Americans and Russians, since retreat for either was unthinkable, just as using submachine guns and automatic rifles at close range was both inconceivable and impractical. Most of the Russians and the commandos resorted to handguns or else used their empty sub-guns and A-Rs as clubs.

In a low, fighting stance, the Death Merchant fired both Auto Mags together and had the satisfaction of seeing the grand-slam slugs explode against the chests of two Russians who were dead by the time they started to sag to the floor. He ducked to one side and a 9mm bullet from a Makarov pistol missed him a foot, struck one of the steel posts supporting the ceiling, and ricocheted. The Russian didn't get a chance to correct his aim. Camellion snapped off a shot with the right AMP and the slug exploded in the Russian's neck, separating his head from his shoulders. The head jumped a foot, fell to the floor, and half rolled toward the body that was slower to go down. Yet Camellion was not out of the woods. KGB guards were all around him, and he wasn't quite fast enough to jerk his left arm back from Leonid Krupska who grabbed his left wrist, tried a sambo[2] snap-kick to his stomach while he swung a Vitmorkin machine pistol at the side of Camellion's head.

2 The Russian version of karate.

Krupska was a head taller than Camellion, outweighed him by thirty pounds, and was very strong. Camellion couldn't do anything about losing the left Auto Mag. Krupska twisted his wrist savagely, forcing Camellion's fingers to relax around the AMP which fell to the floor. But there was a lot he could do about the intended snap-kick and the barrel of the machine pistol speeding toward his temple. He ducked his head, pulled in his stomach, and arched his body. With his right hand he brought up the other Auto Mag. Krupska's knee found only empty space while the barrel of the machine pistol hissed over Camellion's head. At the same time Camellion thrust the barrel of the Auto Mag under his left arm and tilted the AMP downward. Krupska realized his mistake too late. Camellion pulled the trigger and the .357 flat point struck the Russian in the belly, exploded, and ripped him open with all the efficiency of a buzz saw. Krupska's mouth and eyes opened wide. His hand relaxed on Camellion's wrist. He staggered back and began to sag, blue-gray intestines oozing from the bloody slit in his belly.

Camellion straightened his sunglasses, scooped up the AMP he had dropped, stood up, and jumped to the right when he saw another KGB guard aiming down on him with a Stechkin machine pistol. The Stechkin barked on full automatic, the stream of nine slugs passing very close to Camellion. One buzzed within an inch of his right ear and cut through the hood down around the back of his neck. Another 9mm bullet racked across his right shoulder, leaving a rip in the snowsuit. Camellion snarled, *"Idi uv ya belovno!"*[3] dropped the barrel of the AMP to waist level, and pulled the trigger. The big, flat-nosed bullet hit the Russian in the lower cheek, exploded, tore out half of his breast bone, and lifted him 6 inches off the floor before pitching him back almost to Captain Dunmerser who was using his two .45 Enforcers, one of which was empty. The other autoloader had only four cartridges, one in the firing chamber and three in the clip. And he was in trouble. Three KGB border guards were coming at him, one holding a Dragunov submachine gun like a baseball bat. A fierce-eyed pig-farmer with thick bushy eyebrows and a bushy mustache held a 9mm Makarov autoloader in his right hand. The short Rus-

[3] "Go to the devil!"

sian was armed with a Stechkin machine pistol—both men with the autoloaders all set to fire!

Dunmerser fired as he dropped to the floor. and so did Petr Koyan and Efrim Otkin. Andrei Gribski, still holding the Dragunov by the barrel, drew up short, waiting to see the effects of Koyan and Otkin's slugs. He found out.

Both 9mm slugs passed over Dunmerser, who had not missed. One .45 bullet struck Koyan in the groin; the second gave Otkin a second navel, two inches below his natural bellybutton.

Koyan was determined to kill the *Amerikanski*. Although his consciousness was rapidly sinking into a deep, black tunnel, he nevertheless managed to get another round from the Makarov. He pulled the trigger as Gribski rushed forward to smash in Dunmerser's skull with the stock of the jammed Dragunov.

Dunmerser, half blinded by sweat flooding his eyes, fired the Enforcer at the same time he jerked to the right, the compact autoloader roaring as Gribski was preparing to swing the machine gun. Koyan's projectile ripped into Dunmerser's snowsuit on the left side and left a burn mark along his ribs during its passage. Dunmerser yelled in pain and fired again at the swaying Koyan. This time the bullet went up at a steep angle, hit the Russian under the chin, plowed through his mouth, tore off his tongue, and blew out the back of his throat and neck.

Andrei Gribski almost succeeded in smashing Dunmerser's skull like an eggshell. It was Nel Spaulding who saved Captain Dunmerser. After killing a Russian with his deadly Gladiator, Spaulding found that he was only 6 feet in back of Gribski and saw what the pig-farmer was about to do.

Gribski's feeling of elation turned abruptly to astonishment when he felt someone from behind reach out and grab the Dragunov machine gun. He didn't have the time to turn or put up any kind of defense. Spaulding chopped him in the left side of the neck with the razor-sharp blade of the Gladiator, the whack half severing the Russian's head from his body.

"S-Stupid mmmmother-f-f-f-f—" stuttered Spaulding, then found that he was too excited to complete the vulgarism. "The h-hell with-with it!"

His left hand firm around the black micarta grips of the Gladiator, he pulled back the double-edged, fourteen-ounce blade, shook blood from the gutter in the center of the steel, and stepped out of the way to avoid a stream of red spurting from the neck of the falling Gribski.

"Close. Too close for comfort," muttered Dunmerser, getting to his feet and looking at Spaulding. He reached into his bag for another Enforcer magazine. He never got to complete the reloading. Spotting four Russians charging toward him and Spaulding, he yelled, "To your left!"

Amos Huckaba, crouched with his back to several black filing cabinets, was using two Sentinel Mark IV High Standard .22 magnum revolvers, each containing nine rounds, to pop off any Russian trying to get behind any of the commandos. Huckaba wasn't always successful. The fighting was too intense, and he didn't have eyes in the back or the sides of his head. Twice he had saved Lyle Skimbus, once from being stitched across the back from ShKAS submachine-gun slugs, the second time from being stabbed.

Now Huckaba, a grin frozen on his face. shifted the tobacco in his mouth and calmly placed a .22 magnum bullet into the side of a Russian technician doing his best to slip up behind Nick Sternberg, who was trying to get closer to Lyle Skimbus. In turn, Skimbus was attempting to help Bruce Tuby who was engaged in a deadly hand-to-hand struggle with a tall KGB guard.

Using a Quicksilver survival knife with a hollow aluminum handle, Skimbus was struggling desperately to free his right hand from the iron grip of a Ruskie whose other hand held a long-bladed Tartar knife—and Skimbus was losing the battle for life. The much stronger Russian twisted the survival knife from Skimbus's hand and, still holding onto Skimbus's right wrist, began to force the Tartar knife closer to the commando's neck—until Sternberg grabbed the ivan around the neck with his left arm, shoved a knee into the man's back, and, with his right hand stabbed into the Russian's right kidney region with a Colt AR-15 bayonet. The Russian let out a tremendous *"Ahhhhhhhh"* and was sinking when Sternberg pulled out the bayonet, yelled "Watch it!" at Skimbus and ducked in time to avoid a stream of slugs from a Stechkin MP on full automatic. Within seconds the Stechkin was on empty and the Russian was doomed. Sternberg threw the bayonet by the handle. The Russian tried to avoid the blade, failed, cried out in agony, and looked down at four inches of the blade and the handle of the bayonet protruding from his stomach. Quicker than a roadrunner running from a brushfire, Sternberg bent down, picked up the Tartar knife, and threw it at the KGB guard who was about to aim down on Huckaba. Unfamiliar with the weight of the knife, Sternberg didn't succeed. The knife struck the Russian sideways; it did startle him enough to make him forget about Huckaba and swing around toward Sternberg and Skimbus, both of whom were dropping flat and pulling out their 9mm Brownings. The Russian was only a halfsecond from pulling the trigger of the Tokarev in his right hand when there was a loud pop and his right side exploded. The Death Merchant had put a .357 AMP slug into him. The Russian's body jerked. He sighed, died, and his finger pulled the trigger as he fell to the floor. The 7.62mm bullet missed Skimbus and Sternberg, but it did strike the end of the handle of the Quicksilver survival knife. The cap flew off, the knife jumped a foot off the floor, and a pencil, matches, and a length of wire fell out of the hollow handle.

By now, Skimbus and Sternberg had their Brownings out and headed for Bruce Tuby who was in the same kind of predicament that Skimbus had been in. Lazar Zimkolovitch had his right hand around Tuby's right wrist, but he couldn't twist the Browning autoloader from Tuby's hand any more than Tuby, whose left hand was around Zimkolovitch's left wrist, could force the Russian to drop the Stechkin in his left hand. At the same time, as they struggled, each man kept trying to knee the other in the groin or stomp on his instep. Each time each man tried, each man failed. The tug of war came to an abrupt termination when Skimbus shot Zimkolovitch in the right side.

The three commandos saw that while the battle was still raging, the KGB was losing and giving ground. To the southsoutheast, Colonel Gordon and his group had broken through KGB defenses and seemed to be on a killing spree.

Tuby, Skimbus, and Sternberg hurried to the defense of Will Scaggs and Roy Jack Hood, the latter two furiously fighting with four Russians. Three of ivans wore green smock coats and the commandos assumed they were technicians of some kind. The four Russians were dressed in the green and blue uniform of the KGB border guards. The commandos also saw that, to one side of Scaggs and Hood, Richard Camellion was having his troubles with a pig-farmer wearing the red and blue shoulder boards of a captain on his shoulders. They weren't concerned about Camellion, feeling that somehow he had done all this before and was too experienced to let himself be terminated.

The Death Merchant, not having had time to reload, had shoved the Auto Mags in their holsters. Seeing the Russian coming at him with the speed of a high ballin' Texas Special, Camellion pulled the L.E.S. P-18 autoloader from its right shoulder holster, but before he could switch off the safety and blow away the pig-farmer, Captain Valdimir Kakich, who had not found time to reload either, was all over him. Kakich grabbed Camellion's right wrist, twisted, and forced the P-18 to fall to the floor. All in the same motion, he tried to stab Camellion in the side with an AKM bayonet.

The quick-thinking Camellion jerked his body sideways and retaliated with a left-legged *shinto-ryu* karate *mae geri keage.* Due to his delivering the front-snap kick at an angle and while he was in motion, the kick was not very powerful, or it would have made mush of Kakich's intestines. As it happened, the snap-kick only gave Kakich moderate pain and knocked him back long enough for the Death Merchant to regain his balance. Kakich came in very fast, and from the way he handled the bayonet, Camellion knew the pig-farmer was not a stranger to the subtleties of knife fighting.

*"Kav evoi zhennykh, Amerikanski sil'vu!"* snarled Kakich, his large dark eyes glittering with hatred.

"May you get St. Vitus dance of the bung hole, pig boy," Camellion replied in Russian. "You're too stupid to slice a loaf of bread."

The Death Merchant evaded a right-handed straight thrust by backstepping and sidestepping Kakich's attacking knife-hand. Simultaneously he blocked another right-handed thrust and moved his body slightly forward in an effort to lure the Russian in a trap. Kakich fell for it. This time he thrust harder, a jab that was much longer, and this time Camellion was ready. With lightning speed, he grabbed Kakich's wrist with both hands and pulled the KGB officer's arm in an upward and outward motion. Kakich didn't have time to reorganize his thoughts and change tactics.

Camellion stepped under the Russian's arm, rotated and locked the elbow, spun around, jerked the arm over his shoulder, twisted the knife from the hand, bent over slightly, and prepared for a shoulder throw. The frantic Kakich tried to pull away but he was helpless. With any kind of violent movement at all, he would have snapped his own arm; yet he knew that Camellion was about to do just that.

Pulling on Captain Kakich's arm, the Death Merchant lifted the Russian off his feet and, as he pulled the terrified man forward, broke his arm at the elbow a split second before throwing him over his shoulder to the floor, the howling Russian landing on his back with a loud thud. Kakich was as good and knew it. He tried weakly to squirm out of the way—a waste of time and muscle power. The Death Merchant first kicked him in the left temple, a blow that switched off his consciousness. Camellion had only begun. His right foot was only a blur when it stamped Kakich in the throat and crushed his windpipe.

Turning, Camellion heard two muffled explosions from outside the Palace of Laughter, from even beyond the behavior-modification laboratory. *Connery and his boys*. The explosions sounded like RDX packs going off.

Camellion picked up the P-18 autoloader, then spotted a group of Russians coming down the steel stairs to the west. Four were regular KGB border guards. Five were technicians. Two of the technicians were women. Most carried either sub-guns or hand weapons. Camellion ducked behind one of the foot-in-diameter support posts and opened fire with the P-18. At almost the same instant, Captain Dunmerser flopped flat beside two KGB corpses and started triggering a ShKAS submachine gun, the one dropped by a Russian who had tried to snuff Lyle Skimbus.

Slugs rained all over the Russians, 9mm and 7.62mm projectiles cutting off pieces of uniform cloth and cotton smocks before cutting into flesh. One of the women threw up her arms and screamed *"Deistvuyet! Deistvuyet!"*—"Surrender! Surrender!" Her words gurgled off into blood that welled up in her throat when projectiles stung into her breasts and almost cut her head off when they sliced into her throat. Five seconds later it was all over with. The Russians lay crumpled on the stairs, some on top of each other.

Smoke curling from the muzzle of his P-18, the Death Merchant felt like screaming in defiance of the peculiar and grotesque silence, the abnormal quiet that meant the fighting was over, at least for now, in the Palace of Laughter.

Camellion glanced behind him and saw Captain Dunmerser, twenty feet to his right. And there was Lilmuten, Hood, Skimbus, and the other commandos of Delta-Green group. But not Clark Ochsner. To the northeast, Colonel Gordon and his Bravo-Red boys approached cautiously, Gordon's Mossberg .45 automatics in his hands. Gordon and his men moved faster when they saw that Camellion and his group had terminated all the ivans in the south end.

By the time Gordon reached Camellion and Captain Dunmerser, the Death Merchant was reloading his Auto Mags and giving orders to the commandos. "Reload your weapons and start photographing. Take your pick of filing cabinets; they're all over the place. I want each man to photograph twenty-five sheets and put a dozen sheets in his pocket but not the papers he photographs."

"Hold on, dad," growled Lilmuten. He shoved a full clip into his Ingram and grinned at Camellion. "We're not on wheels, you know. We can work only so fast."

"Why only twenty-five sheets?" Dunmerser's snowsuit was cut and ripped in a dozen places; yet he was no worse for wear than the rest of the Delta-Green men and Camellion and Colonel Gordon and his men.

"Because that's all we need to prove that we've been here," Camellion said, "to prove to the Soviets that we know the type of experiments they were conducting on Wrangel Island."

"Just wondering," Dunmerser said and moved off toward the filing cabinets, his hand moving toward his shoulder bag, to the compartment where the camera was snug in its bulletproof, shockproof case.

Colonel Gordon raked his fingers through his dirt-caked hair and looked at Camellion. "We've got three prisoners. Two are psychologists. The third one is a KGB major. He's the son of a bitch that gave me this." Gently he touched the long cut on his left cheek still wet with half-dried blood. "I put a .45 in his gut, but he was still breathing when we headed this way. I've got a dozen men guarding the two scientists."

The Death Merchant's mouth twisted into that special smile. He saw that Bruce Tuby, who had his camera out, was coming toward him.

"We'll take those two psychologists with us," Camellion said. "By the time they get through talking, we'll have enough to write a book about this damned base."

Reaching Camellion, Tuby asked, "What about the launcher and the Homers?"

"You and Scaggs can pick them up on the way back," Camellion said, "after we've planted charges in here and in the other buildings."

Tuby nodded and hurried off.

"We'll have more than enough swimsuits," Gordon said, then finished lighting a cigarette. "I've lost more than twenty men. No telling how many Connery's lost. And don't worry about any Ruskies on the upper floors of this dump." His voice danced with notes of victory. "The three psychologists told us that—"

"I thought you said there were only two psychologists?"

Gordon exhaled smoke noisily. "Three. We cut one's throat to show the other two we meant business. They got the message. They couldn't talk fast enough. They told us there's only a hundred or so test subjects upstairs. That's where the main torture rooms are. It's a goddamn shame those poor devils have to go when the building comes down."

"I quit worrying about such things years ago," Camellion said.

Gordon looked inquiringly at the Death Merchant. "So how do we do it? Of course, we can leave a dozen men here to guard the prisoners while we attack the lab."

Camellion shrugged. "You've answered your own question, Colonel. We take the lab, set the charges, and get back to the south coast. Then on to the SDVs." He smiled again and sniffed at the stale air. "Who knows? Some of us might reach the subs alive and healthy!"

Colonel Gordon wasn't amused at Camellion's macabre humor. There had to be something very wrong about a man who laughed at death and *meant it,* who went about acting as if living and breathing were burdens to be borne like some kind of penance.

Gordon cleared his throat and reached for the PRC-6 on his belt.

"I'll contact Connery."

# Chapter Fourteen

It was not difficult for Colonel John Connery and his Alfa-Blue force to affect linkage with the groups of Richard Camellion and Colonel George Gordon. Connery and his men simply moved from the second laboratory and its ninety-six KGB corpses, raced around the west end of the behavior modification lab and darted to the Palace of Laughter, their only obstacle a dozen or so KGB gunners on the roof of the behavior-modification lab. During the crossover six commandos were killed, and every KGB guard but four. Upon reaching the Palace of Laughter, Connery immediately sent a dozen of his Alfa-Blues to the roof to exterminate the remaining four KGB guards. A dozen of Colonel Gordon's men went to the roof of the Palace of Laughter to kill any stray KGB fighters who might be lurking there. None were. The commandos found only one KGB guard. He had been wounded and was unconscious. A bullet in the head made him unconscious forever.

The next step was preparing for the final attack, the final smash against the behavior modification laboratory, which now took on a new significance. The two Russian psychologists, one of whom was a Ph.D. from the Lenin Institute in Moscow, swore that the leading scientist and the two highest KGB officers on Wrangel Island were holed up in the second lab.

"You crumbs had better be telling the truth," warned Colonel Gordon, glaring at the two frightened psychologists, both of whom had their hands tied behind their backs and were sitting on the floor. "If we find that you've lied, we'll pour gasoline over you and burn you alive."

"They're there," Doctor Yuri Ghantimur said hoarsely, looking up at the circle of hostile faces around him and Vasili Kudmak. He continued, speaking thickly accented English. "Doctor Aleksei Agarev is the senior biologist and

161

psychiatrist. He's in the laboratory with General Vatutin and Colonel Milovanov. On the grave of my mother and father, I swear it."

Vasili Kudmak quickly interjected, "Major Rinchino was in this building. I suppose he is among the dead in here."

A red-faced, half-bald man in his late forties, Kudmak was more than anxious to show his willingness to cooperate.

"I think he's telling the truth." Colonel Gordon turned to Connery. "I put a bullet in a Ruskie wearing a major's insignia."

The Death Merchant looked down at the two miserable Russian psychologists. "How many guards are in the lab?" he asked softly and pulled an Auto Mag which the two Russians regarded with fearful eyes.

"I don't know." Dr. Ghantimur's voice was weak and uncertain. "We don't know how many KGB guards were on the outside or how many of them you killed."

"There are no windows," Kudmak said nervously. "We have knowledge of only what has happened in this place."

"Then how do you know the bigshots are in the other lab?" the Death Merchant said. "You know, when people lie to me, I blow their skulls apart."

"We saw them!" Kudmak's eyes went wide. "When the scouts reported your force was coming, we all took shelter. We saw Colonel Milovanov and General Vatutin walking toward the lab. Dr. Agarev went in behind them. Dr. Ghantimur and I were coming from the mess hall at the time."

"How come none of the big buildings have windows?" Captain Dunmerser stared down at the two psychologists as if they had just crawled out of a sewer.

Neither Russian answered.

The Auto Mag in the Death Merchant's hand roared, the bullet striking the floor and exploding only six inches from Vasili Kudmak's left hip.

Kudmak and Yuri Ghantimur jerked violently in fear and began talking simultaneously. The Death Merchant pointed the barrel of the AMP at Kudmak. "You, shut up!" The barrel swung to Ghantimur, a thin-faced man with a short beard. "Talk."

"The time factor," croaked Ghantimur. "The buildings were designed in such a manner that none of the test subjects would be able to look outside. Without windows, the test subjects would never know whether it was day or night.

Without windows, it was easier to confuse their sense of time. An individual's ego-identity depends in part on his keeping a sense of time." He closed his red-rimmed eyes in anguish.

"Bastards!" spit out Sergeant Virone, his face twisting in anger. "If I had my way, I'd kill you right now."

The Death Merchant holstered the Auto Mag, a cold, calculating look in his blue eyes. "I think it would be more practical to plan how to capture the lab with a minimum of casualties."

Both Gordon and Connery seemed surprised at Camellion's remark.

"Hell, we use explosives, what else?" remarked Connery, hitching up his equipment belt. "We can hardly knock on the main entrance and ask them to let us in."

"Why attack at all?" Dunmerser said with agonizing deliberation. His questioning eyes moved swiftly from Gordon and Connery to Camellion. "We have the General and the rest of them trapped inside. Why not blow up the lab and bury them? Why do it the hard way? Or is the reason the files? Are they really that important?"

"They are," Camellion said sternly, then summoned up a fatherly smile. "The files in the behavior modification lab are especially important. To quit now would be akin to climbing Mount Everest and stopping a few hundred feet from the summit."

"In that case we might as well get on with it," Dunmerser said harshly and looked at his watch. "Right now we're fifteen minutes behind schedule."

The film used by the Delta-Green boys was left with thirty commandos who would remain in the Palace of Laughter. The commandos waited impatiently for twenty other men to do their work, twenty who had left the building to plant blocks of RDX against the north and the south sides of the huge behavior modification lab: three different places against the south wall—one to the west, one to the east, and one in the center.

On the south side, three pounds of RDX were slapped against the wall toward the southeast corner. Last of all, four pounds of the powerful military explosive were stuck against the wall 20 feet west of the main entrance. When the twenty men returned to the Palace of Laughter, the entire force—except for the thirty men who would remain behind—moved out of the building through the large hole in the south wall and took refuge on the west side of the Palace. The Death Merchant and four commandos crept to the southeast corner of the building. Bruce Tuby and Dearl Austin carried the rocket launchers, Gary Mohr and Cliffton Sebastian the Homer rockets.

Tuby and Austin looked along the east side of the Palace. The south side of the laboratory was 30 feet to the north of the Palace's north wall.

"Not quite a hundred feet," Austin said happily. "But if you ask me it's a waste of two good Homers. Them five explosions will rattle the brains of them Rooshians like marbles. They'll be too damned befoggled to know what's happening to them."

When the Death Merchant didn't reply, Austin and Sebastian glanced expectantly at him, then at each other.

"Personally, I think maybe the whole damn building will come down," Gary Mohr speculated. "But maybe not. It's pretty damn big."

He stood waiting, a Homer rocket in his hands.

Camellion, who had taken the remote-control detonator from his pocket, turned and smiled slightly at the four commandos. "Load the launchers, then get down," he said mildly.

Far to the southwest there were three explosions, muffled and rumbling. The cruising SDVs had blown up more patrol boats.

The Death Merchant watched the four commandos load the launchers and move to the south wall. He looked upward, his line of sight traveling through a break in the layers of drifting smoke to the blue sky stationed in the reaches of infinity. He flipped back the cover of the R-C detonator.

*Old friend, what a holiday you are having this day!*

He pressed the red button.

The five individual explosions, sounding like one stupendous blast, shook the ground and blew tons of concrete out of the north and the south walls of the laboratory. Chunks of broken concrete, some the size of washtubs, slammed against the north wall of the Palace and the south walls of the wrecked powerhouse and the second laboratory which the commandos had turned into a bloody mortuary. Behind the tornado of rubble came the smoke and dust and the acrid smell of burnt cyclotrimethylenetrinitramine, the compound composing RDX. And as the echo of the explosion rolled and rumbled across Wrangel Island only Camellion heard the pleased laughter of the Cosmic Lord of Death.

As efficient at the art of killing as two well-oiled machines, Bruce Tuby and Dearl Austin picked up their rocket launchers, moved to the corner, and looked at the south side of the behavior modification laboratory. Gradually as the smoke drifted off and the dust began to settle, they saw that where the southeast corner had been there was now a tremendous hole—big enough to drive a truck through. The ragged cavity to the west was even larger, a colossal opening that extended not only to where the main entrance had been but to 30 feet west of where the RDX had been placed against the wall; and upward, the largest tear in the wall was 25 feet high and shaped like an inverted V, the point of the V taking in a portion of the second story, the floor of which was now exposed.

Bruce Tuby fired first. His Homer stabbed through the gap in the southeast corner and went off with a tremendous roar.

As Dearl Austin lifted his launcher to his shoulder, the Death Merchant took the PRC-6 from its case on his belt. He waited until the rocket had found its target, the area beyond the chasm in the center of the wall, and exploded. He then switched on the PRC-6 and spoke one word—"Go!"

Connery, Gordon, and the commandos went. They poured from around the west side of the Palace of Laughter and ran to the east, to the space between the two buildings, some going to the yawning opening in the center, others to the enormous gap where the southeast corner had been. However, fifteen commandos, under the leadership of Captain Dunmerser, ran along the west end of the lab, turned at the northwest corner, raced east, and stopped by the first blasted hole in the wall. Quietly they waited, Ingrams ready to fire.

On the south side, commandos tossed half a dozen fragmentation grenades through each hole, the blasts tearing apart more of the interior and causing loose chunks of concrete around the top and sides of the two holes to fall. Came the last two grenade explosions and then the commandos did what they had to do, did it the hard way, the only way: they stormed through the holes, Ingram submachine guns firing short bursts into the hazy interior ahead. Lights, powered by reserve batteries, still burned, the white-yellow circles of illumination half-obscured by the dust and smoke generated by the explosions.

By the time the last of the grenades had exploded, the Death Merchant and the four rocket men had reached the area of the southeast corner. All five charged into the building with the other commandos. At the same time, using the last grenade explosion as a signal, Captain Dunmerser and his force of fourteen charged through the opening in the north wall.

Dearl Austin had been proved wrong. The five RDX explosions had shaken and disorganized the Russians. Masses of concrete, flying inward, had killed eighteen of them. Ten more KGB guards had been disabled with broken bones. But the KGB guards alive and in good health had lost none of their ability to fight. Furthermore, they were the cream of the crop of troops on Wrangel Island—tough, well-trained, and filled with hatred for any non-Communist.

A hail of submachine gun and automatic rifle slugs greeted the commandos, most of it coming from the center of the floor, although in the confusion one could not be certain. The RDX explosions had not only demolished equipment and partitions in various rooms, but vast chunks of concrete had even smashed entire walls. The total effect was that the first floor was a nightmare of devastation, of wrecked equipment, smashed furniture, and broken walls composed of snapped off 2" X 4", splintered lumber, and broken sheets of plaster board. The floor was littered with papers, broken glass, and other rubble. File cabinets, covered with dust, stood every which way. Some had even been knocked over on their sides.

The two commando forces on the south side had not advanced thirty feet before PPS and AKM slugs began cutting into their ranks. A Degtyarev light machine gun began its high-pitched roaring, adding to screaming of ricocheting projectiles.

Commandos dived for cover. Chuck Lilmuten zigzagged to the left in an attempt to throw himself behind a large ragged piece of concrete. He was only several feet from his goal when three 7.62mm slugs raked across his right side and terminated his existence. He fell to the left, his face ripped by the twisted ends of steel-strand reinforcing sticking out of the very hunk of concrete he had been trying to reach.

A scathing burst of Degtyarev L.M. slugs ripped across

five commandos, the full-metal-jacketed lead cutting into chests and stomachs. All five, including Roy Jack Hood, were stone dead by the time they crashed to the floor.

A lot more commandos would have died if it hadn't been for Captain Dunmerser and his fourteen men. They opened fire from the north and began tossing grenades—six fragmentation grenades and one thermite grenade. The six frags tore apart more furniture and walls already half-demolished, and killed one Russian with shrapnel.

The single thermite grenade burst into blue-white fire in the middle of a dozen KGB guards who instantly were inundated with molten metal. At once the Russians, turned into human torches, were screaming and dancing a fatal jig of death, their shrieks of excruciating agony ringing out even over the chattering of machine guns.

Paralyzed with horror at the fate of the twelve, the other KGB guards gradually stopped firing and stared incredulously at their comrades who were being cremated before their very eyes. Many of the Russians then ducked down when the molten thermite began setting off cartridges in the ammo pouches of the doomed men that the thermite had splashed over; and this included cartridges in the Degtyarev L.M. whose gunner was already dead. All the flesh left on him was on the lower part of his body. From the waist upward, the thermite had dissolved most of his skeleton. All that was left was half the skull, some of the spinal column, and six ribs.

The Death Merchant had dived down ten seconds after darting into the interior, he had crawled behind what looked like an overturned operating-room table, the steel bed on the other side of him. He looked around, saw a shattered glass-and-wood case and a lot of surgical instruments lying on the floor and decided that he had been right the first time.

On each side of him other commandos had sought protection behind massive chunks of concrete, all of them pinned down by the storm of KGB projectiles first thudding against the concrete, then ricocheting into space, some striking the high ceiling and *zinging* off for a second time. Some of the ceiling had caved in from concussion, the ragged openings edged with broken flooring, the joists splintered. Various pieces of furniture rested precariously at the edges of some of the holes, as if trying to decide whether to topple downward or to remain stationary.

It was one hell of a way to spend an afternoon! Abruptly, the Death Merchant heard grenades going off to his right. *Dunmerser and his troops!* The explosions were followed by a peculiar kind of shrieking, the screeching of men being roasted alive. *My, my. He's given them a thermite hotfoot!*

The firing died down, and the Death Merchant and the commandos took instant advantage of the lull by charging forward as rapidly as was possible under the conditions that prevailed—charged slowly because of the wreckage that they were forced to go around or crawl over. The important point was that they now had the advantage and were able to fire before the KGB had time to line them up in their sights. The instant a Russian reared up to fire, a commando spotted him and cut loose with an Ingram. But not always. Leaning walls made it impossible for the commandos to always see a Russian and vice versa.

Not far from the center of the room, the Death Merchant's Ingram ran out of ammo. He didn't take time to reload the weapon. Still on the dodge, he slung the small submachine gun over his shoulder by its leather sling-strap, jerked out both Auto Mags, switched off the safety catches, and jumped over a chunk of concrete and a chair with a broken back. He saw the dirty face of the KGB man as the man, 20 feet ahead and to his right, was dropping the barrel of the PPS sub-gun in line with his body.

Camellion dove to the left as the weapon chattered and a stream of 7.62mm slugs poked the air to his right, one projectile clipping the bottom of the heel of his right Pakboot while he, in midstride, was throwing himself behind a machine that resembled some kind of generator. Three more slugs *pinged* off the front of the machine, but by then Camellion was safe and analyzing his situation.

The pig-farmer had fired from behind one end of a metal partition that sagged forward. The only reason the partition hadn't fallen to the floor was that it was supported by a motor mounted on four slanting steel legs, the bottom ends of which were bolted to the concrete floor. A circular disk, 5 feet in diameter, was attached to the end of the motor's shaft, portions of the disk of various colors and filled with small holes. *A hypnometer!* When the disk rotated lights in the rear of the spinning circle would affect a specific pattern by which a test subject could be lulled into sleep, in order that his mind could be more easily manipulated.

Camellion toyed with the idea of using a frag grenade. No. There was an easier way. *If the metal is not too thick.* Carefully, he looked around the left side of the machine. There was a 3-foot gap between the left end of the metal partition and the next wall, which seemed to be made of metal also, and padded. *A cell!* the thought came to Camellion. *Either a padded cell or—could it be a soundproofed chamber?*

He picked up a small piece of concrete and tossed it to his right.

Again the KGB guard triggered off a short burst and slugs *zinged* off concrete.

*Yeah, the commie crud hasn't changed his position.*

Camellion moved around to the left side of the machine, leaned out and rapidly fired four rounds from the AMP, spacing the projectiles a foot and a half from the end of the wall and a foot apart from the floor. The thin sheet steel and padding might as well have been cardboard. The four .357 projectiles tore through the partition. One bullet missed the Russian and ended its journey in a Myosone Muscle Monitor. The other three tore out the Russian's liver, blew off his right leg at the knee, and left his right arm dangling. Spurting blood and unconscious from the terrible impact of the lead, he sagged to the floor and started to die.

The Death Merchant tore across the area like the proverbial bat out of Hades. Keeping low, his eyes darting like two beacons, he glanced at the blown-apart pig-farmer, looked around, and saw that he was in what had been a soundproofed chamber whose other two walls had been blown down. *Mind-murder with sound! It figures.* Ahead the area was relatively open, except for masses of concrete, more wrecked equipment, parts of ceiling that had fallen, and flattened walls. He got down by a part of a slanting wall and prepared his next move.

"Hey! Wait for us!"

Turning to the left, Camellion saw Nel Spaulding and Cliffton Sebastian creeping toward him, hunched down like two conspirators afraid they would be caught in the act. Although as grimy as two old-time chimney sweeps, the two commandos were as cheerful as two prostitutes who had the sole franchise at a salesman's convention.

Together, the Death Merchant and the two comrades advanced toward the center of the main floor, Spaulding and Sebastian conscious that at any moment slugs could end their lives. It was different with the Death Merchant. He wasn't too concerned about being the recipient of a KGB slug. Like Time, Death was relative and not at all important in the long scheme of one's total development.

Camellion, Sebastian, and Spaulding moved cautiously through wrecked rooms in which smoke and the sweet smell of death hung heavily. In one room they came across Willie Scaggs, Amos Huckaba, and Gary Mohr.

Scaggs wiped his face, all the while peering closely at the Death Merchant. "Camellion, which way do you think we should go?" he asked warily.

Mohr, shoving a fresh magazine into his Browning, made a motion with his head. "There's a dozen ways to go up there. We can't figure out which way might lead to a stacked deck."

Huckaba, down on his haunches, spit a stream of tobacco juice that smacked the center of a photograph of Leonid I. Brezhnev hanging crookedly on part of a wall still standing. "Most of the firing is going on to the left of us," he said, wiping his mouth with the back of his hand. "We should go to left and get it over with. There ain't no other way."

"He's right," Camellion said. Moving to the left, he edged past a wall that was little more than framework. The rest of the commandos trailed behind him, most of them with handguns. In such close quarters, ricochets from automatic weapons could be almost as fatal as bullets.

It was several rooms and 45 feet later that they came face to face with a group of KGB men who, in a desperate effort, were trying to outflank the American force. Both groups had been moving very quietly, and they came together so unexpectedly—so close they could look into each other's eyes—that for the barest shave of a moment both Russians and Americans were astonished. All they could do was stare at each other in surprise. Not the Death Merchant, who snapped up both AMPS and blew apart two Russians before the other KGB guards had time to recover from the shock.

The crashing roars of Camellion's AMPs snapped both sides into action, both Americans and Russians knowing instinctively that they didn't have time to dive down or seek any kind of cover. In an instant both sides clashed. Now nothing mattered—but terminating the enemy.

One Russian brought up a Vitmorkin machine pistol and was swinging it toward Cliffton Sebastian, who fired first, his 9mm Browning slug hitting the Russian in the chest. Then, when the Russian acted as if he might have the strength to fire as his knees buckled, Sebastian fired again. This time the piece of lead stabbed the KGB man in the throat and finished him off.

An instant of fear flowed through Sebastian, for the slide of the Browning autoloader had snapped back and stayed there. The weapon was empty. At the same time, Ivan Iakinf was shoving out a Stechkin machine pistol toward Sebastian, who knew in that instant his life was balanced more precariously than a ping-pong ball centered on the point of a needle.

Sebastian jerked to one side as Iakinf fired. The stream of 9mm slugs sizzled very close to Sebastian, who twisted his body to the right, struck Iakinf's wrist with his left forearm, and grabbed the front of the machine pistol with his right hand, making sure his hand was not covering the muzzle. At the same time, as the startled Iakinf tried to pull back, Sebastian used a knife-hand karate chop against the side of the Russian's wrist and bent the Stechkin toward the KGB man's body with his right hand, forcing Iakinf to release his grip on the machine pistol, or have his index finger broken.

*"Nyet! Nyet!"* yelled Iakinf in fear, now that the Stechkin was sliding into Sebastian's right hand.

"Your nose in sheepdip, Pig Man!" snarled Sebastian. "You're playing with the big boys now."

He shoved the barrel of the M.P. into the Russian's stomach and pulled the trigger, feeling only intense satisfaction when the Stechkin went *Brrrrrrrrrrrrrrrr* and a dozen 9mm projectiles tore out Iakinf's insides. The Russian went limp and started to sag, his eyes staring, his lips and teeth suddenly red with the blood that was pouring down his chin by the time he hit the floor, only 6 feet from where Will Scaggs had just been grabbed by a Russian in a front choke hold. The KGB guard's thumbs were beginning to dig into Scaggs's Adam's apple when the commando, clasping his hands together, gripped the knife edge of his left hand with the fingers of his right hand and tightly wrapped the left thumb around the right thumb. He did not interlock his fingers. He next drove his hands up between the Russian's arms, forcing the man's fingers from his throat and making the KGB guard's arms fly outward.

Scaggs didn't lower his closed hands. Before the startled enemy could recover, the commando smashed his closed hands on the bridge of the man's nose, a brutal blow that stunned the pig-farmer. He became even more dazed when Scaggs shattered his collarbone with two savage knife-hand *shuto* chops to the side of his neck. The KGB man started to wilt on rubbery legs. A moment later he was choking to death from a right-handed multiple-finger *nukite* stab that Scaggs delivered to his throat. Scaggs next ducked down, snatched up the Browning autoloader he had dropped, and dove far to the left, desperate to shove a full magazine into the weapon.

At least he was safer, if only for the moment, than Gary Mohr. He had snuffed a Russian with his Browning, only to have the weapon knocked from his hand by another KGB guard who somehow had managed to grab him in a rear overarm body hold, the pig-farmer's right arm tightening around his neck, the Russian holding his right wrist in place with his left hand.

"Son of a bitch!" muttered Mohr and lost his temper. First of all, he felt ashamed that he had permitted the Russian to get such a hold on him. Secondly, he didn't like anyone touching his neck. With a bellow of rage, he used his left foot to stomp the Russian's left instep, a vicious smash that caused the Russian to grunt in pain and to loosen his grip. Mohr raised his elbows shoulder high, quickly lowered his body by bending his knees, and, turning his body slightly to the right, drove his right elbow into the Russian's stomach with all his might. The wind knocked out of him, the Russian yelled again and threw up his arms reflexively, helpless during those few moments. Mohr was very fast. His right hand shot out and grabbed the man's right upper arm above the elbow. He gripped the Russian's right wrist with his left hand, spun, pulled, and threw the disorganized man over his shoulder, the man's legs striking Walter Czaplicka, who was lunging toward Nel Spaulding. Knocked off balance, Czaplicka now decided he would first put a Tokarev bullet into Mohr who was about to kick in the other KGB man's neck with a savate kill-kick. It didn't work out that way. Scaggs, having reloaded his Browning, put two 9mm slugs into Czaplicka's right side and pitched him to the left. The dying man fell in back of another KGB border guard who turned around, saw what had happened, and discovered that from his position he could use his Stechkin to kill not only Mohr but Spaulding and Amos Huckaba as well. Spaulding had just broken the neck of a Russian and Huckaba had killed two Russians by stabbing one in the gut with his big-bladed buck knife and shooting the second one in the face.

Only a bolt of lightning could have killed the KGB guard with greater speed. One of the Death Merchant's Auto Mags roared and the head of the KGB man exploded with the kind of sound a hammer makes when it hits a watermelon.

The battle had not lasted two minutes. The Russians were dead. Standing were the five commandos and the Death Merchant, all six bathed in sweat and powdered with smoke and dust.

Spaulding stooped and picked up his Browning Hi-Power, saying in a nervous voice, "If I w-were a re-re-religious, I'd s-say a per-prayer to the Ba-Big F-Fellow up-upstairs."

"Let's finish it," Richard Camellion said.


The entire commando force closed in on the remaining Soviet forces, overrunning their positions like a flowing tide of death. Colonel Connery and his men came in from the west; Camellion and the five men with him from the southeast. Captain Dunmerser and his group came from the north. Gradually the opposing forces merged until it was not one group fighting another, but men fighting each other in groups of twos and threes and men fighting man to man.

Angry at himself because he had broken his sunglasses, Camellion had exhausted the ammo in the two Auto Mags by silencing the Degtyarev light machine gun and the Russians clustered around the weapon. The KGB had tried to protect the weapon and themselves by surrounding it with steel sheeting hastily pulled from wrecked walls. More than several dozen times the sheeting had deflected pistol and Ingram projectiles, but the .357 Jurras flat points stabbed through the metal and blew the Russians apart.

With both the AMPs out of ammo, Camellion shoved them into their hip holsters and pulled the L.E.S. P-18 autoloader from its right shoulder holster. Close by, Colonel Gordon and Sergeant Virone were also being surrounded by desperate KGB border guards.

*"Dominus Lucis vobiscum!"* Camellion snarled and started to raise the P-18. A hand instantly closed around his wrist and twisted, the strength of the Russian forcing Camellion to drop the P-18 autoloader and to turn his body to the right to prevent his arm from being broken. His situation worsened as three more KGB guards came at him, two from the left, one from the right.

Colonel Gordon and Sgt. Virone were in the same kind of predicament. Gordon had emptied his Mossberg .45s and was using them, in conjunction with karate kicks, to slam-out Russians with blows to the head, the groin, and the stomach—until the weapons were wrenched from his hands. Gordon then resorted to a defense that was all karate. He employed a *hiza ate* knee lift to the groin of one man, ducked another KGB man's straight-in fist-punch, slammed out the fellow with a *haito uchi* sword-hand ridge-strike to the side of the neck and, with his left hand, stunned into partial unconsciousness an enemy by using a *tettsui uchi* hammer-hand blow that caught the Russian squarely on the end of the chin. The Russian that Gordon had struck in the side of the neck went down choking and gasping, yet still trying to pull a Makarov pistol from a belt holster. The Russian stopped trying when Sergeant Virone threw a Marine combat knife that buried itself in the Russian's back, between his shoulder blades.

Varone then had to concentrate on saving his own life and defending himself from Afanase Bezak and Enver Galden coming at him from the front and from Gorki Mundov charging from the rear, Mundov reaching him ahead of the other two guards, a Russian bayonet in his upraised hand.

Reasoning that it was better to have one man to his rear than two, Varone knew he did not have time to turn around. He bent his body forward and kicked back with his right leg, catching Mundov with a savate rear-crotch-with-heel kick, his heel connecting solidly with Mundov's sex machine. Mundov let out a choked cry of intense agony, dropped the bayonet, and started to sink into unconsciousness from shock.

By then, Bezak and Galden were at him, Bezak to the left, Galden to the right. Sergeant Virone jumped high and used his right leg in a spinning savate kick to Bezak's stomach, a slam that made the Russian's eyes almost pop out of his head. Bent almost double, his hands over his stomach, he

174

started to stumble back toward Colonel Gordon while Enver Galden, catching Virone off balance, chopped him across the face with a *sambo* ridge-hand, tripped him to the floor, and pounced on top of him, pinning Virone's left forearm with his right knee. In pain, Virone suddenly found Galden's hands on his throat and his air being cut off as the Russian applied pressure. Virone attempted to throw up his legs and grab Galden's head with his feet. He couldn't. He didn't have the strength and the KGB man was bent too low. Virone was still not helpless. With his right hand he reached into the top of his right boot and pulled the Sportman's Pencil from its sheath, pressed the "eraser," releasing the 6″ steel needle, and stabbed Galden in the left armpit. Galden screamed, jerked, and automatically released his hands from Virone's throat. Virone's right hand was only a blur as it stabbed the needle into the left side of the KGB man's beefy neck. Then he stabbed him a second time. Starting to gurgle blood that poured out of his mouth and fell all over the commando's chest, Galden started to fall, but Virone pushed the dying man from him and, panting heavily, got to his feet. Getting his breath he saw that Colonel Gordon had caught Afanase Bezak, had spun the Russian around, pulled back his arms and, while holding him by the wrists, was breaking his back with a ball-of-the-foot-kick to the spine.

Keeping one eye on the three KGBs charging him from the front, the Death Merchant prepared to terminate Alexei Brudov who had grabbed his left wrist and was aiming a closed-fist blow at the side of his head. Camellion easily ducked the blow, turned more to the right, and countered with a right-handed *shuto uchi,* the deadly sword-hand chop thudding against Brudov's left temple, the strike of such penetrating power that it cracked not only Brudov's temporal bone but also shattered the sphenoid bone, that small patch of bone on the side of the head about an inch in back of the eye. Slammed into unconsciousness, Brudov went down, the Death Merchant spinning around to meet the other three men before Brudov's head hit the floor with a loud crack.

Camellion noticed that the man farthest to his left wore the insignia of a KGB colonel in the border guards. Serge Roshgin and Stephan Timofeevich were also officers—both lieutenants. Of the three, Roshgin had to be the dumbest.

He rushed in trying for a closed-fist blow to the face and a spear-hand stab to the stomach. The sleepy looking Timofeevich advanced more cautiously, with the stance of a professional *sambo* fighter, both hands raised for knife-hand strikes. Colonel Josef Milovanov was the more prudent of the three. He hung back slightly, waiting to see how Roshgin and Timofeevich would do. He saw!

The Death Merchant blocked Roshgin's closed-fist blow with a right *hiji uke* elbow block and the intended *nukite* stab with a left *sukui uke* scooping-hand sweep. Coordinated with the two blocks, he executed a *yoko geri keage* side-snap kick aimed at Timofeevich. Camellion's foot smashed into Timofeevich's stomach, just below the navel. Timofeevich had rushed right into the vicious kick—the last mistake he would ever make, a fatal one. His bladder, femoral arteries, and a profusion of spinal nerves were crushed beyond repair. Only moments from hell, the Russian started to sag at the same time that Camellion disposed of Serge Roshgin before the KGB officer could reorganize his defenses. The now startled Russian, who knew he was on the defensive, was about to attempt a knee lift but quickly changed his mind when Camellion employed a left-legged *chimku* block.

The Death Merchant's hands and arms moved with such blinding speed that the Russian couldn't realize what was happening. Roshgin could only gag from the agony of Camellion's *otoshi hiji ate* downward elbow-strike that broke his nose and made blood spurt from both nostrils. Camellion's *koko-i* tiger-mouth kill-clutch to Roshgin's throat ended his life by crushing his voice box and the upper part of his windpipe. He was choking to death, velvet falling over his mind, by the time the Death Merchant turned and used a right-legged knee shift as a defense against Colonel Milovanov's left-foot stamp that was intended to shatter his knee cap; and a double *ko uke* arch block to wreck Milovanov's double-piercing-finger strike aimed at the side of his neck.

Milovanov was very fast and very good at *sambo*. His only flaw was that he wasn't good enough. He jerked back from Camellion, feigned a left foot kick to the groin and a right-handed fist-strike to the side of the neck. With his left hand he attempted the real McCoy, a vicious spear-hand thrust to the Death Merchant's solar plexus.

Camellion, who had fought far better men than Milovanov, wasn't fooled by such tactics. He blocked the spear hand by sweeping aside the Russian's arm. Simultaneously, he used an *ippon ken* single-knuckle punch to shatter Milovanov's front teeth. A very fast *haito* ridge-hand to the Russian's left cheek sent him staggering, his senses reeling, his befuddled condition giving Camellion time to pull the small but very wicked Dwarf and swing it toward the Russian in a sideways slicing motion. Colonel Josef Milovanov never saw the triangular shaped blade, and he would never know which side of the blade cut across his throat and gave him another half-moon mouth in the vicinity of his Adam's apple. It wouldn't have made any difference: all three sides were twice as sharp as a straight razor.

The Death Merchant jerked his hand and body back in time to keep from getting a bath in the dying Milovanov's blood that gushed from his throat. Arms as limp as sails on a dead calm sea, Colonel Milovanov toppled to the floor in a wide spray of blood.

*Never send a little boy to do a man's job!* Camellion glanced down at the dead KGB officer, then ducked low, moved to one side, and picked up the L.E.S. P-18 autoloader that Alexei Brudov had forced from his hand. All around him was a sea of bodies, mostly Russians, but there were also dead commandos.

The firing had decreased, and, getting down behind a massive lump of concrete, he saw that the Russians still alive were holed up behind a barrier composed of furniture, various pieces of equipment, and parts of walls.

To his left, he noticed Colonel Gordon, Sergeant Virone, and other commandos creeping toward the area. And as they and the Death Merchant closed in, Colonel Connery and other commandos stormed the barrier, firing handguns and Ingram SMGs. General Vatutin and the KGB guards with him used PPS sub-guns and machine pistols.

*A mistake! Connery is too damned anxious!* Listening to the staccato explosions of cartridges, Camellion knew that now it was a matter of which side had the most nerve and the edge on the firing.

And the most luck. . . .

Commandos began dropping, their insides torn apart by KGB slugs. But KGB fighters died even faster and in greater numbers. The reason was that, while the Russians had a lot of nerve, none had any practical experience in fire-fighting, unlike the commandos, most of whom had seen action in the stinking hell of Vietnam.

A grimy General Vatutin was down on both knees, a PPS submachine gun in his hands and two Vitmorkin machine pistols, with full magazines, on each side of him. With him were three other KGB men, determined to die fighting, and Doctor Aleksei Agarev and two lab technicians, all three determined to live, if possible. The General and his pathetic group were surrounded on three sides by overturned metal desks and tables faced with sheets taken from blown-in walls. In front of Vatutin and the others was a short wall built of chunks of concrete.

All around, Death was celebrating.

Colonel Connery finished the last of his Ingram cartridges on two Russians who jumped up from behind a mass of rubble and tried to trigger off bursts. He ducked down, tossed away the Ingram SMG and pulled the two .45 Mossberg autoloaders which he had reloaded before charging the last pocket of resistance.

The firing had died down to almost no shots at all. Connery and the other men looked around.

"Hell, I guess we got 'em all," said Amos Huckaba, who was squatting to Connery's left.

"Can we be sure?" asked another commando.

"Negative," growled Connery, squinting. "See that three-sided deal beyond that pile of concrete up ahead. About thirty feet up and to the left? They didn't put it together for their afternoon's exercise."

The mound of concrete rubble was situated between Connery and the small, makeshift fort of General Walter Vatutin and his group, the concrete 20 feet in front of the forts opening. Since the mass of concrete was higher than the short wall in the opening of the square shed, Connery and his men could see only that the front of the shed was open. They guessed the rest: that the last Russians alive were waiting behind some kind of small, protective barrier.

The plan was a simple one. Four commandos would creep up one side of the concrete mound and, staying down out of the line of fire from the Russians, would rake the inside of the rear wall. Colonel Connery and other commandos would charge from both sides of the mound.

Ingram slugs from the four commandos set up a screaming nightmare of ricochets that must have been heard all the way to Moscow, the four stopping the barrage when Connery, Amos Huckaba, and two other men charged from the left and six other commandos stormed in from the right.

Ricocheting projectiles had killed one technician and two of the KGB guards. But General Vatutin and Lieutenant Boris Kasimov were very much alive. Vatutin raised the PPS machine gun concurrently with Connery who began triggering the Mossberg .45s and with Kasimov who jerked up two Stechkin machine pistols.

Kasimov never got the chance to use the M.P.s. Huckaba spit a stream of tobacco juice that hit him in the left eye and blinded him. Before Boris Kasimov could fire the two Stechkins, Huckaba began to pump .22 Magnum slugs into him from his two Sentinel Mark IV H.S. magnum revolvers.

Kasimov jerked, dropped the machine pistols, and started to do the soft-shoe shuffle of the dying. In another second his chest exploded in a spume of flesh, blood, and patches of cloth as another commando stitched him vertically with a long burst of Ingram SMG slugs.

Four of Colonel Connery's .45 slugs bored into General Walter Vatutin: one that blew the end of his chin off, one in the lower throat, and two in the chest. As Connery fired, Vatutin triggered the PPS submachine bun. During that infinitesimal point in time, Vatutin knew that he was right on the brink of infinity. So be it. But the *Amerikanski* would go with him.

Dead within a second, Vatutin's massive chest dissolved in dozens of spurts of bloody debris from 9mm projectiles fired by a commando who had jumped to the side of Connery, and who had died at the same time as General Vatutin. The Mossberg .45s fell from his hands. He stood there, swaying, the front of his snowsuit hanging in tatters . . . a few tiny pieces of nylon drifting to the floor. Blood poured from each side of his mouth; and, while his eyes were wide open, they were sightless and staring past everything. His eyes closed. He toppled forward, hit the floor on his face, and lay still.

"No shoot! No shoot!" screamed Oskar Zintotrekei, the technician who, with Dr. Aleksei Agarev, was flat on the floor.

"We surrender!" yelled Dr. Agarev, shaking so much that he could hardly talk. "We surrender. I am Professor Agarev. Please don't shoot, Americans."

Captain Dunmerser was very worried about the time

schedule. He had lots of company worrying with him—Camellion and the rest of the men. Of even bigger concern was the report that Colonel Gordon had recieved by radio from Commander Ledbetter and Lieutenant Ed Percy. *Sea Tiger* had destroyed seventeen Russian fighter jets and two Ilyushin IL-76 troop carriers. Another IL-76 had gotten past *Sea Tiger* but had been destroyed by missles from *Foxfire*. Worse, the Soviet Navy was coming in force and was less than 75 miles to the west in the *Sibirskoje More*. It was obvious what the Soviets would send by air: high-altitude fighters and troop carriers that the short range ground-to-air missles carried by the subs could not reach.

"Those destroyers will have the latest electronic detection gear," said Dunmerser. "And they're sure to have automatic homing torpedos."

"It's twenty-three hundred hours right now," Colonel Gordon snapped, stepping close to the Death Merchant. "I say we get the hell out right now and move back to the coast. We don't have time to set charges or even take a crap. Every minute counts."

"All the files and photographs in the Soviet Union won't help nobody if we get snuffed," said Lyle Skimbus. He looked at the Stechkin machine pistol he had picked up as a souvenir.

"Right on all counts," conceded Camellion. "Let's move and get back to the subs as quickly as possible."

"That's more like it," Gordon remarked judicially. He pulled the PRC from his belt. "I'll contact Ledbetter and Percy."

Hours earlier, 140 commandos had moved inland against the Soviet base. Now, fifty commandos, with their four Russian prisoners, raced for the south beach of Wrangel Island, an onrush that was a speed contest between life and death. Even the four Russians kept pace, panting, gasping, and at times stumbling, forever conscious of the Death Merchant's warning: "If you don't keep up, I'll personally kill you." The four prisoners knew that he meant it.

Twelve of the men were wounded, nine only slightly, three so seriously that they were half-conscious and had to be carried, a task that kept the force from moving at maximum speed. The strongest of the commandos carried the wounded on their backs. Every ten minutes the commandos rotated, a technique that enabled the carriers to keep up their strength and not lag behind from weariness. There was little conversation.

Each step was a risk. Gordon and Camellion had taken the shortest route, one that did not involve going over hills or through tiny valleys but led for the most part over flat tundra —straight to the beach.

Muscles crying out in protest, lungs gasping, the commandos reached the tall stacks on the south beach. There was no rest period. Moving quickly, men reached for deep-dive suits, including the forty men who had remained on the beach. Commandos dressed the wounded men in diving suits and checked the equipment, especially the gas flow and the closed-circuit breathing system.

Under the watchful eye of commandos the four Russian prisoners got into swimsuits. Before the faceplates in the helmets were secured, the Death Merchant rattled off a final warning in Russian.

"Down below, you'll be surrounded by commandos. Try to escape and you'll be executed instantly."

Eyes wide, the Russians nodded.

One commando, screwing down the faceplate of Dr. Agarev, spoke in annoyance to Camellion. "You're always referring to the Russians as 'pig-farmers.' I don't get it. My dad's a farmer in southern Indiana and he raises hogs. There's nothing wrong with that."

"Naturally there isn't," Camellion replied spiritedly, understanding why the man felt insulted. "But your father doesn't get down in the mud and wallow with the hogs. When I call the Russians pig-farmers, I mean that I consider them liars and moral filth and trash." He added in heartfelt tones. "Granted that the term is a rather poor choice of words."

The commando turned to Camellion and smiled. "But it makes sense the way you explained it."

At last it was time. The commandos began wading through the surf toward deeper water.

They could hear the sound of enemy planes very high overhead.

Soon the water was covering the force and they were swimming to the SDVs. Now it was only a short step to home.

# Arrière-Pensée

Captain Coffey finished pouring his coffee and returned to the ward room table where Richard Camellion and Colonel Gordon were sitting. Having showered, shaved, eaten a hot meal, and changed into clean clothes, the two didn't look like men who had just returned from hell.

"It's like I said earlier," Coffey reiterated, approaching the table. "The only thing that saved all three subs was the Gf-Mechanism. Since heat and sound couldn't get past the barrier, the Ruskies were convinced that there weren't any submarines in the area." He pulled out a chair and sat down, his face very thoughtful. "Gentlemen, I tell you, we were very fortunate. As close as the Russians were, they could have blown us right out of the water."

The Death Merchant's face did not register emotion. "Sooner or later, some Russian scientist will guess the secret and realize that Big Uncle has a device that makes his subs invisible."

Coffey sipped his coffee, then put the mug on the table. "Speaking of scientists, I don't suppose you've had time to learn anything from the prisoners?" He looked from Camellion to Gordon. "Or shouldn't I have asked?"

"You shouldn't have, but since you have an A clearance, I'll tell you," Camellion said affably. He pretended not to notice Gordon's disapproval. "I cornered Doctor Agarev the minute we got on board and told him that if he didn't answer my questions I'd break every bone in his body. I wanted to know about that wide road in the middle of Wrangel Island."

Coffey's eyes flashed interest. "Did he tell you?"

"The highway leads to an underground installation that contains what Agarev referred to as a 'Cosmic Generator.' We missed those Russians in the center of the island. They were in the underground installation."

"We still don't know what a Cosmic Generator is," Gordon said crisply, toying with a cigarette lighter. "Agarev's not a physicist. He's a mind-bender and a biologist."

"All Agarev could tell us was that the Cosmic Generator generates a very strong magnetic field. This is accomplished by means of magnetic generators or degaussers. He said he thinks pulsating and nonpulsating generators are used. As far as he knows, the experiments are far from complete. The whole deal is a problem for the Company's technical people. Our scientists can figure it out, as well as evaluate the progress the pig-farmers have made in Psychopolitics, the KGB name for brainwashing."

"How far are we from Alaska?" Colonel Gordon asked the skipper of *Tirante,* abruptly changing the subject.

"We're right on top of Alaska," Coffey replied. "We'll be going through the Bering Straits in another hour. By the way, so far there hasn't been a single word about Wrangel Island in any radio transmission from the Soviet Union, either in regular or short wave."

The Death Merchant gave a remote smile. "There won't be. We clobbered the hell out of the Russians. The Soviet Union won't want the world to know about its terrible defeat."

"And what they were doing on Wrangel," added Gordon, his face sullen. "It's just too bad that Connery had to go the way he did. I guess it was his time to buy the farm."

"Connery should have waited," Camellion insisted stubbornly. "He acted too rashly. He was too anxious to take prisoners, or he could have used a grenade. He died for nothing."

"I don't think so." Gordon didn't look at the Death Merchant. "If Connery had tossed a grenade, we wouldn't have Dr. Agarev. Our side will learn more from him about Soviet brainwashing than from all the files put together—and don't forget his tipoff about the Cosmic Generator."

"If Connery had used a grenade, he'd be alive and we wouldn't know the difference," responded Camellion. "It's useless to discuss the pros and cons. What it boils down to is that some men have to die in order that others might live, sometimes in order that entire nations can continue to exist."

"Unfortunately you're right." Colonel Gordon sighed deeply. "All we can do is accept what is. . . ."

Once again the Death Merchant thought of the radio message the Center had squirted to *Tirante* days earlier, a coded message that only he could decipher.

Camellion had the feeling that very soon he would be involved in a massacre in Rome.

*But I enjoy Italian food and the girls are pretty. . . .*